Cat's breath ~~~~~~~~~~~~
him from time ~~~~~~~~~~~~~~~
for her father, but those occasions had been
fleeting, and she had done her best not to let
them affect her. Now, as she stared at him
across the room, she became aware of the rush
of heat through her body and the sudden rapid
beating of her heart.

"Is something wrong?" the young man she had
been dancing with asked. The music had just
stopped, and couples were drifting back to the
refreshment table.

"No, of course not," she assured him with a brilliant smile. "But if you would excuse me a moment, I see someone I really should speak with."

She left him before he could reply and boldly
made her way toward Evan. In the back of her
mind she knew she was being foolish.

Proper young ladies did not go anywhere near
men like Evan O'Connell.

MAURA SEGER

Catherine

W🌐RLDWIDE.

TORONTO • NEW YORK • LONDON • PARIS
AMSTERDAM • STOCKHOLM • HAMBURG
ATHENS • MILAN • TOKYO • SYDNEY

CATHERINE

A Worldwide Library Book/April 1988

ISBN 0-373-97067-6

For C.M.,
with thanks for the hours of good humor
and wise advice.

_____ *Part One*

Boston, December 31, 1899

"YOU CAN'T MEAN IT, Catherine," Olivia Sherman insisted. Her sallow face reflected astonishment as well as a hint of envy. She cast a narrow glance at her cousin standing next to her in the upstairs hallway of the Benningtons' Louisburg Square house.

Downstairs, a ball was in progress. Catherine's slender foot tapped in time with the music drifting up the curving marble steps. Her white silk gown swirled around her, its modest lines in keeping with what was expected of a girl of seventeen, not yet officially in society. The glow from the newly installed electric lights caught the bright gleam of her golden hair, dressed in soft curls that framed her oval face.

"Why not?" she asked, a flush of excitement warming her high-boned cheeks. "I've danced twice with Father and the same with Jimmy. That's quite enough, especially since I'm not allowed to dance with anyone else. If we hurry, we can be back in time for the champagne at midnight."

"Even you wouldn't dare to go to Carmody's," Olivia asserted. "You say you would, but you won't."

"Don't be so certain of that," Catherine said. Her silver-gray eyes gleamed with inner excitement as she glanced at the grandfather clock near the stairs. "In another few hours it will be midnight. A whole new century will have begun. I certainly want to remember more about tonight than sipping lemonade and making polite conversation with boys who stumble over every word and blush every time I look at them.''

Olivia had to almost bite her tongue to keep from pointing out that she would give anything to have the same problem. Boys did not react that way around her; rather, they seemed virtually oblivious of her existence. The only consolation was that they had much the same attitude toward almost every other girl, except Catherine.

But then, Catherine was beautiful. Not merely pretty or pleasing to the eye, but quite genuinely beautiful. Everyone said so. The grandes dames of Boston society murmured about her, shaking their heads and nodding wisely. The women of Olivia's mother's generation maintained a more stoical front, tolerant if they had no daughters themselves, otherwise tight-lipped and watchful.

The girls a few years older than Catherine who were already in society tried to dismiss her as being too young to count, but they kept an eye over their shoulders and were somewhat more anxious to be safely married than they might otherwise have been. It was rumored, though no one would admit it openly, that several gentlemen who might already have wed had decided that they preferred to wait.

The following year Catherine Bennington would be officially presented. She might then be said to be, if not precisely available, at least no longer locked up in the safety of the nursery. There was no reason to believe she wouldn't be as beautiful then as she was at the moment, perhaps even more so. There was every reason to know that she would be rich.

Olivia sometimes thought that she hated her cousin. "Go ahead, then," she said. "If you're so daring, go to Carmody's. But I'm not going with you. Your father thinks you can do no wrong, but mine will take a strap to me if he knows I even thought of it."

Catherine's smile faded as she looked at her cousin sympathetically. She knew Olivia wasn't exaggerating about her father's wrath or its consequences. Strappings were no rarity among her acquaintances. An upper-class environment and all its supposed advantages in no way diminished the notion that to spare the rod was to spoil the child.

She and her brother were highly unusual in never having experienced such punishment. Not that they hadn't been clearly given to understand what was and was not acceptable behavior.

Drake and Elizabeth Bennington brought up their children with loving firmness. Aside from those few occasions when a quick swat on the bottom kept small fingers out of the fire or equally dangerous situations, they relied on patience, clarity and ample expressions of affection. They preferred to encourage their children's spirits rather than crush them. There was, of course, a certain risk in that.

"There's nothing terrible about Carmody's," Catherine said with the easy self-assurance of the privileged young. "It's simply a place to meet friends and have a good time. Why, we've both been past it in the daytime, and you'll admit it hardly looks sinister."

"People go there unchaperoned," Olivia said. "It's scandalous."

Catherine's slanted eyebrows rose. They were slightly darker than her hair, which was the shade of antique gold. Those who knew her well considered them an accurate barometer of her emotions. "Why?"

"Because . . . because it just is, that's all. Such things aren't done."

"Weren't done," Catherine corrected. She gave a small laugh, filled with anticipation. "That was in the old days. This is now. Think of it, Olivia. An entire new century, a hundred years to fill up with wonderful things. My father says a new age is beginning, when people will live as they have never done before. You need only look around you to see that he's right."

Olivia's mouth pursed into a thin line. For a moment she took on the look of the maternal grandmother she shared with Catherine. Abigail Bennington's stern and unbending portrait hung downstairs next to a painting of her husband. It was difficult to imagine a more unlikely couple.

Catherine's grandfather had been a handsome, dashing young man who lived life to the fullest, to the intense irritation of his puritanical wife. He had died long before Catherine was born, so she had no actual memories of him, but she often thought that she would have liked very much to know him.

Her grandmother was a different matter. Abigail had lived until Catherine's eighth year, though she had been incapacitated for some time before then by a stroke. Catherine remembered the guilt she had felt for being glad when her grandmother could no longer speak, because she had never done so except to complain.

Elizabeth had gone once a week to visit her, taking Catherine along perhaps one visit out of four, which was all she thought the child should have to endure. A long-suffering nurse tended Abigail, and toward the end a doctor had been present. Everything possible had been done for her comfort, though she had never acknowledged it by so much as a word or a gesture.

Catherine had the sudden, disquieting thought that Olivia might become like that. She pushed it firmly aside. At seventeen, she never thought very long about anything that displeased her. There were far too many happy alternatives to consider.

"Are you sure you won't change your mind?" she asked. "We'll be back before anyone even knows we've gone. Besides, Jimmy's coming along."

Olivia wavered for a moment. She was terribly sweet on her handsome young cousin and was almost tempted to put caution aside in order to be with him. Almost, but not quite. Resolutely she said, "That's fine for him. He's a boy and can get away with it. You shouldn't even try."

Catherine shrugged. She didn't see what the fuss was about. They would go to Carmody's, have a sarsaparilla, take a turn around the floor and be back before midnight. Nothing could be safer.

After Olivia had returned downstairs, Catherine made her way quickly to her room on the third floor. Her maid would not be expecting her for several hours and would therefore still be belowstairs with the other servants.

In the back of the dresser drawer she found the tiny purse filled with coins and a few folded bills. It was all the money she possessed—at least in cash—and the rest didn't count, because she never thought of it. She wouldn't have any at all if she hadn't carefully husbanded it over the years, squirreling away a dime here and a quarter there.

Her only opportunity to handle money came when her mother asked her to run some little errand for her. The family had accounts everywhere, but Elizabeth wanted to give her daughter some experience with actual money, so that she would at least know what it was. She also always told Catherine to keep the change.

Hence the tiny collection that she looked forward to squandering at Carmody's. With a smile, she wondered if any of the other bold souls who had agreed to the expedition had given a moment's thought to how they would pay for it.

The boys all received allowances at their boarding schools, but these were simply kept on account for them; no money changed hands. For the girls there wasn't even the pretense of such an arrangement. They were never expected to have any need for money and therefore never received any.

She jangled the purse, which had a satisfying weight, before slipping it into her pocket. Even if she had to spend every penny, it would be well worth it.

Excitement spurred her on as she left the room and made her way to the back stairs. She slipped down them quietly, to find her brother waiting for her.

"Where have you been?" Jimmy asked. "I was beginning to think you had changed your mind."

Catherine shot her twin an affectionate look. They had been born minutes apart and had rarely been separated until Jimmy went away to St. Alban's at fourteen. The hurt of that parting still lingered and gave a bittersweet tang to every reunion, no matter how brief.

"You know perfectly well I wouldn't do that," she said. "I just had to get something. Where are the others?"

"Getting their coats. We didn't think of that, you know. Smithers is on duty at the cloakroom."

Catherine made a face. She didn't dislike the elderly servant, who was being gradually eased into duties less taxing to his waning strength, but she knew that he unfailingly took his responsibilities seriously.

He would be certain to ask why the young gentlemen wanted their coats when their parents weren't leaving. When he wasn't provided with a satisfactory answer, he would send them packing.

"Charles will think of something," she said hopefully. "He always does."

Jimmy grimaced, which gave him the look of a vexed angel. He was fairer even than she, with hair that had darkened little from the white blond of infancy. His eyes were a warm, rich brown, unshielded as yet by the slightest subterfuge. His features were not identical to his sister's, his being rather squarer than hers and more suited to a masculine face. But a girl blessed with them would still have been considered very pretty.

When he grew a little in years and experience, Jimmy would be as handsome as their father. But at the moment he was burdened by the awkwardness of youth and tended to look to his more assured sister for guidance. That did not, however, mean that he always agreed with her.

"Charles is an ass," he said. "He thinks he knows everything."

"The van Rhyses have always been like that," Catherine said, unperturbed. "They think they own the world, and in fact they do have title to a large chunk of it."

"He's already claiming that going to Carmody's was his idea."

"Let him," Catherine said. "I don't care who takes the credit so long as we go." She looked up and down the hallway impatiently, seeking some sign of their fellow conspirators.

Jimmy had already gotten their own coats from the back closet where they were kept. He had also thought to bring along a pair of boots for Catherine, pointing out that she could hardly expect to slosh through Boston's snowy streets in her dancing slippers.

With a grateful smile for his foresight, she sat down to put them on. The process took several minutes, involving as it did the laborious hooking of more than two dozen small buttons. Jimmy helped, so by the time a trio of young men appeared at the end of the hallway, she was ready.

"We got them!" the tallest of the three exclaimed.

Charles van Rhys was a large, fair-faced young man with light brown hair, amber eyes, and the sort of features found in portraits of the landed aristocracy. His nose was sufficiently Roman that when he looked down it, the view was impressive. Heavy lids fringed by pale lashes gave him a slumberous appearance he cultivated assiduously. Under almost any circumstances, he affected to look bored. He was doing so even now, despite his obvious excitement.

Charles brandished his overcoat with its rich beaver collar as though it were a trophy seized from the enemy. "Old Smithers was sitting right there, smack in front of the door. We would never have gotten past him, except I got John and Peter here to stage a diversion. Had the old boy jumping, they did."

Beside him, a pale, red-haired boy blushed as he addressed Catherine. He was quite in awe of her, as was his younger brother at his side. Had she suggested a jaunt to the ends of the earth, both would have gone along.

"W-we pretended to be fighting, you see, off to one s-side. Nobody else was around, so he had to go see to us. W-we got the back of his tongue, all r-right, but by the time he had f-finished, Charles had snuck in and s-snitched all our coats. C-clever, don't you think?"

Before Catherine could reply, Charles said, "I didn't sneak, you lout. I walked right in. A gentleman doesn't stoop to subterfuge."

"What was the diversion about, then?" Jimmy demanded. He and Charles didn't precisely dislike each other, but there was an antipathy between them that came out from time to time in various ways.

"That was strategy," Charles informed him loftily. "You would understand the difference if you paid more attention on the field." Charles had also attended St. Alban's, graduating the previous spring, much to Jimmy's relief.

"I pay attention in *class*," he murmured. "In the hope that I won't go up to Harvard entirely ignorant."

Charles had taken over the task of helping Catherine into her coat, having all but seized it from her brother. Now he turned and glanced at him haughtily. "You're bidding to be a grind, Bennington. Keep up and you'll find yourself shut out by those who count."

Jimmy stared back at him evenly. "If you mean yourself and those louts you go around with, I'd just as soon be blackballed. It's no loss, so far as I'm concerned."

The other boy's face turned ominously dark. He took a step toward Jimmy before Catherine laid a hand on his arm.

"If you both don't mind..." she murmured admonishingly. She sympathized with her brother, even if she didn't quite understand why he always had to provoke

Charles, but she wasn't about to have her adventure spoiled by unwanted arguments.

When she said as much, the two had the grace to look abashed, though she suspected that Charles, at least, was not over his pique. However, he immediately adopted an air of gallantry, while her brother rolled his eyes. Peter and John followed at a suitable remove, grateful simply to be included.

"What happened to Davis?" Jimmy asked after they had slipped out the back door and were making their way down a narrow path.

Charles shrugged and answered without looking at him. "He remembered a previous engagement."

Catherine laughed, but softly. They were still too close to the house to risk alerting anyone. The sounds of the party spilled out even though the high French windows were closed against the winter cold.

With a slight shiver, she turned up the collar of her black velvet evening coat. It was snugly fitted across the bodice and secured with frog closings. In the pocket she found a pair of leather gloves lined with mink and slipped them on.

The path had not yet been sanded, so it was slippery. She took Jimmy's arm as they hurried along. Her stays made it difficult for her to move as agilely as she would have liked, but at least they were laced loosely enough to allow her to keep up.

There had been some brief discussion of trying to hire a hack, but few frequented Beacon Hill, where they were rarely needed by residents who maintained their own carriages. Charles had been in favor of persuading one of the drivers waiting for guests to drive them, but Catherine had refused.

She would not drag a man from the warm kitchen simply for their convenience, and she would not implicate anyone in their romp—especially not someone who could lose his job in the process. Old Smithers was safe simply because it would never occur to the Benningtons to dismiss a servant who had been so long in their employ. But others were not so considerate.

With any luck, that would not be a concern. For all its vast social divisions, Boston was a small city; everything tended to be close together. Carmody's was little more than half a mile away. Even in the cold, they could walk that easily. She tightened her hold on Jimmy's arm, trying without great success to contain her eagerness.

THE COBBLESTONED STREETS were all but empty. They passed several houses where other parties were under way, but otherwise there was little sign of life. A cold dank wind blew off the bay, carrying flecks of snow.

"This is such a stodgy city," Jimmy murmured to her, "I'll bet most people are already asleep, the New Year be damned."

"But we're not," she whispered back. "That's what counts."

The walk to Carmody's took longer than she had expected. In the carriage it had seemed such a short way to go, but on foot the distance felt longer. Her toes were beginning to turn numb by the time they spotted the rows of colored lights and heard the gay voices of the crowd.

"Look," Catherine said, "isn't it wonderful?"

Through the open doorway, they could see couples clustered together near a long wooden bar or gathered at the railings off the great center rink, the installation of which had endowed Carmody's with instant fame. A band played jaunty ragtime tunes as patrons hurried to get into their rented skates and join those already circling the floor.

"We should be ice-skating this time of year," Charles said as he glanced around. "Not this—what's it called?— roller-skating."

"You're just afraid you won't be any good at it," Catherine told him gaily. She tugged Jimmy along in her eagerness to get inside. "Come on. It's getting crowded."

The arrival of four young men and a beautiful girl caused only a small flurry of interest, but that increased drastically when they handed their coats to the checkroom attendant.

It had not occurred to Catherine—or any of the others—that they would stand out so glaringly in their evening clothes. Only when she became aware that people were staring at them did she realize how differently they were dressed from the rest of the patrons.

For all its proximity to Beacon Hill, Carmody's catered to a largely working-class clientele. The young men and women gathered there worked in the nearby offices and shops. They were neatly and quietly dressed, as was expected of them.

Beside them, the four young men in their exquisitely tailored evening clothes looked like sleek birds of prey dropped in amid a group of drab pigeons. But it was Catherine who stood out the most.

Her golden hair, the radiant white of her gown, the gracefulness of her face and form—all set her apart. She looked like a statue cast in ivory and precious metals, a statue that had miraculously come to life.

Instinctively Jimmy moved closer to her. He was aware of the scrutiny they were receiving—especially her—and he did not like it. As he took her arm protectively, his gaze fell on a young man standing off to the side with a group of friends. When he met Jimmy's eyes, his broad, freckled face broke into a sneer.

"Just what we needed, lads," he said with an Irish brogue, "a bunch of fine toffs with a yen to go slumming." His eyes lingered on Catherine as he spoke. The smile he gave her was bold and challenging, on the far side of impropriety.

Jimmy stiffened and would have said something if Catherine hadn't murmured, "Don't. There's no harm done. Besides, they have a right to resent our being here."

She was surprised by her own words. She had never stopped to think that their presence might not be welcome at Carmody's, or anywhere else, for that matter.

The idea that people such as herself were a source of resentment to others was such a novelty that she turned it over several times in her mind before she felt she had even a slight hold on it.

She had always understood that her family and acquaintances were far better off than most people, but she hadn't really considered what that meant to those on the other side of the fence. Now she did so for the first time—and felt uncomfortable as a result.

So did Jimmy. He had gone along with his sister when she announced that she wanted to visit Carmody's, simply because he almost always fell in with her plans. It was a habit ingrained from their childhood, but one he was now wondering if he shouldn't have tried harder to break.

Still, he hadn't really seen any harm until he caught the look on the young Irishman's face and realized what a combination of passion and envy Catherine could so unwittingly provoke. He was half tempted to insist that they leave immediately, but pride and a lingering disinclination to disappoint her stopped him. Frowning, he turned away and began guiding his sister to a table near the railing.

The others followed, except Charles. His resentment over Jimmy's earlier comment still festered. The store of anger in him demanded an outlet.

Haughtily he eyed the Irish boy. "Somebody ought to teach you how to behave around your betters, Mick."

The boy stiffened as though he had been struck. His friends gathered around him did the same. They all stared at him to see what he would do.

Slowly and clearly, without taking his eyes from Charles, he said, "I don't see any betters. Just four toffs and a right pretty piece."

Charles's fists clenched at his sides. "What did you say?"

Mockingly the boy raised his voice as though he thought Charles might be deaf. "I said she's a right pretty piece."

He glanced at his friends, all of whom were listening avidly, egging him on.

"I think I'll go over and introduce meself. You never can tell, she might have a soft spot for a bold son of Erin. Considering the lot she goes around with, I could get lucky."

He grinned broadly as his friends laughed and urged him to go ahead.

"You damned, impudent lout," Charles said. "I'll teach you to entertain even the notion of such a thing."

Before the other boy could move or so much as brace himself, Charles hurled himself at him, fists flailing.

The boy, no stranger to street fighting, responded in kind. They hit the floor together with a crash and rolled across the wooden floor as their stunned audience jumped hastily out of their way.

"Bastard!" Charles shouted as he got the boy under him and began pounding at him. Blood splattered from the Irish lad's nose, further firing Charles's anger. "Damn Irish bastard! This will teach you."

Catherine had been unaware of the confrontations until the noise alerted her. She whirled at the sound, her face turning as white as her gown. Her only thought was that somebody had to stop them. Jimmy grabbed hold of her and pushed her back.

"You can't! Stay here, don't move!"

Dimly she nodded, then watched in horror as her brother flung himself into the melee. He intended only to try to separate the two, but the Irish boy's friends thought he had something else in mind.

Instantly several of them flung themselves at him. Catherine screamed as Jimmy went down beneath swinging fists.

She remembered very little of what happened next. Peter and John hesitated a moment, then loyally hurled themselves into the fray. Several more joined in from the other side.

Tables and chairs were overturned and went skittering across the floor. People on the rink stopped where they were and stared at the fracas. A few came over to the railing to get a better view.

"Stop them!" Catherine screamed, but no one seemed to be paying any attention. She had a sudden glimpse of Jimmy being held down by two burly young men who were pummeling him. She heard the sickening crunch of breaking bone, then felt a wave of dizziness that threatened to carry her away.

Rather than give in to it, she did the only thing she could and grabbed hold of one of her brother's assailants. Clinging to his jacket, she tried frantically to pull him away. With an angry curse, he pushed her off. She fell heavily against the opposite wall and lay there, stunned.

Her vision was only beginning to clear when she became aware of the sudden silence. The shouts and thuds of the melee had stopped. In their place was an abrupt, tension-filled hush.

"What in bloody hell," a deep voice demanded, "do you lot think you're doing?"

Where moments before there had been a writhing mass of bodies, a solitary man stood. His ebony hair gleamed with silver in the light. A strand of it had fallen over his high forehead. Crystal-blue eyes gleamed beneath his sweeping black brows.

He was well over six feet tall, with a broad chest and shoulders that tapered down to a narrow waist and hips. His long, heavily muscled legs were clad in homespun wool trousers. He wore a collarless work shirt, open at the neck, with the sleeves rolled up to the elbows. His brawny forearms were crossed over each other as he surveyed the scene before him with blunt contempt.

"Fine way to welcome the New Year, acting like a bunch of whiskey-sodden hooligans. You know Carmody doesn't go for this sort of thing."

One of the boys who had been beating Jimmy stood up and dusted off his hands self-consciously. He studied the floor as he said, "Sorry, Evan. It just happened, it did."

"I can see that," the tall man said derisively. Catherine stared at him a moment longer, caught by the hard, square features bronzed by the sun and radiating an overpowering strength.

With a wrenching act of will she tore her gaze away and found Jimmy lying on the floor. She gave a small, strangled cry as she jumped up and ran to him.

"What the . . . ?" Evan muttered as he saw the slender, golden-haired girl in the white gown dart past him. Carmody's got its share of pretty young females, but never one like this. It took him only an instant to realize two things: that she was extraordinarily beautiful, and that she was "quality," a combination that unfailingly spelled trouble.

As she knelt beside the unconscious boy and cradled his head in her lap, Evan cursed under his breath. He was Carmody's right-hand man, his troubleshooter, and he was good at his job. But he hadn't counted on having to handle anything like this. The boy, and the other three who presumably were with him, were bad enough. But the girl was bidding to be a disaster.

"All right," he said in the quick, decisive tone that served him at least as well as his size and strength. "The show's over."

He made a quick sign to the bandleader, who immediately struck up a jaunty reel. Within moments, couples were once more circling the rink, murmuring about what they had seen but already forgetting it.

"Let me have him, miss," he said as he bent over Jimmy and quickly lifted him into his arms.

"He's hurt," Catherine choked. "Oh, God, he's hurt." She had stumbled up and was staring at her brother, her face ashen and her full mouth trembling.

Evan did his damnedest not to stare at those soft, ripe lips. Instead he glanced at the boy, and his features hardened. "He'll be all right," he said with an assurance he was far from feeling. "There's a room in the back. We'll see to him there."

She followed mutely, glad only that there was someone who knew what to do. When Jimmy had been carefully laid on a bedraggled couch, she knelt beside him again, holding his hand tightly and willing him to come to. As though in direct response, his eyelids fluttered and, after a moment, opened. He stared at her, dazed and uncertain.

"W-what happened...?"

"The fight," she said on a long breath of relief undercut by the realization that he might still be seriously hurt. "You were injured. But you'll be all right."

He had to be. As though to confirm it, she turned to the man who had gone to the door to get the basin of water and towels the bartender had brought.

Evan carried them over to the couch and looked down at the boy lying there. His color was bad, and he didn't seem to know where he was, but the blood had stopped oozing from his nose, and he was breathing regularly. Evan put down the supplies and moved a gas lamp closer to the couch. By its pale light, he looked closely at Jimmy.

"You're lucky," he said, the words blurred slightly around the edges and the cadence melodic. "With the pack you had on top of you, you've got no right to be in such good shape."

Jimmy grinned, then winced as the movement hurt his torn lips. "I gave as good as I got."

Evan sighed. It was always this way, whether in the harshly beautiful hills of Connemara, from which he had come, or the vital, treacherous streets of America, where he was struggling to make a new life. Young men would always fight, with even the losers boasting of their prowess.

He looked at the boy stretched out on the couch, realizing that he was only a few years older himself, but feeling every one of those years as though it had been a decade.

"Sure, and you taught them a thing or two," he murmured as he wet the cloth and began cleaning the blood from the young man's face. Jimmy flinched, wringing a soft moan from Catherine.

"His nose is broken," Evan told her bluntly. "No man ever died of that."

"I didn't think—" She broke off, torn between the desire to defend her perfectly legitimate feelings and the determination not to do so.

"You can get a doctor to fuss with it if you like," Evan told Jimmy. "But there's little enough he can do, and it'll heal on its own anyway. Of course," he added with a slight smile, "You'll not be quite so smooth faced and innocent looking as before."

"That's fine with me," Jimmy said decisively. "I won't mind looking as though I've been around a bit." Silently he reflected that the man taking care of him certainly had that appearance.

His own nose looked to have been broken at least once, and there was a thin white scar running from his left eyebrow across his forehead into the hairline. If whatever had caused that had gone half an inch or so lower, the man would have lost an eye.

As it was, he had undoubtedly been in more than a few fights, though Jimmy ruefully suspected that he had acquitted himself somewhat better than he himself had managed.

"Who are you, by the way?" he asked as the man dabbed something stinging on his cheek. He had to grit his teeth to keep from jerking back, but he was determined to show no further sign of weakness.

Evan hesitated a moment. He was still clinging to the idea that he might be able to get rid of the pair without revealing anything more about himself than he had already done.

Long-imbued habit made him cautious of all those
who possessed wealth and power. These two fledglings
most certainly had both, albeit indirectly, through their
elders. Elders who would be eager for retribution when
they discovered what had happened to them.

Yet he could hardly refuse to tell the boy his name, and
pride prevented him from inventing an alias on the spot.
"O'Connell," he said at length. "Evan O'Connell."

When the boy continued to look at him, he added
grudgingly, "I work for Carmody, supposedly keeping
the peace in this place." A low, hard laugh broke from
him. "Sure, and didn't I do a good job of it tonight."

He glanced over his shoulder at Catherine, who was
sitting white and still on the edge of the couch. His voice
hardened as he added, "But then, I didn't expect a major bit of disruption to come strolling through the door."

She lowered her eyes for a moment, then raised them
to stare at him directly. "You don't think we should have
come here, do you?"

He gave a derisive snort and turned back to Jimmy. "Is
there any doubt of it? Light a fire under the most placid
donkey and he's going to jump. Probably kick, too, in the
process. And who's to blame him?"

"You can't mean that you think what those . . . those
ruffians did was right?" Catherine demanded, outraged.

He shrugged his broad shoulders with infuriating calm.
"I can't say if it was or it wasn't, since I didn't see what
started it. But I do know the lads who were messing it up,
and they aren't bad sorts."

Catherine's gray eyes turned smoky. She leaned toward him, her hands clenched in her lap. "Not bad sorts!
Look what they did to my brother! They should be

locked up somewhere. People like that shouldn't be allowed to—''

"That's enough, Cat," Jimmy broke in with a firmness she wasn't accustomed to receiving from him. For just an instant, he reminded her of their father. While she was still digesting this unaccustomed behavior on his part, he turned to Evan.

"My sister is understandably upset. I think the best thing is to get her back home as quickly as possible."

He glanced down at his stained and torn clothes and shook his head ruefully. "As it is, there's going to be quite a lot of explaining to do."

Evan nodded absently. He sympathized with the young man, but not to any great extent. It was beyond him to believe that the very rich could have any real problems.

"What about the others?" Catherine murmured. Evan had risen from the couch and was clearing up the soiled bandages. She moved to help him, though she kept her eyes studiously averted.

"If you mean the other three young gentlemen," he said with a slight edge of sarcasm, "I told the bartender to send them on their way. One didn't seem to think he should go, but Sean convinced him otherwise."

"That would be Charles," Jimmy murmured. "He's got something of a temper."

Evan brushed that off. The unknown boy didn't interest him, but these two did, one of them only too much. Deliberately addressing Jimmy, he said, "I've told you who I am, but you haven't returned the favor."

"I'm sorry," Jimmy said, genuinely contrite. Good manners had been bred into him, but beyond that, he was also innately considerate. He sat up and managed to get his legs over the side of the couch, though the effort cost him.

Holding out a hand, he said, "I'm James Bennington, and this is my sister, Catherine. We really are very grateful for your help."

Evan resisted the impulse to wipe his own hand on the seat of his pants before taking the hand the boy offered. Inwardly he was cursing his own bad luck. Getting mixed up with the gentry was unfortunate enough, but why did they have to be Benningtons to boot?

The name was well-known to him, as it was to anyone who had been in Boston more than the shortest time. The Benningtons were part of the handful of families who were set apart from all others by virtue of their immense riches and authority.

They lived in a world so vastly different from his own that he could barely imagine it. He was certain of only one thing: the sooner he saw the back of them, the better.

Outwardly he gave no sign of his concern as he said, "We'll be getting you home then, James. You, too, miss. Come along."

He eased an arm under Jimmy and helped him up. The boy was good-sized, but Evan barely felt his weight. His attention was on Catherine, who had hurried to Jimmy's other side.

"Lean on me, too, Jimmy," she said softly, her eyes wide with concern. "You mustn't do anything to strain yourself further."

"Don't fuss, Cat," the boy said, not unkindly, but with that same note of firmness Evan had heard in his voice before. The girl seemed startled by it again, but then, he supposed very few ever took that tone with her.

Slowly they made their way out of the back room. The bartender, Sean, saw them coming and went to get their coats. Evan put Jimmy's over his shoulders, while Catherine slipped into hers.

Meanwhile Sean had gone to summon a hack. When it pulled up in front, Evan helped Jimmy into it, then assisted Catherine in beside him.

As he was about to shut the carriage door, she leaned forward slightly, compelling his attention. Very softly she said, "Mr. O'Connell, we really do appreciate everything you've done. It was foolish of us to come here, I admit that, and I'm sorry for the trouble we precipitated, however inadvertently."

Evan stared at her for a moment, drinking in the moist smoothness of her mouth, the slight upturn of her nose and the wide, thick-fringed eyes that seemed more brilliant than he imagined molten silver could be.

She had left the velvet evening coat unfastened. Between its lapels, he could see a tantalizing hint of alabaster skin above the silk and lace that covered but did not conceal her high, full breasts.

His body hardened, reminding him—if he had needed any further proof—that his manhood was without reason or contrition. It simply *was*, and growing more so by the moment.

Angered by his reaction to a girl he expected never to see again and by rights could never even dream of possessing, he spoke more harshly than he had intended.

"Then perhaps you'll think before you do something so stupid again. Rich and poor get along only when they keep their distance. Remember that and don't go trespassing where you don't belong."

Before she could reply, he shut the carriage door and gestured to the driver. As the wheels began to turn, he caught her gaze through the window.

Her eyes looked hurt, but also something more. There was a hint of wistfulness in them, as though she, too, regretted the realities that locked them forever in separate worlds.

EVAN PUT A HAND to the back of his neck and rubbed it wearily. It was getting on for four in the afternoon, late enough for the light already to be fading. He'd been bent over the ledgers longer than he cared to remember and was only beginning to make some headway with them.

With a sigh, he stood up and went over to the cabinet where Carmody kept his private stock. His employer wouldn't begrudge him a wee nip after his endeavors, and the devil take anyone who did.

It was Carmody's idea that he learn the ledgers, all part of his grand plan to educate Evan.

"Rise above yourself, me boy," the stocky, red-faced ward leader had said shortly after they met. "No man knows his own limits. Why presume that yours are less than they may be?"

Evan didn't presume that. He was ambitious, which was part of the reason Carmody took an interest in him. It didn't hurt that he was also smart, tough and not overburdened by scruples.

His mother, peace be with her, had brought him up to be God-fearing and law-abiding. And he might have remained so if the conditions he had witnessed in Ireland hadn't fired him with rage at an uncaring deity and the determination to escape the brutal life for which he seemed destined.

A rueful grin lifted the corners of his firm mouth as he glanced back at the ledgers. He wasn't about to let them defeat him. They were nothing compared to some of the challenges he had faced in his twenty-two years, chief among them simply staying alive.

But the neat rows of columns wouldn't succumb to a strong back or a ready fist. They would yield only to the power of his mind, which just then seemed to be wanting.

He took the whiskey back to the table and sat down again. Carmody was at the ward office; he rarely dropped by the dance hall that bore his name.

"That's for the voters, lad," he'd explained. "They come to Carmody's, have a good time and go away thinking kindly of me. Since I got talked into installing that damned rink, I also get credit for being modern. None of which means I want to spend any time in the place.

"Times are changing, lad," Carmody claimed. "Not on their own, mind you. There's nothing magical about crossing into this new century. It's what we make of it that counts." His blunt features had twisted into what could pass for a smile. "And we'll be making plenty, boyo. You can be counting on that."

Evan shook his head at the memory. Carmody had grand plans. His own were a bit more mundane. During the interminable voyage on the leaky scow that had brought him to America, he had made himself two promises. The first was that he would never be hungry again. The second was that he would never again be humbled by any man.

"We were bloody slaves in Ireland," he had said to Carmody shortly after they first met. "The English treat their dogs and horses better than they do us." Bitter and self-conscious, he had felt compelled to add, "But the day will come when Ireland's shame will be washed away in blood."

Carmody had scoffed outright, sadness shadowing his derision. "We're a race of martyrs, boyo. If you've got a brain in your head, you won't be planning to become another of them. It's power that counts, and money makes power. The two are like a man and woman intertwined. You can't say where one ends and the other begins."

Thinking of that image, Evan stirred uncomfortably. Since his brief meeting with Catherine Bennington two days before, she had flitted constantly through his mind.

His best efforts to dislodge her had failed, to his intense and growing irritation. He was a damn fool to be remembering her at all, let alone dwelling on the perfection of her face and form.

With a low growl of impatience, he slammed the ledger shut and stood up. There was an easy remedy for his problem. He could take himself over to Molly Burke's, pick out a likely girl and make an evening of it. But somehow the prospect didn't have the appeal it should have.

He pushed his hands into his pockets and walked over to the single window. It was uncurtained and looked out on a scraggly back-lot dotted with broken bottles and other unidentifiable effluvia. The winter grayness was unrelenting.

He shut his eyes for a moment, seeing behind them the lush green beauty of Ireland. Tragic, haunted beauty that followed her children wherever they went and left a yearning in their hearts that could never be satisfied.

He was staring out the window again at the gathering darkness when the door behind him suddenly opened.

Evan turned quickly, in time to see a tall, blond man entering the room.

He wore a double-breasted suit of gray flannel that, even to Evan's untutored eye, was meticulously tailored. His white dress shirt did not appear to have a single crease, so perfectly starched and ironed was it. A conservatively striped tie was knotted in the precise center of the wing collar. The man's square jaw was smoothly shaven. His thick blond hair, shot through with strands of silver, was brushed back from his high forehead. The eyes that studied Evan were a rich brown. Finely drawn lines around them deepened as the man smiled.

"You must be Evan O'Connell." There was a watchful composure to the man's rugged features that bespoke keen intelligence and strength of will. It was also distantly familiar.

Evan inclined his head very slightly. "Would you be Drake Bennington?"

His visitor looked surprised to have been recognized, but nodded. "I've come to thank you for your assistance to my children. You extricated them from a difficult situation, I understand."

"You could put it that way," Evan said absently. His mind was whirling with the implications of this visit. Men such as Drake Bennington did not customarily pay calls on anyone outside their own very select social class. If they wanted to see somebody, that person was summoned at the appropriate time to the appropriate place.

But Drake Bennington seemed to find nothing peculiar in his presence in Carmody's. On the contrary, he glanced around with interest, noting the ledgers on the desk and the glass of whiskey.

"I'm interrupting your work."

"It's of no matter." Evan got hold of himself and gestured to the chair opposite the desk. "Would you have a seat?"

Drake did as he suggested, and Evan, after a moment, resumed his own seat behind the desk. He felt very odd to be in that position but was glad of it, since it gave him at least the illusion of being in charge.

"Is there something I can do for you?" he asked.

Drake smiled slightly. "You can accept my thanks, for a start. Catherine and James have a tendency to support each other in mischief. It's been that way since they were born. At any rate, this time they realize that they were in over their heads, and they've promised to be more sensible in the future."

Evan was surprised by the mildness of the other man's tone. He got the impression that while Drake was sincerely glad that his children had escaped relatively unscathed, he also didn't especially regret their having had the experience.

As though to confirm that, Drake said, "They've both led rather sheltered lives. Too sheltered, I sometimes think. It doesn't hurt them to learn something about the real world and the people in it."

Evan kept silent. He was suspicious of the instinct that urged him to relax with Drake Bennington, even to like him. Nothing in his experience indicated that the wealthy and powerful were ever trustworthy, let alone deserving of affection.

Yet Drake Bennington seemed different. Watching and listening to him, Evan had the sense of a man who refused to be limited by other people's expectations, a man who faced the world on his own terms and reserved his respect for those who did the same.

At length he said, "I take it they told you all about their adventure."

"Not quite all. Catherine has admitted to having come up with the idea, but I suspect that there were others besides the two of them involved."

He waited, giving Evan a chance to confirm or deny that suspicion. When he declined to do either, Drake shrugged.

"At any rate, I'm not unmindful of what could have occurred had you not intervened when you did. I would like to find a more concrete way to show my appreciation."

Evan stiffened. If the man offered him a tip, he was going to toss it back at him, however much he needed the money. But Drake seemed fully aware that no such gesture would be appreciated. He eyed Evan for another moment before he said, "I'd like you to think about coming to work for me."

Evan stared at him, uncertain that he had heard correctly. "Work . . . ?"

"I run a large company," Drake said mildly. "Actually, a group of companies. I don't imagine it would be very difficult to find a place for a man of your sort."

He paused slightly, then rose and slipped a hand into his breast pocket. The card he placed on the desk was thickly embossed. On it was printed an address in Boston's financial district. There were initials in black ink in the upper right-hand corner—D.B.

"Come and see me when you've made up your mind."

Evan picked up the card slowly. The smooth, creamy paper felt cool between his fingers. Like the man who had handed it to him, it was discreetly understated but also extremely expensive. Deep within him, a hard, gnawing hunger stirred.

"I'll give it some thought." He put the card in his pocket.

Drake nodded pleasantly. He turned and left the office as quietly as he had come. Evan stared at the door long after it had closed behind him.

In his mind he saw not the man who had just departed, but the girl who was his daughter—the living vision of what Evan had not even permitted himself to think of possessing.

Until now.

DRAKE SAT BACK in the carriage and glanced out the window. If the sky was anything to go by, there would be more snow that night. It was just as well he would be getting home a bit early. He had left the office slightly before the usual hour in order to pay his call on Evan O'Connell.

The man had surprised him. He was younger than Drake had expected, and more self-contained. With a smile he realized that he had instinctively presumed his children's description of Evan to be exaggerated. Now he wasn't so certain.

His smile faded slightly as he considered whether or not he might have made a mistake in offering Evan a job. It hadn't precisely been a spur-of-the-moment decision; Drake had not done anything impulsively in a good many years. But he had been undecided until he met the man.

The younger man was carrying around a good deal of anger inside him; Drake was certain of that. Considering where he had come from, it was hardly surprising.

Conditions in Ireland were appalling by any standard. Most of the people lived in brutal poverty, denied even the rudiments of education and hope. Their every attempt at political freedom was either stymied by the English or adroitly compromised.

Drake had heard it said that the Irish were the niggers of the British Empire. While he despised that word, he had to admit it was accurate in this case. Nothing else quite expressed the status of people whom many still felt weren't quite human.

None of which explained why he was willing to take Evan into his own organization. Of course there was the fact that by doing so, he would be taking him from Carmody.

The old pol wouldn't like that, not one little bit. Drake had nothing in particular against Carmody—he understood that the man performed an important function—but he also wouldn't mind ruffling him a bit.

He was still contemplating that mildly amusing possibility when the carriage pulled up in front of the Louisburg Square house. As he stepped out onto the sidewalk, Drake glanced up at the building he had purchased some eighteen years before.

It was a three-story stone mansion in the Federalist style, with gracefully high ceilings, and stone moldings over the double doors. He had bought it because he wanted to bring his bride to a home of his own. His, not theirs. Back then, Drake had presumed a great many things about marriage that had turned out to be incorrect.

There was a tolerant gleam in his eyes as he remembered his younger self. Lord, he had been foolhardy in those days! Sometimes he thought it was a wonder that Elizabeth had stuck with him. But she had, thank heaven, and he was confident that she didn't regret it.

Certainly there was no sign of regret in the woman who greeted him at the front door. She was tall and slender, like her daughter, with blond hair lightly touched by silver, and deep gray eyes.

She was in her mid-thirties, and age had lightly traced thin lines around her eyes and mouth, but had in no way detracted from her beauty. As always when he looked at her, Drake forgot everything else. He bent and dropped a tender kiss on her mouth.

"Everything all right?" he asked.

"Fine," she assured him as she laid a gentle hand on his arm. "Jimmy has been persuaded to stay in bed, although he insists he feels fine. Catherine is practising her music."

Drake became aware of the somewhat faltering piano notes emanating from a room on the far side of the entry hall. He chuckled softly. "Is that her punishment?"

Elizabeth shrugged and drew him farther inside. They walked arm in arm together toward the parlor, where an inviting fire burned. Elizabeth was wearing a slate-gray velvet and brocade gown with a silver lace collar that framed her oval face. Her golden hair was swept up and secured by diamond clips. As she turned away from Drake, he caught a scent of her perfume, a blend of jasmine, hyacinth and sandalwood.

His eyes lingered on her as she moved gracefully across the room, opened a chinoiserie cabinet that concealed a small bar, and poured a measure of brandy into a crystal snifter. When she turned back and saw him watching her, her eyebrows rose slightly.

"How was your day, darling?" she asked, her voice soft and throaty with the slight Virginia accent that remained even after all her years up North.

He took the brandy from her and sipped it before he said, "Profitable. It's the unusual day that isn't."

She laughed and took his arm again, drawing him to the couch in front of the fire. "How fortunate for us. I was thinking today about Catherine's debut later this year. It isn't too soon to begin planning her wardrobe."

He smiled at her ironically. "Is that your way of telling me that household expenses will be going up?"

"Hmm, I should say so. Why, I remember what it cost to outfit me eighteen years ago. Of course," she added a bit wickedly, "I was also shopping for my trousseau, even if I didn't know it at the time."

"There are times when I wonder if your father still thinks me guilty of cradle snatching."

She tilted her head to one side and looked at him from beneath her thick lashes. "He didn't then, although I'll admit he had some reservations about you. They were thoroughly erased long ago."

Their eyes met in understanding. Neither had to speak of the difficulties that had strained their early marriage. It was enough that they had survived and gone on to savor a union that grew stronger with each passing year.

"I hope," Drake said teasingly, "that you aren't suggesting a similar economy for Catherine?"

"Combining a coming-out wardrobe with a trousseau? Certainly not. Besides, there's no one she's interested in."

Drake hesitated a moment. Quietly he said, "Are you sure?"

Elizabeth looked genuinely puzzled. "Of course. You know how close we are. If she cared for someone, I would at the very least be aware of it. What makes you think otherwise?"

"I don't," he assured her. "I'm merely exercising a father's prerogative to worry."

She laughed and shook her head. "Worry more about her tendency to mischief. Did you see the Irishman, by the way?"

Drake nodded. "I offered him a job." Dryly he added, "He said he would think about it."

Elizabeth shook her head wonderingly. "Most men would jump at the chance to work for you."

"You flatter me, my love. I have something of a reputation as a taskmaster, though I don't believe that would frighten Evan O'Connell off. No, I think he merely distrusts so sudden and unlooked-for an opportunity and wants to make sure that the ground is solid beneath his feet before he jumps."

"Always a wise policy," Elizabeth said. "I wouldn't mind if our children were to adopt it."

"Not anytime soon, I expect." He loosened his tie slightly and draped an arm over the back of the couch. Elizabeth moved closer and put her head on his shoulder.

They stared at the fire for several minutes before he said softly, "Sometimes, when I really think about it, I'm astonished at how quickly the years have passed. It seems like only yesterday that they were being born."

"Remember how red and squalling they were? Both so mad at being ejected into the world. Thank heaven my mother knew what to do. I certainly didn't."

"They adjusted quickly enough," he said. "So did you." He turned to her as he added, "I don't think there's been a better mother. The children are very lucky."

She colored faintly, as she always did when he praised her, and touched a soft finger to his face. "What a lovely thing to say, Drake. But you must know that they wouldn't be nearly the people they are if you hadn't been such a loving father.''

He dropped a light kiss on the tip of her nose and grinned. "We have to face it, we're a pair of paragons. Now, if only our children would be suitably grateful."

She let her finger drift to his mouth. "We've been very lucky, you know. With them and with ourselves."

He nodded, put the brandy snifter down and gathered her to him.

Moments later the butler who put his head in the door to announce that dinner was ready withdrew hastily when he saw the master and mistress locked in what gave every evidence of being a prolonged embrace.

The sight was not particularly surprising to him. It was well-known that Elizabeth and Drake Bennington were deeply in love and expressed it in very romantic fashion. Cook would simply have to hold dinner back a bit, hardly for the first time—or the last.

Chapter Four

CATHERINE KNOCKED LIGHTLY at the door of her brother's room, waited until she heard a murmur, then went in.

Jimmy was propped up in bed. A nightshirt was tied across his chest, and he was covered by a quilted comforter.

There was a stark white bandage across the bridge of his nose and another tied around the knuckles of his right hand. In addition, livid bruises and abrasions marred his face. When he saw her and moved to sit up farther, he grimaced.

"Take it easy," she said, going quickly to his side. "Smithers hasn't announced dinner yet, so I thought I'd come by and see how you're feeling."

"Embarrassed," he said with a wry grin. "I thought I'd have bounced back by now."

"It's only been two days," she reminded him. "Besides, Dr. Haley said you'd feel worse before you felt better."

Unlike Evan, who had doubted a physician's usefulness, Elizabeth and Drake had insisted on summoning one as soon as they saw their son's condition. Dr. Haley had agreed that there was no point in trying to set Jimmy's nose, but he had insisted that he stay in bed until his other injuries began to heal.

"Do you have everything you need?" she asked, glancing at the pile of books, newspapers and magazines strewn across the bed. There was a silver jug of water on a side table, along with an empty teacup and a plate that had held some of his favorite brownies. Only crumbs remained.

Jimmy followed the direction of her gaze and laughed. "My only problem is going to be stuffing dinner in. Cook has been sending up treats since yesterday, and Smithers drops by every hour or two with whatever he's found to amuse me."

"Everyone's been very worried about you," she said.

He looked at her strained face with the too-large eyes and sighed deeply. Of all the people who were concerned about him, Cat was at the top of the list.

She was blaming herself for what had happened and, he suspected, feeling guiltier by the minute. He shook his head slightly as he reached out and took her hand.

"You've got nothing to be sorry about, Cat. The situation just got out of control, that's all."

"I still feel it was my fault." She spoke very low, reluctant to impose her guilt on him, but not knowing who else to turn to. Softly she added, "Mother and Father do, too."

"They haven't said that," he reminded her gently. "And they never would. All Father said was that we should have had more sense than to go there. *We*, not just you."

He smiled crookedly. "If you want to know the truth, I think he's just waiting for me to get better before he gives me holy hell for letting you walk into a place like that."

"He'd better not," Catherine said, suddenly fierce. She adored her father, but for her brother's sake, she would defy even him. "It was my idea all along. I'll tell him that again if he tries to blame you."

"I don't think he's really interested in blaming anyone. He just wants to make sure that we have more sense in the future."

"I suppose..." She looked away for a moment, then turned back to him. "I had a note from Charles."

Her brother's eyebrows rose in surprise. "What about?"

"It was very formal. He said that he deeply regretted the incident and hoped we were well. He also informed me that he had not mentioned his involvement to anyone. I gather he'd like it to stay that way."

Jimmy nodded, unsurprised. "He would be more concerned about that than anything else. I didn't notice him staying around to make sure we were all right."

"I gather Mr. O'Connell had him removed."

At the mention of Evan's name, Jimmy brightened. "He's really something, isn't he? The moment he showed up, nobody moved. They're all scared of him, I suppose. He certainly knows how to handle himself."

"He's all right," Catherine said with studied casualness. "Men like that must see a lot of violence. He would be used to it."

"What do you mean," her brother asked innocently, "'men like that'?"

She shrugged, hoping he wouldn't notice how flustered the mere mention of Evan made her. For two nights she had lain awake staring at the canopy above her bed but seeing him instead. In the course of many a long, wakeful hour she had replayed the scene at Carmody's over and over again.

Repeatedly she remembered his calm strength, his instant ability to take charge and determine what needed to be done, even the gentle, competent manner in which his large hands had touched Jimmy, caring for him with practical efficiency underlined by kindness.

Not, of course, that he had been particularly kind to *her*. He had made it clear that he felt nothing but derision for any female foolish enough to provoke such an incident. His contempt stung, almost as much as her own remorse.

"I hope Father thanks him properly," Jimmy was saying. "That's the only reason I thought he should have Evan's name. He didn't say so exactly, but I got the impression he'd do the right thing."

"I'm sure he will," Catherine murmured. She didn't want to talk about Evan O'Connell. The sooner she forgot he so much as existed, the better.

"Can I bring you anything from downstairs?" she asked.

"No, but come back after dinner if you can and play cards with me. I'm going out of my mind stuck in here."

"All right," she promised as she heard the soft tone of the gong announcing dinner. At almost the same moment, there was a knock at the door. Catherine stood up, smoothed the skirt of her apricot silk gown and went to answer it.

A young maid stood in the hall, loaded down with a tray from which succulent aromas wafted. She smiled at Catherine, then gazed shyly at Jimmy. "I've brought your supper, sir, if that's all right?"

He grinned and gestured to the table beside him. "If you can find some place to put it, Mary."

"Oh, I'll manage, sir," she assured him as she slipped into the room. She set the tray down on the dresser temporarily, then began briskly straightening up. Her cheeks were flushed as she did so, and she kept glancing at Jimmy out of the corner of her eye.

Catherine suppressed a grin. "Well, I can see you're in capable hands, so I'll be getting along."

He rolled his eyes wryly. "Don't forget you promised to come back."

"I will," she assured him, then took one more look at the maid who had placed the tray on the table and whisked off the napkin to reveal at least half a dozen different dishes.

"Now Cook says you're to eat all this, sir, otherwise you won't be recovering as quick as you ought to."

Jimmy groaned softly, but looked as though he might be talked into it. He glanced again at the pretty maid. "I'm just not sure I can manage on my own...."

"Oh, sir, I'll be glad to stay and help—"

"I don't think that's really necessary," Catherine said briskly. "Come along, Mary. Cook undoubtedly has things for you to do downstairs."

The maid flushed but did as she was told, allowing herself only a single backward glance at the chagrined young man. Jimmy shot a mock glare at his sister as she laughed and shut the door behind her.

HER PARENTS WERE ENTERING the dining room arm in arm as Catherine joined them. She took the seat Smithers held out for her as her father assisted her mother. When they were all seated, Drake looked across the table at his daughter. "How is Jimmy doing?"

"Fine. When I left him, he was starting his own supper. Cook sent him up at least one of everything."

"Good," Drake said. He let the matter drop. Catherine's remorse over the incident at Carmody's had not escaped him. "Your mother had a letter from Calvert Oaks today,'' he mentioned in passing, hoping to take her mind off things.

Elizabeth recognized her cue. She was also concerned about their daughter, who seemed oddly preoccupied and somber, even given what had occurred. Seeking to distract her, she said, ''Your grandmother and grandfather are both well. They'd like to see you soon.''

Catherine brightened. She had not seen her grandparents in almost a year, since her family's most recent trip to the Virginia plantation that was her mother's birthplace. Calvert Oaks was a second home to her, almost as much as Quail Run next door, where her uncle and aunt lived with their children.

''I wish they could come for my debut,'' she said. ''That's the only thing that would make it seem worthwhile. Although I know,'' she added, ''that they can't leave the plantation at that time of year.''

Elizabeth and Drake exchanged a puzzled glance. Catherine had never before expressed any reluctance about having the standard coming-out party that young women in her position were treated to. On the contrary, they had had the impression that she was enthusiastic about the idea.

''I thought you were looking forward to a party,'' her father said.

Catherine shrugged. She waited until the junior butler, carefully scrutinized by Smithers, had ladled a serving of lobster bisque into the Limoges bowl in front of her.

When he had gone on to serve her father, she said, ''It just doesn't seem very important anymore.''

''What's happened to change your mind?'' Elizabeth asked. She picked up her spoon and took a sip of the bisque without tasting it. Her attention was on her daughter.

"I don't know," Catherine admitted. She could hardly explain that the incident at Carmody's had disturbed her in some way she couldn't define.

Her encounter with Evan had made her vaguely ashamed of both herself and her class. But more than that, she was suddenly self-conscious about assuming the official status of a marriageable young woman, which her coming out would make her.

"Perhaps you're simply tired," her mother ventured. "What happened was a great shock to you."

"Yes," Catherine said quietly, "it was."

Again her parents glanced at one another. After a moment Drake said, "It would be a mistake to exaggerate the incident, Cat. Jimmy's going to be fine, you've both learned an important lesson, and that's that. It's time to get on to other, more pleasant things."

She looked up, meeting his eyes. Through all the years of her childhood she had been able to go to him as much as to her mother. He had soothed her hurts, cherished her confidences and always wrapped her in all-encompassing love. But he could not prevent her from growing up. Nor, she knew, would he try.

"What lesson have I learned? Simply to be more careful? It seems to me that there was more to it."

"Such as?" her father asked softly.

She took a deep breath and spoke in a rush. "Those people hate us. I saw how they looked when we came in and when they were hitting Jimmy. You would have thought we were their worst enemies. I've never seen anything like that in my life before, never even imagined it."

Unconsciously she shivered. "It was horrible but it was also... I don't know... understandable, somehow. I've been wondering how I would feel if I were poor, with no real chance of improving my lot in life. I think I'd be very angry, too."

"Now wait a minute," Drake said. "Those people in Carmody's can hardly be called poor. If they were, they wouldn't be able to patronize such a place. If you want to see actual poor people, I'll arrange it for you. Believe me, you'll notice the difference."

"That isn't the point," Catherine said firmly. "Compared to us, almost anyone is poor. We take things for granted that most people can't even dream of having."

She glanced around her at the room furnished with exquisite French and English antiques. The table was laid with heavy silver, crystal, and china edged in gold. A magnificent chandelier hung over the center of the table. Its light was reflected a thousand times over by the diamonds in her mother's hair and on her fingers.

"Somehow it doesn't seem right," she said softly.

Drake was about to reply when Elizabeth sent him a cautionary glance. He shrugged and let her handle it. "Darling, what do you imagine would happen if we sold everything we have, took the money and gave it to the poor?"

Catherine hesitated. She had never had such a discussion with her parents, had truthfully never really thought of such matters before. She had the distinct feeling that she was out of her depth, but she didn't want to make that too obvious.

"I suppose they would be glad to have it," she said at length.

"Possibly, but it's at least equally likely that they would simply resent us for being the source of such wealth. People are rarely grateful for charity. That's why it's always best to give anonymously."

Catherine nodded, well aware that this was her parents' practice. The Benningtons funded schools, hospitals and old people's homes throughout Boston and far beyond. But their name appeared on none of these institutions, and their involvement was kept strictly private.

"Besides that," her mother went on, "how long do you imagine such a sudden influx of money would make a difference to those people? They would spend it soon enough, perhaps sensibly, perhaps not, and then they would be in the same position as before."

"What your mother is saying," Drake broke in, "is that it isn't enough to simply give money to the poor. You have to create jobs and housing, provide good education and the opportunity for people to advance themselves. To do that, money must be accumulated and put to work, not merely given away."

"How much opportunity is there?" Catherine asked. "The Irish are not welcomed in many occupations, any more than the Italians or other immigrants. What are such people to do?"

"Work harder," her father said quietly, "and smarter. People who do that get ahead no matter where they come from. It may not be a very pleasant prospect, but the fact is that this country was built by the toughest and the most determined. Not too surprisingly, they like to keep the fruits of their labor for themselves. But that doesn't mean someone else can't plant his own tree, and in time, harvest it."

"In time," Catherine repeated softly. It was not her habit to disagree with her father. On the contrary, she was inclined to believe anything he said.

But she had a sudden vision of Evan O'Connell and felt again the driving, burning energy within him. He was not a man to wait, to bide his time patiently and hope that tomorrow would be better. On the contrary, she thought him much more inclined to seize the day, no matter what the consequences.

But she did not say so, and the conversation moved on to other things. Her mother described a mix-up that had occurred at her Ladies' Auxiliary meeting the previous week and soon had them laughing.

Catherine glanced at her parents, thinking how extremely well suited they were to each other. She couldn't remember a time when they hadn't seemed perfectly happy and in love.

A wistful yearning filled her as she wondered if she would ever experience anything as idyllic. Not, she reasoned, if she was doomed to be attracted to a singularly inappropriate Irishman who had nothing but contempt for her and everything she represented.

EVAN STRETCHED OUT his long legs under the table and leaned back in his chair. He looked at the man across from him, trying to guess what was in his mind.

Reading Fitz Carmody's face was never easy. At first glance, he looked not unlike many another square-jawed, snub-nosed Irishmen who had been in one too many bar fights. He had wide blue eyes that could look innocent or mean depending on his whim. His once black hair had long since turned to a nondescript gray. It was thinning on top, and he was vain enough to comb it to the side.

"I didn't think you'd be one for doing business with the likes of Drake Bennington," Evan said quietly.

Carmody laughed. He took a long, noisy swallow of his beer and set the mug down with a thump.

"Laddy, the meek may inherit the Earth, as the good book tells us, but in the meantime it's the rich and powerful who are running the place. That means we do business with them. Drake Bennington's hardly the worst of the lot. Fact is, he's better than most."

Evan lifted his broad shoulders and let them fall. His eyes scanned the barroom absently. Long experience had taught him to pay attention to his surroundings.

A pretty girl in a frilly skirt that ended just below her knees and a tight bodice that did nothing to conceal the fullness of her breasts caught his glance and smiled. Un-

der other circumstances, he would have smiled back. As
it was, he looked away.

"I'm not sure what he wants with me."

"A job, he said. That could mean anything."

"Or nothing."

Carmody shook his head. "Not with Bennington. If he
wants to hire you, he'll have something in mind for you
to do. He didn't get where he is today by wasting talent."

"What do you mean? I presumed he was born rich."

"Oh, he was," Carmody confirmed. "But there's rich
and there's *rich*. Bennington's a whole lot wealthier than
he was when he started out. You don't hear about him as
much as you do the Lodges and Cabots and their crew,
but they've got nothing on him. He's just quiet about it,
is all."

"Where does his money come from?"

Carmody shrugged. He finished his beer and raised a
hand to summon another before answering. "Shipping,
to start with. He controls a good piece of the China trade,
not to mention a fair amount of what goes between here
and Europe. Then there are the railroads and banks, plus
interests in oil, steel, gold, a diamond mine in South
Africa, and a few other nits and nats. When you come
down to it, you'd have a hard time finding something
Drake Bennington doesn't have his finger in. He's one
hell of a smart bastard and plenty tough, but they say he's
also fair. Maybe that's his Achilles' heel."

"Is that what you're looking for?" Evan asked. "A
way to get to him?"

Carmody took another swallow of beer and leaned
forward. His voice was low and hard. "Not just him,
laddy, all of 'em. I said it before and I'll say it again: our
time is coming."

Evan sighed deeply. "I'd like to believe you, but I've heard it too often. 'Ourselves Alone,' we say in Ireland, as though just the speaking of it makes us free. But it doesn't, not there and not here. No man gives up power willingly, or even shares it. What we want, we must take."

"And we shall," Carmody said softly. "But at the right time and in the right way. We've an opportunity here, one we'll never have in Ireland. We can win through the ballot box what we'll never hope to win at the end of a gun."

"You've more faith in the system than I do. From where I sit, it looks as though men like Bennington will do anything they have to in order to keep us in our place."

"Maybe," Carmody said with a shrug. "But if you're right, then you'll agree it would be damn useful to have somebody on the inside, keeping an eye on things, so to speak."

Evan gave a short, hard laugh. "Bennington would never let the likes of me get near anything that counted."

"Maybe not at first," Carmody said. "But that doesn't mean you can't convince him to make an exception where you're concerned." He grinned and hoisted his mug once more. "Use your imagination, boyo. That's what the good Lord gave it to you for."

Evan pondered that a short time later after he had parted from Carmody and returned to his lodgings. He had a room to himself in a run-down building in the North End. He paid twenty dollars a month for the privilege of living there, an exorbitant sum compared to what it would have cost him to share a room, as most single men did.

The accommodations were hardly luxurious, but the privacy alone made them worth the cost. For the first time in his life, he had a place to himself. Within its four walls, cracked and peeling as they were, his spirit could expand.

He lay on the narrow iron bedstead for a while, staring up at the ceiling and considering what Carmody had said. After a time, he stopped thinking of the Irishman and thought instead of Drake Bennington.

He looked like what Carmody had called him—tough. There was nothing soft about the man, not in his body or his mind. Evan respected that, though at the same time he knew enough to be wary of it.

The other men of Bennington's class whom he had seen were different. There was a meanness about them and an arrogance that spoke clearly of both their pretensions and their fears.

They believed themselves superior to other men, but they were also afraid that their superiority was self-imposed, not natural, and that one day it would be overthrown.

To Evan's way of thinking, they were right to be afraid. Drake Bennington, however, had no such fear. That made him both stronger and more dangerous than the others.

Evan's wide brow was knitted in a frown as he angled his long body off the bed and went over to the rickety bureau. There were a chipped china bowl and pitcher on top of it. The water in the bowl was very cold, but he washed his face and hands in it vigorously.

After he had dried himself, he took his only suit off the wall peg where it had been hanging, laid it on the bed and stripped. He dressed slowly, preoccupied with his thoughts.

When he was ready, he left the room, pocketing the key, and made his way down the narrow flight of stairs to the street. A gaggle of grimy children was playing out in front.

They turned to look at him as he passed by, but made no attempt to get him to part with a few pennies, as they usually did. Instead they stood staring at the tall man in the roughly made suit as he strode purposefully away.

Drake Bennington's office was located on the corner of State and Congress streets, in the heart of the city's financial district. Evan approached the marble-fronted building warily, conscious of feeling out of place.

Around him the narrow sidewalks were filled with men in dark suits hurrying back and forth from one building to another, carrying packages that could contain anything from a simple note to important documents and large amounts of cash.

Other men dressed with equal formality but greater elegance alighted from carriages at the curbs, perhaps pausing to chat with a colleague before going on about their business.

Nowhere within Evan's view was there a woman to be seen. He knew that they could be found a short distance away, where the more luxurious shops were located, but here in the heart of the business center, men reigned.

In a few hours, when the businesses closed, females would filter in, but only to scrub the floors and empty the wastebaskets. They would be gone well before daylight and the start of the next business day.

Before then, he intended to see Drake Bennington and discover for himself what the man had in mind for him to do. Taking a deep breath, he entered the building whose address was on the card Bennington had given him. Barely had he gotten inside the front door before a uniformed guard approached him.

"May I be of assistance...sir?" The marked delay in applying that courtesy revealed the guard's suspicions as clearly as the assessing glance he gave Evan.

The man's disdain angered Evan, but he was careful not to show it. Instead he smiled lightly and said, "I'm here to see Mr. Bennington."

The guard's eyebrows rose. "I suppose you'll tell me he's expecting you?"

"Well, now, as to that, I can't say, but I do know that he told me to come by, so here I am."

Evan reached into his pocket and produced the card Drake had given him. "This is the place, isn't it?"

The guard scrutinized the card, taking particular note of the scrawled initials D.B. in the upper right-hand corner. His manner underwent a change. When he handed the card back to Evan, his face was carefully blank.

"Mr. Bennington is on the second floor. You can use the stairs over there."

Evan nodded once at the man. He crossed the marble lobby, climbed the stairs and looked up and down the hallway. At the far end was an open set of double doors. Beyond them was an elegant furnished reception room, where a young man sat at a leather-topped desk. He looked up as Evan entered.

"I see," he murmured as he glanced at the card. Slowly he stood, looking at Evan cautiously. "Won't you have a seat, Mr...?"

"O'Connell," Evan said. He made himself comfortable in an overstuffed chair and relaxed marginally. The magic card had gotten him this far. He was content for the moment to see what else it could do.

An older man appeared at the door between the reception room and the inner offices. He was over fifty, slightly stooped, with a kindly, intelligent face.

"Mr. O'Connell," he said, "I'm Jacob Stein, Mr. Bennington's assistant. He is in a rather important meeting at the moment, but he should be free in about a quarter of an hour. In the meantime, if you would come with me..."

Evan nodded and stood up. He studied Jacob Stein surreptitiously as the older man led him inside. Beyond the reception area was a large open space crowded with rolltop desks at which several dozen young men worked, many with their sleeves rolled up and eyeshades in place. A Teletype clattered away in the background. There were telephones on several of the desks.

Aside from Carmody, who kept one in his office as much for show as for anything else, Evan had never known anyone who owned one of the newfangled devices before. He glanced at one suspiciously as it gave a shrill ring.

"Through here, Mr. O'Connell," Jacob Stein said. He stood aside to admit him to an inner office. The noise outside dimmed as soon as the heavy mahogany door was closed.

"If you would make yourself comfortable..." He gestured to a horsehair sofa set against one wall.

Evan sat down again. The older man went over to a large desk and took his own seat. He quietly and efficiently began reading through a stack of papers, making occasional notes in the margins as he did so.

Evan glanced at him, trying to assimilate the fact that Drake Bennington's top assistant was a Jew. He had no particular feelings about that one way or the other, except to know that it was highly unusual.

If prejudice against the Irish was bad, the Jews faced even worse. At the very least, Jacob Stein might have felt compelled to change his name. Instead he had it engraved on a brass plaque on top of his desk. Evan remembered what Carmody had said about Bennington not being one to waste talent. He decided that Carmody had been right.

A door near Jacob Stein's desk opened suddenly and a group of men emerged, talking quietly among themselves. One or two of them glanced in Evan's direction with some curiosity, but they continued on their way without pause. Several spoke to Jacob, murmuring urgently and nodding when he did.

When they were gone, Jacob smiled. "Just another moment, Mr. O'Connell." He went into the inner office; true to his word, he emerged almost at once. "Mr. Bennington will see you now."

Evan stood up, took a deep breath and followed him. Drake Bennington was seated behind a desk of gleaming black wood incised in the Chinese style. On the other side of the room there was a large round table surrounded by chairs that had been pushed back.

Across from it was a couch, and above it, directly in the line of sight from the desk, hung the portrait of a beautiful woman with blond hair and dancing gray eyes. She had been painted in an evening gown; diamonds hung at her throat and were sprinkled through her upswept hair. She was staring directly out of the picture, her expression alive with happiness.

It took Evan a moment to realize who she must be. For an instant he had thought that he was looking at the girl he had helped in Carmody's—Bennington's daughter. But the features were not the same, although the aura of

feminine beauty and strength certainly was. This must be
Catherine Bennington's mother.

With an effort he turned away and gave his attention
to the man he had come to see.

Drake Bennington had risen from behind the desk.
Evan had not expected any such courtesy. He responded
to it instinctively by stepping forward and offering his
hand. "I hope I haven't come at a bad time, Mr. Bennington?"

"Not at all," Drake assured him as they shook hands.
His gaze was steady and direct as he studied Evan.

He was not surprised to see the Irishman; on the contrary, he had fully expected him to come. What pleased
him was the speed with which Evan had responded. That
suggested to Drake that he was ambitious and confident, two traits he could make use of.

"Please sit down, Mr. O'Connell," he said, joining
him on the couch. He reached into his breast pocket and
withdrew a flat silver case. "Do you smoke?"

"I wouldn't mind," Evan said. He helped himself to
one of Drake's thin Cuban cigars. They went through the
ritual of lighting up and taking the first few satisfying
puffs in silence.

Only then did Drake say, "I gather you're interested in
my offer of a job."

"I am," Evan confirmed. "Though I need to know
what you have in mind."

Drake looked at him thoughtfully for a moment
through a haze of cigar smoke. Quietly he said, "Rather
than my suggesting something to you, suppose you tell
me what you're interested in doing?"

Evan was caught off guard. He couldn't remember
anyone asking his preference before about anything, unless he counted the girls at Molly Burke's.

Especially when it came to work, he'd never thought about what he did or did not want to do. He simply took whatever was available. But with Drake he suddenly had a chance to improve on that.

After the barest hesitation, he did so. "I'm interested in making money, Mr. Bennington. Preferably a significant amount of it."

Drake looked surprised for a moment, then laughed. "A worthy enough ambition, Mr. O'Connell. One a great many people share, though few state it as frankly. All right, you want to make money. In that case, I think we can be of use to each other."

He propped a foot on the opposite knee and went on. "You may know that I own a shipping line. We move quite a bit of cargo in and out of Boston Harbor. There's always been something of a problem with pilferage, but that's to be expected, and I don't really mind so long as it doesn't get out of hand. The problem is that it's done exactly that. For the last six months I've been losing an intolerable amount. Goods are disappearing right out of the warehouses and off the docks. So far, I haven't been able to learn who's responsible."

"What have you done to find out?" Evan asked quietly.

"I sent in two men, first one of my own, then one from Pinkerton's. The man who worked for me has disappeared. Perhaps he ran, perhaps he didn't. The Pinkerton's man was waylaid in a dark alley and badly beaten. He's still in the hospital, though he's expected to recover. And no," he continued before Evan could ask, "He didn't get a look at his assailants. They were masked."

"I see..." Evan said slowly. "So you want to try again?"

Drake nodded. "That's right. If you're interested, I can get you a job working undercover. See what you can find out and report back to me."

Evan puffed thoughtfully on his cigar for a moment. "And if I do, what's in it for me?"

"I've been losing an average of five thousand dollars a month, Mr. O'Connell. You bring me the name of the person responsible and that's what I'll pay you. Five thousand dollars."

Evan was hard-pressed not to let his mouth drop open. Five thousand dollars was an enormous sum. A family could live on it comfortably for a year or more.

He had never in his life seen so much money, far less possessed it. Hunger gnawed at him, but he fought it back as he looked at Drake directly.

"Let me be sure that I understand you, Mr. Bennington. I bring you the name—nothing more—and the money is mine?"

"That's correct."

"It's a great deal of money."

"It's a very difficult and dangerous job," Drake countered.

Evan shifted slightly on the couch. He stared at the glowing tip of his cigar. Softly he said, "I wouldn't want you thinking you'd be getting more than you would. I'll find your thief for you, all right, but I won't kill him." With a slight smile he added, "Much as I want money, there are limits to what I'll do for it."

"I'm glad to hear that," Drake said calmly. "Paid assassins come cheap, Mr. O'Connell. If I want somebody killed, I can get it done for a hundred dollars. There are men who will kill their mothers for that."

"True enough, Mr. Bennington," Evan murmured. "But one hundred or five thousand, it makes no difference to me. Just so long as you understand that."

"I do," Drake said. "I take it you're accepting the job?" When Evan nodded, he said, "Then I'll get Jacob busy arranging your cover and a means for us to stay in contact."

"No," Evan said, shaking his head. "I've nothing against your Mr. Stein. So far as I know, he's as honest as the day is long. But the fewer people who know about something like this, the better. I'll get my own job on the docks. You'll hear from me when I have results. Until then, there's nothing to be said."

Drake nodded slowly. He stood up as Evan did so and went over to his desk. When he returned, he held out a number of bills in large denominations. "Consider this an advance, Mr. O'Connell, the balance to be paid upon successful completion of the job."

Evan took the money and slipped it into his pocket without counting it. He nodded curtly to Drake. "I'll be in touch, Mr. Bennington."

He walked quickly through the outer office, past the young men at their desks and out through the reception room. Not until he was back on the street did he pause to let his satisfaction flow through him. He had a job with Drake Bennington. Moreover, a job with possibilities.

He might be inexperienced in the ways of big business, but he was certain that no one like him could get to the top by any ordinary means. But that didn't mean that a man with intelligence and determination couldn't rise as high as his ambition would take him—provided he was willing to take some risks along the way.

He would be risking his life. Briefly that thought darkened his mood. He shrugged it off, reflecting that he was hardly a stranger to such peril. His life had certainly been in jeopardy often enough in Ireland, where every day could be a gamble. At least this time it would be by his own choosing and for his own benefit.

He put his hands in his pockets, feeling the crisp bills, and smiled. A new world was opening up for him. All he had to do was live long enough to enjoy it.

He was starting down the street, back in the direction from which he had come, when a carriage rolled to a stop in front of the building he had just left. Through the window he caught sight of an oval face framed by soft golden hair and the hood of a fur evening cape.

Catherine stared back at him, her eyes wide with surprise. Instinctively Evan took a step toward her, only to catch himself and stop where he was. He saw her full lips part slightly as she continued to gaze at him and felt his own body stir in response.

She was even more beautiful than he had allowed himself to remember. There was a feminine quality about her that went beyond the strictures of the time or place. She was everything he had ever imagined in a woman, and more that he hadn't even dreamed of.

She was also absolutely forbidden to him. He hardly needed to know Drake Bennington well to be aware of how the other man would react if he had even a hint that Evan was attracted to his daughter, much less that she returned his interest.

Evan would be lucky to suffer only an abrupt end to all his aspirations. He might conceivably find himself a good deal worse off, depending on exactly what form Drake's wrath took.

Oh, no, my girl, he thought as he deliberately turned away. Lovely you are, and under different circumstances... But I've a life to make and you've no place in it. I had my fill of hopeless dreams in Ireland. I'm not about to go chasing after one here.

He quickened his stride, mindful of the gathering winter darkness and the cold that bit through his suit. He wanted a meal and a drink. And he wanted to talk to Carmody. He needed the other man's advice before he pursued the business for Drake.

There was a great deal he had to think about. He had no time and no energy to give to the contemplation of Miss Catherine Bennington, lovely though she might be.

Evan grinned wryly to himself. He was also one bloody great liar if he thought he could keep her out of his mind. She was as firmly lodged there as he would like to be within her body.

Which was a damn crude thing to think about such an innocent young lady. But then, he was a crude man, made so by the rough-and-tumble of his life.

She would marry a gentleman, one of the fine toffs he saw strolling about the town. Perhaps even one of those who had stumbled into Carmody's with her.

The thought of her with such a man, with any man other than himself, vexed him so that he clenched his fists in his pockets. The money crinkled in his grip.

He held it tightly, telling himself that it was all that mattered. Knowing all the while that he was wrong.

"YOU LOOK ABSOLUTELY beautiful, my dear," Elizabeth said. She stood back to get a better view of her daughter, who was gazing into the full-length mirror. Their eyes met in the glass. Elizabeth's were full of admiration and love. Catherine's were wary.

"I suppose I really have to go through with this," she said, smiling ruefully.

Her mother laughed. "Only if you want to avoid disappointing a hundred or so people who will be showing up downstairs."

"Heaven forbid," Catherine said. She glanced at herself again in the mirror, thinking that the girl before her looked like a stranger.

Certainly she herself had never looked so beautiful and elegant, not to mention so grown-up. But then, she had never before been eighteen and about to be presented to society.

Her gown was white, as tradition required. It was by Worth, her first such creation by that august designer. She was more tightly laced than usual; her waist appeared infinitesimal, emphasizing her breasts and hips. The creation of white batiste and Valenciennes lace was flounced and pleated in graceful folds that ended in an abbreviated train. It was worn low on the shoulder, revealing a tantalizing expanse of alabaster skin.

Her golden hair was swept up in an elaborate French twist. Around her slender throat she wore a collar of pearls secured with diamond clasps.

There was the lightest dusting of cornstarch powder on her nose and brow, but no other makeup. The high color of her cheeks was purely natural, as were the rosy fullness of her mouth and the thick, bristly spikes of her dark lashes.

"I guess I'm as ready as I'll ever be," she murmured.

"Come along then, dear," Elizabeth said with a smile. She blinked back the tears that had briefly formed as she gazed at her daughter, looking suddenly so much a woman.

Pride and love overflowed in her. She exchanged a quick glance with her maid, Tilly, who had been with her since Elizabeth was a young bride and mother. Tilly smiled wistfully as she opened the door for them.

"Have a wonderful time, Miss Catherine," she said. "This is a night to remember forever."

Catherine laughed a bit nervously. She gathered up her courage along with her skirts and followed her mother.

Drake was waiting for them at the foot of the stairs. His expression was solemn as he watched his wife and daughter descend. Not for a moment did his gaze waver from them. When they reached the bottom, he put an arm around Elizabeth and kissed her gently.

"You look beautiful, sweetheart. As lovely as I've ever seen you."

She flushed at his praise. Catherine watched her parents with gentle amusement mixed with wistfulness. She adored them both, but the evidence of their love for each other was an ever-present reminder that her own future was as yet unformed.

Perhaps, she thought as she gazed at them, she would meet the man of her dreams that very night. Her mouth curved up at the thought. Unlike most girls her age, she wasn't given to such romantic fantasies.

There was a broad, practical streak in her, possibly the legacy of her Yankee grandmother, who as a young woman had kept a plantation running in the midst of the Civil War. Yet Sarah Calvert was no more a stranger to love than her daughter, Elizabeth. Catherine had two indomitable women to look to as examples she could only hope to equal.

Her thoughts broke off as Drake put his hands on her shoulders and smiled. Softly he said, "I'm very proud of you, Catherine. When you were a tiny girl, your mother and I had great hopes for you. I think I can safely say that you have more than fulfilled them."

Catherine swallowed hard. His wholehearted love and approval touched her deeply, all the more so because she knew that her mother felt the same way.

She was among the fortunate ones, from every possible perspective, and she was deeply grateful for it, even if she did sometimes feel a tiny shiver of almost superstitious fear as she wondered what the price of such blessings would turn out to be.

"You aren't nervous, are you, Cat?" her twin asked. Jimmy had joined them at the foot of the stairs, looking very handsome in his evening clothes. When she said as much, he flushed.

"Forget about me. This is your night."

"It doesn't seem quite fair that I should have a coming out, but not you," she said with a laugh as she took his arm. They moved into the parlor, where they would await the first of their guests. Smithers stood ready with a silver tray upon which rested four tulip-shaped glasses filled with pale gold champagne.

Drake took one of them and handed it to Cat. He gave another to Elizabeth and the third to Jimmy before taking the last for himself. As he raised his glass, he said, "To beginnings. This is a special one for Cat, but I hope she'll know many more, all of them as happy."

They drank, Catherine wrinkling her nose slightly at the bubbles. She had tasted wine before, including champagne, but the sensation was still unsettling. She felt torn between pride at her newly acknowledged maturity and doubt about her ability to live up to it.

There was very little time to dwell on that. They had barely finished their champagne before the first carriages began to roll up in front of the house.

Catherine stood with her parents and brother in the entry hall to receive each guest. She smiled and nodded, exchanging polite chitchat, thanking each person for coming until her face was stiff and aching.

By the time she at last entered the ballroom on her father's arm, with Jimmy escorting her mother, she was already weary. She longed to escape to the tranquillity of her room but knew that she could not.

Her lassitude alarmed her, since it was far from characteristic. But the significance of the occasion weighed on her, damping her normal enthusiasm and making everything she did an effort.

It had been her prerogative to choose the music for the first dance. She had selected a Strauss waltz that she particularly loved. When her father led her out to the empty dance floor, her spirits lifted.

She looked around at the smiling faces of the elegantly dressed men and women and told herself she was a fool to be anxious. This was her world, where she belonged, among people who knew and liked her.

As her father had said, this was a beginning for her. If she had any sense at all, she would make the most of it.

After she and Drake had danced alone for a few minutes, Jimmy led Elizabeth out. Soon they were joined by other couples as the party got under way.

Catherine shortly forgot her self-consciousness and gave herself up to the pleasure of the evening. She chatted with the matrons who sat on gilt chairs along the edge of the ballroom, thanking them for their compliments without particularly noticing the watchful looks in their eyes.

Several girls her own age or slightly older came up to congratulate her. She thanked them, too, danced with their brothers and had another glass of champagne. By the time dinner was served, she could honestly say that her earlier hesitation was gone. She was having a thoroughly good time.

Until she discovered that Charles van Rhys had somehow contrived to be seated next to her. Her mother had laid out the seating chart in consultation with Catherine. So far as she could recall, a male cousin was supposed to be at her right.

"I couldn't resist," Charles murmured when he saw her surprise. "Say you don't mind."

Actually Catherine did, but politeness prevented her from making an issue of it. Instead she smiled coolly. "It makes no different to me where you sit, Charles. None at all."

His long, angular face darkened. They had seen each other on several occasions since the incident at Carmody's, but Catherine had kept her distance from him.

She was certain he had been responsible for precipitating the violence that erupted that night. He was arrogant and spoiled, with a volatile temper that made him dangerous. He was also very stubborn.

"You shouldn't be like this, Catherine," he said quietly when they were seated. As he leaned closer to her, he smiled. To all appearances they were simply a young couple having a pleasant chat. "There could be something very important between us. You know that."

His audacity shocked her. Gentlemen simply did not make such statements, at least not to ladies. But Charles didn't seem to care about such proprieties. He regarded her coolly, as though challenging her to disagree.

"I have no idea what you mean," she said and looked away.

He laughed—a low, odd sound that sent a shiver down her back. There was a light in his eyes that she had never seen before and did not like.

"I think you do and just don't want to admit it. But that's all right. You're entitled to all the steps in the game. I'm willing to be patient . . . up to a point."

"What you are is presumptuous," she muttered under her breath. The waiters were beginning to circulate with the first course. All around her the guests were talking and laughing.

Two long tables had been fitted together and covered with snowy linens, then set with the finest crystal, china and silver. Behind every two chairs stood a liveried waiter who anticipated the guests' needs before they even became aware of them.

A string quartet played off to one side. The tall French doors were thrown open to admit the scents from the garden. Honeysuckle and roses mingled with the perfume of the hothouse flowers strewn in profusion around the room.

At one end of the table Drake was deep in conversation with a banker friend. At the other, Elizabeth was chatting with a gentleman who had recently returned from the Orient.

Jimmy sat across the table and down from Elizabeth. She could see him laughing with a very pretty brunette who was clearly much taken by him. Their eyes met briefly over the girl's head, and Jimmy grinned.

Catherine suppressed a sigh. It would look very odd if she refused to talk with Charles, yet she briefly considered the alternatives. The table was too wide to talk across comfortably, and the elderly gentleman on her other side was nearly deaf.

That left Charles, who was well aware of her predicament. He looked at her smugly when she turned back to him.

"Aren't we having lovely weather?" she asked, deliberately picking the most boring and impersonal topic she could think of.

He stared at her a moment, then laughed loudly enough to attract a few startled glances.

"I'm going to miss you when I'm back at Harvard, Catherine." Significantly he added, "But there are breaks often enough. We'll be seeing each other."

"Don't count on that too much," she advised him coolly.

He put down his fork and stared at her. "What do you mean?"

"It's obvious, isn't it? After all, the whole point of this is to get me married off."

She didn't for a moment believe that; her parents had made it clear that, far from being anxious for her to leave the nest, they expected her to give very thorough and prudent consideration to any such decision. But it served her purpose to let Charles think otherwise.

"I might choose someone who isn't from Boston," she added, as though the idea gave her no particular concern.

"Don't." He picked up his wineglass and drained it in a single swallow. "That would be a mistake."

"Really, Charles," Catherine said as lightly as she could manage, "you do go beyond anything. I'll marry whom I please, when I please. You have nothing to say about it."

"Perhaps not, but do you really imagine that you have such freedom? Your father will never permit you to marry anyone who isn't suitable."

"He happens to be very broad-minded."

He laughed again, derisively. "Don't fool yourself. When it comes to selecting a husband for you, he won't consider anyone who isn't part of our own little set. Besides the fact that he wouldn't trust anyone else, he most certainly won't want you to go very far from home."

"My mother moved to an entirely different part of the country when she married," Catherine reminded him. "She was born and raised in Virginia, yet she's lived here for almost twenty years. Perfectly happily, I might add."

"Not at first. But that's beside the point. The fact still remains that your parents will never allow you to—"

"What do you mean, not at first?" Catherine asked. It wasn't like her to interrupt, but she was so struck by his comment that she couldn't resist. "My parents have always been extremely happy together. Theirs was a true love match."

He looked at her from beneath half-lowered lids. "If you are truly that innocent, Catherine, then far be it from me to disabuse you."

She sucked in her breath, wanting to question him further, but too proud to do so. "I think it's just as well that you're going back to school in a few days, Charles. Your company is wearing very thin."

He flushed again and was clearly annoyed, but the rest of the dinner passed without further incident.

At the meal's conclusion, the waiters wheeled in a large cake decorated with curlicues and roses. As the musicians struck up a lively tune, Jimmy rose and came around the table to where Catherine was sitting. He took her hand and led her into the center of the room, where the cake waited.

With a teasing grin, he said, "Ladies and gentlemen, if I might have your attention for a moment... Our father would normally perform this part of the evening's celebration, but I asked him to accommodate me, and he very kindly agreed. Eighteen years ago tonight, my sister and I arrived in the world. Ever since then, she has been the bane of my existence. We had our first fights in our cribs, and we haven't stopped since. But tonight—" He turned to look at Catherine, his eyes suddenly very tender. "Tonight I see her in a new light. My sister has grown into a beautiful woman, and I am very proud of her."

Catherine felt a sudden rush of tears. As much to conceal them as anything else, she held out her arms to Jimmy. He embraced her tenderly as the guests laughed and applauded.

Over Jimmy's shoulder, she caught a glimpse of her father and mother. They had gone to stand together, their arms around each other, their eyes full of love.

Sometime later, after the cake had been cut and more champagne consumed, the dancing began again. Charles had the sense not to ask Catherine to dance, though she could see that he was tempted. There was no opportunity for him, however, since she was in constant demand.

She was just beginning to think that she had never danced so much in her life, and probably never would again, when her gaze happened to wander to the ballroom entrance.

Evan O'Connell was standing there. He was dressed in a dark suit of good cut that in no way concealed the breadth of his shoulders and chest. His feet were planted slightly apart, his long legs braced, as he scanned the assembled guests. His firm mouth quirked slightly, as though he found the scene amusing.

Cat's breath caught in her throat. She had seen him from time to time since he had gone to work for her father, but those occasions had been fleeting, and she had done her best not to let them affect her. Now, as she stared at him, she became aware of the rush of heat through her body and the sudden rapid beating of her heart.

"Is something wrong?" the young man she had been dancing with asked. The music had just stopped, and couples were drifting back to the refreshment table.

"No, of course not," she assured him with a brilliant smile. "But if you would excuse me a moment, I see someone I really should speak with."

She left him before he could reply and boldly made her way toward Evan. In the back of her mind, she knew she was being foolish.

Proper young ladies did not go anywhere near men like Evan O'Connell. He was a roughneck, a rebel, and just plain trouble. That her father found him useful was all well and good, but that most certainly did not mean that she should pay him the slightest mind.

Except that she couldn't resist the compulsion that drew her to him. Before she could even try, she found herself standing in front of Evan, smiling far more confidently than she felt.

"Why, Mr. O'Connell, what a surprise! I had no idea you were coming to my party."

His crystalline blue eyes gleamed mockingly. "Why, Miss Bennington, I had no idea you were having a birthday. May I offer my congratulations?"

Stung by his mockery, she shrugged. "If you must. What brings you here, anyway?"

The look he gave her suggested strongly that he didn't think it any of her business. Nonetheless he said, "I'm here to see your father. My apologies for intruding on so grand an event, but I need a word with him."

He looked over her head, scanning the ballroom for some sign of Drake. He could not have made it clearer that she was of no interest to him.

"I believe my parents are in the garden," she said quietly, wishing that she could fade back into the crowd of guests and not go anywhere near him again.

Only a few minutes in his company were enough to remind her that the strange yearnings he set off in her could not have been more misplaced. She was a fool to forget the gulf between them, even briefly.

"Will they be returning soon?" he asked.

"I imagine so." As coolly as she could manage, she said, "In the meantime, please make yourself comfortable." When he looked at her, surprised, she added, "I'm sure Father would want you to."

Evan had no such confidence. He took it for granted that there was a gap between himself and Drake Bennington that his employer would not be pleased to have him cross. Still, a mutinous spark ran through him, prompting him to act with uncharacteristic impulsiveness.

"Thank you," he said with a slight bow. "I believe I will join the fun."

Catherine nodded. She stood for a moment, half hoping that he would ask her to dance, half afraid of his doing so. When he did not, she told herself she was glad.

Charles saw her and hurried to her side, taking advantage of her preoccupation. She hardly noticed as they began to dance, so absorbed was she with the tall, bronze-faced man who glanced her way from time to time and frowned.

WHEN DRAKE RETURNED from the garden he was startled to find Evan O'Connell lounging near the refreshment table, having a drink and watching the party. Despite his relatively informal dress, which made him stick out among the elegantly clad guests, he looked perfectly at ease. Drake was amused by that, even though he had no intention of inviting Evan to linger.

"Will you excuse me a moment, my dear?" he asked Elizabeth. "There seems to be a business matter that needs taking care of."

"Tonight?" Usually Drake was scrupulous about keeping business and family separate. If he was allowing anything to intrude on Cat's party, it must be very important. "Is there a problem?"

"No, of course not," he assured her. "This won't take very long."

She watched as he crossed the room to speak with a tall, black-haired man. Elizabeth had seen the man before—once when she dropped by to pick Drake up at his office when they were going out to dinner, and again when they had passed him on the street, and he and Drake had exchanged greetings.

She assumed he was simply another of her husband's employees, though she had the niggling feeling that he couldn't be written off so easily. There was something about him—a sense of uncanny strength and determination, perhaps—that set him apart from ordinary men.

With a shrug she turned away and went to join a group of guests. Whatever had brought the man to their door, Drake would undoubtedly deal with it.

No one would ever accuse Drake of being an open book. He was said to confide in his wife, though no one knew that for sure, since she had never confirmed it. But apart from her, he kept his thoughts strictly to himself.

"Let's step into the library," Drake said, congenially enough. He made no comment about Evan's sudden appearance in the midst of the party, but merely led the way across the marble entry hall to his private sanctum. Once there, he shut the door and gestured to the chesterfield couch along one wall.

Drake opened a silver box on the desk and helped himself to a cigar, but did not suggest that Evan join him. That was the only reminder he offered that the younger man should not make himself too much at home in the Bennington residence.

In the months that Evan had been in his employ, Drake had come to genuinely like and respect the Irishman. He had no illusions about Evan's ambitions, but he also found nothing wrong with them.

Since cracking the pilferage ring on the docks, Evan had undertaken a number of other sensitive assignments for him, all successfully. He had been engaged in one such while away from Boston.

"Roscoe is definitely doctoring his reports," Evan said. "He doesn't want to discourage you completely, because that would cause you to withdraw your financial support. But he also doesn't want you to know that the prospect of finding oil in Texas is actually very high."

"That's not the impression I've had from him," Drake said quietly. "He's been presenting it as possible but dubious."

"While he's telling you that, he's running around on his own buying up all the land he can get his hands on. Moreover he isn't even being very discreet about it. He's boasted that he's getting rich as your surveyor because you're not smart enough to catch on to what he's doing."

Rather than being offended by this last remark, Drake merely laughed. "Too bad for Roscoe that he's wrong."

Evan nodded, his eyes on the other man. "What do you want me to do?"

Drake shrugged, as though the answer should be self-evident. "Nothing. I'll telegraph Roscoe and tell him I want to see him here in Boston. I'll suggest that I'm considering increasing my investment significantly and want his advice. He's greedy enough to go for that. Once he's here, he'll be given the opportunity to sign over the land he's bought to me. Then he'll be free to find some other means of employment."

Evan didn't ask what would happen if Roscoe refused. The man wouldn't. After the initial shock of being caught wore off, he would be glad enough to escape with only the loss of his illicitly gotten gains.

Drake wouldn't even have to suggest that some dire fate would await him unless he complied. Roscoe would simply assume that was the case and behave accordingly.

It had been the same with Latimer, the dock foreman behind the pilferage. When Evan brought his name to Drake, he had briefly wondered if he was sending the man to his death.

Only the fact that he owed nothing whatsoever to Latimer, who delighted in mistreating the men who worked for him, had stopped him. That and the five thousand dollars.

Latimer had been gone from the docks the day after Evan spoke to Drake. In the harborside bars, it was whispered that he had been murdered, his body taken out to sea and dumped. But there were also rumors that he had developed a sudden desire to travel and had last been seen heading west, toward California.

Evan suspected that the latter was true. Drake didn't much care what happened to those who crossed him, as long as they never did so again.

"You did a good job in Texas," Drake said. He went over to the safe that stood in one corner of the room, behind a Chinese lacquered screen, and withdrew an envelope, which he handed to Evan. "I'll have something else for you shortly."

Evan nodded. He slipped the envelope into his breast pocket. Inside, he knew there would be several thousand dollars, his agreed-upon fee for the Texas job.

Tomorrow he would visit the bank where he had opened an account. It already held a sizeable amount, to which he would be adding. There was a property on Prince Street he was thinking of buying, and another closer to the river. Carmody was advising him. Soon he would be making his first investments.

"I'll be going then, sir," He turned to leave.

Drake followed him to the library door. In the entry hall, he said, "Today is my children's birthday. We had a family party for the two of them, but this is Catherine's formal debut."

He gave a short laugh. "The young men are flocking around her like the proverbial bees to honey. But she has a good head on her shoulders. I don't worry about her doing anything foolish."

"I'm sure she won't, sir," Evan said. He wondered why his employer saw fit to mention his family to him at all, but concluded that Drake was merely in an expansive mood. He had every right to be.

"If there's nothing else..." He was anxious to be gone. After an absence of several weeks, a great many matters demanded his attention. Matters Drake Bennington knew nothing at all about.

But most urgently, he felt the need to put distance between himself and Catherine Bennington. She most certainly did not figure in his careful calculations. On the contrary, she was a liability he could not afford.

"Go on, then," Drake said with a smile. "But keep in touch. As I said, there will be something soon."

Evan nodded and took his leave. He turned back for a moment after the butler closed the door, hearing the music coming from the ballroom and picturing in his mind's eye the beautiful girl he had encountered there.

With a muffled exclamation of annoyance, he started briskly down the street. He was ten kinds of fool to be thinking of her. Carmody would be the first to tell him so.

BUT CARMODY HAD other things on his mind, none of which had anything to do with Miss Catherine Bennington.

"Good thing you're back," he said when Evan walked into the small office at the rear of the grocery store that Carmody had owned and operated for some three decades. It was where he had gotten his start and where he preferred to stay, keeping in touch with his roots.

Throughout the day, a steady stream of people flowed into and out of the back room. Widows came to ask for help feeding their children; men with promising sons came seeking entry into the colleges that were the surest route out of the North End; those in need of housing came, as did the sick, the old, and those straight off the boat, desperate for a toehold in their new land.

For those who couldn't come to Carmody themselves, there were the ward heelers who fanned out through the neighborhood, discovering who needed what and seeing that it was provided.

The system was straightforward and simple—assistance in return for votes. Through it men like Carmody had risen to great power, though the wisest of them were careful never to flaunt it.

With his rolled-up sleeves, his rumpled hair and his bloodshot eyes, Carmody looked like the hardworking grocer he had been for the better part of his adult life. Now he sighed as he pulled off the eyeshade he had been wearing to study his accounts and gestured to a bottle of Scotch on a nearby shelf.

"Pour us both a wee drop, will you? Then have a seat. We've some talking to do."

Evan did as he was told, though he made Carmody's "wee drop" a good deal more generous than his own. The long trip from Texas had left him tired. He wanted a hot bath and a decent night's sleep, but they would come soon enough.

Carmody took a long swallow of his drink, closing his eyes as he did so to better savor the smoky taste. He smacked his lips appreciatively as he put his glass down.

"There now, that's better." He sat back in his chair and studied Evan benignly. "You're looking good, boyo. I'd say those duds you're wearing strike just the right note—elegant, expensive, but understated. You keep dressing like that and the Brahmans will start thinking you're one of their own."

Evan laughed. "Not much danger of that. I've only to open my mouth to tell them I didn't go to Hah-vahd." He deliberately exaggerated the broad New England accent, so at odds with his own far softer Gaelic inflection.

Carmody grinned. He finished his drink and wiped his mouth with the back of his hand before getting down to business.

"All right, then. Remember that property you were interested in down by the river?"

Evan nodded. "Don't tell me somebody's bought it?"

"Of course not. I told you I'd keep an eye on it for you, didn't I? But somebody else is interested, all right. An outfit calling itself the Porcellian Consortium has been showing signs of making an offer. And not only for the piece you want; for the whole stretch of the waterfront along there."

Evan whistled softly. "Then they must be talking about a great deal of money. Who are they, anyway?"

"I thought you might want to know that, so I've been asking around. Seems like behind that fine-sounding name there's a bunch of boys from the Beacon Hill families and the Commonwealth Avenue crowd. A half dozen or so have set themselves up in the investment business, naming it for some club at Harvard most of them belong to. Sort of a trial run, I suppose, for when they come into their own."

"Do you have any names?" Evan asked.

Carmody shuffled a pile of papers on his desk. He pulled one out of a precariously balanced stack and screwed up his eyes to look at it. "There's a Lodge, a Cabot, a van Rhys, three others. Here, see for yourself."

He passed the list to Evan, who studied it carefully. His face was thoughtful as he returned the list to Carmody. "Are they prepared to move soon?"

"Within a week or so, I'd say. And remember, they're looking to buy the entire property. That's an offer that will be hard to turn down."

"Not if I make a better one first. Do you know what they're planning to pay?"

Carmody named a figure that made Evan flinch. "Sweet Lord, where am I going to get that kind of money, plus more to top it?"

Substantial though his bank account had become, it was nowhere equal to the amount he needed. For a brief moment, he saw his hopes fading, but determination stiffened his resolve.

"You won't need to top it," Carmody said. "Not if you get there first."

Evan shook his head. "Don't kid yourself. If it comes to a choice between selling to me and selling to a bunch of fine toffs, you know who'll win. Unless I can offer more than they can. Right now, I can't even offer as much."

Carmody sighed. He rubbed his red-rimmed eyes and stared up at the ceiling, seeking inspiration that was not there. "I'm stretched thin right now meself, laddy, or I'd help you out. Still, it'll be a bloody shame if you miss this chance. There won't be another stretch of property like that coming up for sale in many a year."

"I have to get it," Evan said grimly. "Somehow, I've got to find a way."

The older man hesitated a moment, then said, "There's always Bennington."

Evan's thick straight brows rose. "Are you suggesting I ask him to come in with me as a partner?"

"Why not? He can certainly afford it."

For a moment, Evan was tempted. It would certainly be the solution to his problem. But after brief reflection, he shook his head.

"Bennington is accustomed to being in complete control. When he is partner on a deal, he always holds the majority interest, and that's exactly what *I* want. Besides," he added, "I'd just as soon not have him knowing what I'm up to."

"You really think you can keep it from him?" Carmody asked.

"Not forever, certainly. But the longer he doesn't know, the better. Working for him gives me access to information that's very helpful in deciding on investments. I want to hold on to that advantage as long as possible."

"It's your decision," Carmody said with a shrug. "I'm just going to say again that it will be a shame if you lose out."

Evan agreed with him, but at the moment he had no idea how to prevent it. He sat with Carmody a while longer, talking of happenings in the ward. There was an election coming up later in the year for the Common Council. It was not precisely a foregone conclusion who would win, but some very educated guesses could be made.

They had put a further dent in the whiskey bottle and were beginning to wax philosophical when a slender, red-haired girl stuck her head in the door.

"I might have known," she said with a stern look. "Who else would my da be sitting up drinking with than the likes of you? Don't you have a home, Evan O'Connell, or are you too busy working for Mr. High-and-

Mighty Bennington to concern yourself with such things?''

"It's nice to see you, too, Maude," Evan said with a grin. He had stood up as Carmody's daughter entered the room. As always, she looked very fine, dressed in a plain white blouse and navy blue serge skirt, her Titian hair pulled back severely from a face with classic features and honey-toned skin.

At sixteen, Maude Carmody was by any standard a fine-looking girl. But she also had a settled air of maturity unusual for her age. It came from being the eldest of six children left motherless when Maude was eight. She'd had the keeping of them ever since, as well as looking after her father, who she often said was harder to take care of than any of the little ones.

On impulse Evan said, "I swear it's true, Maude, you get prettier every time I see you."

She flushed, but waved him away with the back of her hand. "Go on with you. Do you think I'm some little flibbertigibbet to have my head turned by that kind of talk?"

He flashed her a teasing grin. "If there's any head turning to be done, it would hardly be in front of your da."

Carmody laughed. He stood up with some effort and eyed the pair indulgently. "Go on with you, then, Evan. You're in need of rest, and if I don't come upstairs soon, it'll be my head that's turning."

He made his way around the side of the desk and let Maude take his arm. "Think about what I said," he told Evan as he turned toward the door. "There's got to be some way to make it work."

Evan nodded. He wished the older man a good-night, nodded to Maude and took himself off. Though the day had been warm, with sunset the air had turned brisk, and low clouds had blown in from the west. Fat drops of rain were falling as he stood for a moment on the sidewalk in front of the grocery.

Common sense told him he should return to his room. Instead he turned south toward the river.

The stretch of property that he was interested in included three warehouses, a saloon and a dilapidated boardinghouse for sailors awaiting their next berths. It was not a place to be wandering around alone at night. But he was a large man whose aura of strength and will deterred most who might have thought of importuning him.

It did not, however, deter the streetwalkers who were out even on so inclement a night. He ignored their invitations and stood staring at the buildings. He had no interest in the saloon or the boardinghouse. As for the warehouses, he wanted to own one, two at the most.

But the owners would be approached to sell as a package, surely the easiest and most attractive deal for them to make. He could hardly blame them for agreeing to it.

His fists clenched at his sides as a feeling of helplessness washed over him. The Porcellian Consortium— grand name for a bunch of snot-nosed boys that it was— had resources he couldn't approach. It seemed a classic case of those who already had being able to get more without difficulty, while those who had little or nothing, were left out in the cold.

Except that this time he was determined to challenge the hand fate had dealt. He was going to find a way, whatever it took.

With that conviction firmly implanted in his mind; he left the warehouses behind and walked to his room. There he spent the night stretched out on his bed, refining his strategy and convincing himself that it would work.

Chapter Eight

"I'M SORRY, TOO, OLIVIA," Catherine said into the telephone. "But I hope you'll feel better soon. Spring colds can be awful."

She listened as her cousin croaked a few more words, commiserated with her again, and was relieved when she was finally able to hang up. She hadn't been looking forward to seeing Olivia and felt only mildly guilty about being glad that their plans had to be canceled. Family obligations could be a tremendous bore when one had relatives such as her waspish cousin.

Being unexpectedly free for an entire afternoon did not distress her. On the contrary, she was delighted by her sudden autonomy. Her father was at work, her mother was meeting with a group of ladies from their church, and Jimmy was off with friends.

No one would be looking for Catherine until it was time to dress for dinner. She smiled to herself as she considered all the things she might do until then.

"I'm going out now, Tilly," she called down the stairs to the kitchen where her mother's maid was busy ironing. "I won't be late."

"You and Miss Olivia have a nice time," Tilly called back.

Catherine felt the slightest twinge at not telling her that Olivia wouldn't be coming along, but she knew that Tilly would raise a ruckus about her going out on her own. And in this day and age, too.

It was 1900, for heaven's sake, long past the time when young ladies required chaperons. She felt perfectly confident about her ability to deal with anything she might encounter as she closed the door behind her and set off.

She window-shopped along Newbury Street, not feeling the urge to venture into any of the stores where her family had accounts and where she could purchase anything she liked without question. Constant shopping did not appeal to her; she was all too conscious of how much she already had.

Olivia, on the other hand, was far more typical. She couldn't pass a shop without going in and rarely emerged empty-handed. Often her purchases were so numerous that Catherine grew weary waiting for them to be completed. Her pleasure in her solitary state redoubled as she passed by the shops and headed east toward the Public Garden.

A warmer-than-usual spring had caused the roses to bloom early, perfuming the air with their scent. She breathed in appreciatively as she wandered along the gravel paths laid out between the formal flower beds.

She was dressed in a neatly tailored two-piece suit of soft blue-violet linen the same shade as the hyacinths that clustered along the edges of the paths. Beneath the jacket she wore a high-necked blouse of ivory silk embroidered with lace medallions.

A wide-brimmed hat shaded her face from the sun. She wore patent leather shoes with a high cloth top completely concealed by the ankle-length sweep of her pleated skirt.

Her outfit was not markedly different from that worn by most of the women she passed. She was, however, vastly more beautiful, almost ethereally so to the man watching her.

Evan had decided to cut through the Public Garden on his way to see Carmody. Upon awakening that morning, he had discovered that spring had settled firmly over the city. Rather than let it go by without his acknowledgement, he had decided to take the long way through the park and enjoy himself, however briefly. If everything went as he planned, there would be little enough opportunity to do so in the near future.

Encountering Catherine Bennington was an unlooked-for bonus, one he hesitated to accept. Prudence dictated that he turn around and walk away. But he was not by nature a prudent man. Audacity suited him far better.

With a smile he crossed the path and greeted Catherine. "Miss Bennington, a pleasure to see you."

"Mr. O'Connell..." Cat was flustered by his sudden appearance and hoped that it didn't show. The sun was in her eyes, and she shaded them as she looked at him.

If possible, he seemed even handsomer and more compelling than the last time she had seen him. His ebony hair had been stylishly trimmed, and he was clean shaven, like her father and brother, but unlike many other men, who favored elaborate sideburns and mustaches.

The suit he wore was in no way remarkable to her, suggesting that it could hardly have been cheap. He was bareheaded, and his skin was darkly tanned. She remembered hearing her father say something about Texas recently and wondered if he had been there.

"How are you?" she asked courteously.

"Very well, thank you. And you?"

She assured him that her health was excellent as they fell into step together. "Lovely day, isn't it?" he said.

"Delightful."

From beneath the wide brim of her hat, Catherine glanced at him surreptitiously. He was smiling slightly, and his eyes were alight with strength and confidence.

She felt a flare of warmth within her that undermined her caution. Above all, she wanted to know him better, to understand what went on behind those rugged features.

"Are you happy working for Father?" she asked.

He raised a quizzical brow. "Happy? Yes, I suppose I am. It's challenging, and it pays very well."

"Is that what's important to you?" Lest he think her curiosity out of place, she added, "I only ask because most young men seem more interested in security and stability."

Evan laughed softly. "Having never had either, I suppose I don't miss them. Besides, I don't think I'd do well being bound to a desk, slaving over ledgers and the like."

"No," Cat murmured, glancing at him again. "I don't suppose you would." His tall, hard body radiated energy and a certain restlessness. She could well imagine how much he would hate being restrained in any way. Not for the first time, she wondered what he did for her father that afforded him a release for that energy. She had never felt able to inquire without revealing a degree of interest that might have aroused suspicion.

She did not wish to give her parents the idea that she was harboring any inappropriate attachments. Not only could that cause problems for her, but it would be utterly unfair to Evan, who, heaven knew, had never done anything to remotely encourage her feelings.

The frequency with which she had to remind herself of that mocked her efforts. He would pop into her mind at the most unlikely times, usually when she was in her bath or after she had gone to bed.

Her thoughts on such occasions embarrassed her deeply. She was profoundly grateful that he could have no notion of them.

Evan glanced at the young girl beside him as he might have a rare and beautiful object unexpectedly come into his line of vision. To him, women such as Catherine Bennington were intended to be protected from the rougher and more sordid side of life.

She wasn't like Maude, who knew her father's business as well as Carmody himself did and couldn't be surprised by any aberration of human behavior. On the contrary, Catherine was an innocent, sheltered all her life, kept pure and unsullied. Above all, he wanted her to remain that way.

Had Cat been privy to his thoughts at that moment, she would have been thoroughly offended. She considered herself an excellent example of the new woman—independent, self-reliant and open-minded.

The fact that she lived in a cocoon of luxury did not, in her estimation, change any of that. If the day came when she had to cope with the real world, she would be more than able to do so.

They were coming to a fork in the path they had been following. In one direction was the exit from the park. In the other was the lake dotted by boats. Evan was reluctant to part from Catherine. Without caring to examine the wisdom of his action, he smiled and gestured toward the expanse of water.

"It's a perfect day to go rowing. Would you care to join me?"

Cat hesitated. She was more prudent than he, if only marginally. Common sense told her to refuse politely, take her leave and go home. But the blue water beckoned, as did Evan.

"Yes, I'd like that very much."

In the cool shadows of the old wooden boathouse, Evan concluded negotiations. The ancient, gnarled boatkeeper handed him a pair of oarlocks and gestured vaguely.

"Help yourself, sir. Not too much custom at the moment. Middle of the day and all."

Evan nodded. He picked the boat he liked from among the dozen or so pulled up on the edge of the lake. After fitting the oarlocks, he removed his jacket and laid it over one of the seats.

He handed Catherine in and pushed the boat into the water. He climbed in quickly, avoiding getting so much as his pant-cuffs wet, and slid the oars into place. As they rested across his knees, he rolled up his sleeves and grinned at her.

"It's been a long time since I rowed."

She couldn't help but smile back. "Does that mean I'm likely to be pressed into service if we go very far?"

He pretended to be horrified by the notion. "Don't tell me you can row."

She nodded. "And swim, ride a horse, play tennis and ski."

"Ski? What's that?"

"They do it in Europe, in the mountains. It involves going downhill with one's feet attached to... well, I suppose you could describe them as sled runners. Anyway, it's very exhilarating. I learned several years ago during a vacation in Switzerland."

"Sounds tiring," Evan said. "Not to mention cold. I can't say that I think much of snow. We hardly ever have it in Ireland. I'd barely seen the stuff until I came here."

"How long ago was that?" she asked. Eager though she was to know more about him, she didn't want to be too obvious. In addition, she was aware that he might consider his background a sensitive point and wasn't sure that he would be willing to discuss it.

Evan did feel some reluctance. But he put it aside as he looked at the beautiful girl seated opposite him. Simply to be there with her, alone and in a situation that had to be described as friendly, was so unlikely as to prompt him to put aside his usual caution. He felt himself opening up, responding like a flower to the sun.

"Three years," he said as he plied the oars smoothly through the water, carrying them toward the middle of the lake. "Though there are times when it seems longer."

She trailed a hand over the side, catching the glistening water between her fingers and letting it trickle back. "What made you decide to leave?"

"Hunger," he said succinctly. At her startled glance he added, "And I don't mean of the body alone. True, things are better than in the famine years when millions died or fled. But a man can't nourish his soul on potatoes alone. Nor dreams, for that matter."

Catherine nodded. She thought she understood. "You left to find a better way of life."

Evan glanced at her without appearing to do so. It would have been easy enough to leave her with her tidy explanation. Certainly that was what people wanted to believe, and there were even times when it was true. Not, however, in his case.

"I left," he said slowly, "because I was angry, and I knew that if I stayed where I was, eventually my anger would lead me to do something that would cost me my life. Furthermore, I realized that the very men I was fighting against, the men who drain Ireland of her substance and her pride, understood that better than I did. They were only waiting for another generation to hurl itself at them and be crushed in the process.''

The bitterness in his voice dismayed Catherine. She had no idea how to respond to it. ''I don't know very much about the situation in Ireland,'' she admitted self-consciously. ''Only that there are people who think the English don't belong there.''

''Ireland must be free,'' Evan said flatly. ''England must get out altogether. But they've been in control for almost eight hundred years, and they won't leave easily.''

''It sounds as though you're advocating violence.''

He gave her a crooked smile that caused her heart to turn over. ''Does that shock your fine sensibilities, Miss Bennington? We happen to live in a violent world. The English are fighting right now to take over South Africa from the Boers, and the Chinese are fighting for their freedom against the Europeans and Americans. Heaven only knows how many other little wars are going on all over the world. Ireland's only one small part of it.''

''Just because violence is commonplace,'' she said softly, ''that's no reason to advocate it. Surely there's a better way to get what you want.''

''What way? Negotiations? Compromise? That's been tried, and it's led only to betrayal. To give John Bull his due, he's managed to take over a good chunk of the world by being willing to use force, more force, and still more. That's what he understands and respects. If we don't meet him on the same ground, we can't win.''

Cat raised her head. She looked at him directly, her gray eyes candid. "If that's truly what you believe, then why are you here?"

Evan winced. She had touched a nerve, whether she knew it or not. For a few brief moments he had allowed himself to forget that he was talking with Drake Bennington's daughter. Now he cursed himself for doing so.

At length he said, "I saw opportunities here that don't exist in Ireland, so I decided to take them."

"Surely no one can blame you for that," Cat said, though inside she was a little disappointed. He had spoken so fiercely about his people's need to be free, yet he seemed completely content to leave them behind while he got on with his own life.

Looking at him, she wondered how he intended going about that. Clearly his job for her father was important to him, but she had the sense that he would never be satisfied to be merely an employee, no matter how trusted or well paid. Nothing he had said indicated that to her, yet she was as certain of it as she was of her own most secret inner yearnings.

Evan wanted far more. The only question was how he intended to get it.

She could hardly ask him that, much as she longed to. But watching the smooth flexing of his muscles beneath his bronze skin as he rowed them across the lake, she was certain that whatever he set his mind to, he would be likely to achieve.

She envied him that; her own life seemed far more complex and disorganized. She had no clear-cut goals, no shining objectives at which to hurl herself.

Not even the proper aspirations of every young girl of her class—marriage and motherhood—appealed to her overly much. She supposed they would simply happen to her, as had everything else so far.

She was grateful to the loving parents who protected and guided her, but she was also beginning to chafe at their control, however well-intentioned. Watching Evan, she felt a restless need to take charge of her own fate, whatever it might be.

EVAN LEFT CAT at the edge of the park. She politely refused his offer to escort her home, something they both knew would have been unwise. He watched as she walked away. Her head was proudly tilted beneath the jaunty bonnet, and her hips moved most enticingly. Evan grinned to himself, but there was an element of keen frustration behind his amusement.

Since first meeting Cat and becoming aware of his desire for her, he had consoled himself with the thought that while she was beyond his grasp, her type of woman was not.

If he rose as far as he planned, he would have his pick. The problem was that he already seemed to have made his choice.

Resolutely he turned his mind from her and strode off in the opposite direction. He could have taken one of the hacks lined up near the park, but decided instead to walk.

It was a pleasant day, the heat abating as the afternoon waned. He strode briskly, busy with his own thoughts.

When he reached the North End, he became more attentive to his surroundings. Although the crime rate in this section of the city was down, thanks in large measure to the efforts of ward leaders such as Carmody, it was still wise to be alert. The streets here were much narrower than in the affluent area around the park.

Shops that were steadily replacing the old-time push-cart peddlers spilled out onto the sidewalks, their exteriors festooned with goods. Women were out in large numbers, carrying their baskets as they shopped for supper. Children darted among them, the more daring snitching an apple from a bin, then running wildly from the fist-shaking shopkeeper.

Evan loosened his tie as he walked. For all his alertness to potential dangers, he felt more at home as soon as he entered the North End. Unlike Beacon Hill and the downtown business district, this was the world he knew and where he had already begun to make his mark.

Several people nodded to him respectfully as he passed by. He returned the greeting, but kept going, not disposed to linger when he considered the work awaiting him.

He didn't regret taking a few hours off. They had cleared his mind and clarified his intentions. Further, the fortuitous meeting with Cat had banished any lingering doubts he might have had. He knew better than ever what he wanted—and what he would have to do to achieve it.

He was whistling as he entered the grocery store. Maude was behind the counter. She had her red hair pinned up in a knot on the crown of her head but left soft and loose around the sides in a style he thought became her quite well. As usual, she was simply dressed in a striped blouse and navy blue skirt. She looked up as he entered and sighed.

"You again. Just when I was hoping to coax Da upstairs for a rest. He's had a busy day, in case you're interested. People in and out of here since early morning. There's a limit to what a man his age can handle."

"Don't let himself be hearing you say that," Evan told her with a grin. "Besides, I've got good news for him."

She looked at him skeptically. "What does that mean, then?"

"Come along while I tell him," he suggested. "I wouldn't mind hearing what you think of it."

Maude pretended to hesitate, though he could tell that she was pleased. She was a bright girl, with a sharp, practical mind. If there was a hole in his plan, she would spot it as readily as either he or Carmody. Perhaps even more so.

But when he had explained to both father and daughter what he intended to do, neither of them could think of an objection, beyond the obvious.

"It won't be easy to arrange," Carmody said. "Especially not in so little time."

"Which is why I'm bringing it to you," Evan said. "No one knows the North End better. I need half a dozen men like myself with the means to buy a small business. Separately we wouldn't stand a chance against the Beacon Hill lot, but together we can beat them at their own game."

"You mean form a consortium," Maude said, "just as they did?"

Evan nodded. "That's right. We'll give it a fine-sounding name, too. What do you think of the 'New England Investment Association'?"

Carmody laughed. "That has a solid Puritan ring to it. You know, laddy, the more I think about this, the more it seems you may be onto something. Granted, the Irish have traditionally been a contentious bunch, not overly given to cooperation, but there's nothing to say that can't change." His eyes gleamed sardonically. "Especially here in this grand New World where we find ourselves."

"We have to be realistic," Evan said. "For all that there are Irish lads going to Harvard now, and one or two even buying homes on Beacon Hill, there's still an inner circle in this town that's as closed to us now as it was fifty years ago. Working for Drake Bennington, I've had a chance to see how it operates. There's a lot to be said for a group of men similar in outlook and objectives banding together to further their mutual interests."

"In this part of town," Maude said, "that's called a gang."

Evan shrugged. "And on Charles Street it's called a consortium. Beyond a few extra syllables, I'm not sure there's much difference."

Maude made no further attempt to dissuade him, if indeed that was what it had been. She listened attentively as her father began naming men who might join the effort, and even suggested several herself. By early evening a list of a dozen had been compiled.

Carmody surveyed it with satisfaction. "I should have thought of this meself. Every man on here's solid, hardworking and just looking for the right opportunity to better himself. O'Reilly, for instance, has been managing a saloon for going on ten years. Knows the business better than anybody I can think of and has been wanting to buy a place of his own."

He gestured to another name on the list. "Donnelly's retiring from the force next month. He's put away a nice nest egg, and with his pension, he'd have enough to live on. But he's the type who needs to be busy. He can make something of that boardinghouse."

"I'll have to meet with each of them in the next day or so," Evan reminded him. "There's no time to waste."

Carmody nodded, then thought for a moment and frowned. "Only one thing, laddy. Once you've got the money together, how are you going to approach the owners without tipping your hand? You said you wanted to keep your part in this quiet, didn't you?''

"I did, and I still do," Evan affirmed, "but that isn't a problem." He grinned at Carmody's perplexity. "If there's one thing Boston's got more of than bankers, it's lawyers. I'm going to find myself a nice, fresh-faced one to represent the New England Investment Association. He'll do the up-front work while I stay in the background. With a bit of luck, we can close the deal with no one being the wiser."

"You have learned a thing or two working for Bennington," Carmody said. "But to tell you the truth, if it were me doing this, I'd want the whole world to know."

"It will," Evan said quietly. "In time." He stood up to go. "I'll be back in the morning, early. Do you think you can have the first of them in here by then?"

Carmody nodded. He stared at the young man thoughtfully before he said, "It's a shame you're so drawn to business, Evan. You have all the earmarks of a natural-born politician. Maybe you ought to reconsider and stand for the council instead."

Evan laughed and shook his head. "That's your bailiwick, not mine. Besides, if there's anything Boston has more of than lawyers, it's Irish politicians. I'd rather stake my future on fresher territory."

"You're doing that right enough, lad, when you take on the Beacon Hill bunch. If they get any idea that you're too big for your britches, they'll be looking to cut you down to size in record time."

"Let me worry about that," Evan said, knowing that he wouldn't. Confidence flowed through him, drowning out any apprehension he might have felt.

All his life he had been moving beyond the limits fate seemed to have imposed upon him. Now, at last, the re-

wards were within his grasp. He had no doubt that he
would achieve them, even as he had begun to suspect that
they would no longer be enough.

The image of Catherine Bennington shimmered in his
mind—beautiful, innocent, unattainable.

For the moment.

"WHAT IS the New England Investment Association?"
Drake asked. He was standing at his office door, about
to leave. Through the high windows fronting on the
street, the late-spring twilight filtered in softly.

It had been a pleasantly warm day. He was eager to get
home. For a change, there was no social engagement to
attend.

The children, however, would be going out to a young
people's party, where they would be well chaperoned. He
was looking forward to an evening alone with Elizabeth.
Compared to that, the matter Jacob Stein had just mentioned seemed inconsequential, yet his curiosity was
aroused.

"I don't know," Jacob said. "All I've heard is that
they're a newly formed group that purchased a stretch of
waterfront property a few days ago. It appears to have
been a hastily arranged deal, one step ahead of the young
chaps behind the Porcellian Consortium."

"Must have been a disappointment to them," Drake
murmured absently. He went through a quick mental re-
view of who might be interested in the property but came
up dry.

Most of the likely candidates already had ample such
holdings. It had been a logical purchase for young men
striking out on their own.

"Whoever got it, I suppose they'll make themselves
known eventually."

"As you say, sir." Jacob hesitated a moment. "Will there be anything else?"

Drake shook his head. "No, I don't think so. Unless, of course, you'd like to change your mind?"

The older man smiled regretfully. "I'm afraid not, sir. If I did, my wife would never forgive me."

"I can't say I blame her," Drake said. "After all the years of hard work, the two of you deserve an easier life."

"I'm not sure retirement will suit me," Jacob admitted, "but the idea of more time to spend with my family, especially my grandchildren, is very appealing."

"I can hardly blame you. Still, I have to admit that I'm not looking forward to having to find a new secretary. You've done an outstanding job all these years, Jacob. In a very real sense, you can't be replaced."

"That's very kind of you, sir. I must say, there is no one I would rather have worked for. But we both know that no one is truly indispensable."

"Perhaps not," Drake said. "But you're the closest thing to it. If you have any recommendations as to your successor, I'd be pleased to hear them."

"I'll give it careful thought," Jacob promised. "There is time, after all. It's not as though I'm leaving tomorrow."

"No," Drake agreed. "It was very decent of you to give me so much notice. Still, January will be here before we know it. I'd like to have someone in place before then, so that you can break him in properly.

Jacob inclined his head in agreement. "It will be my pleasure, sir."

Drake was smiling to himself as he left the office. In the twelve years that Jacob had worked for him, they had maintained a formality that in no way belied the strength of their mutual respect and affection.

He had known for some time that the older man was considering retirement, but it had still come as a shock to learn that he had decided to leave. He would be sorely missed, but Drake was confident that he would bequeath his position judiciously.

"We must do something very nice for him," Elizabeth said when Drake told her the news. "More than the usual testimonial dinner."

"Jacob has always had a secret passion for racehorses. I thought of presenting him with a promising yearling."

"That's a marvelous idea. With the horse to interest him, he shouldn't be bored."

"Oh, I don't imagine he would be anyway," Drake said. "He's amassed considerable business interests of his own over the years that will keep him occupied."

In the course of his employment, Jacob had become a wealthy man, something Drake had never begrudged him. He would receive a more-than-generous pension, but even without it, he would have been well-off.

"I suppose you'll be giving careful consideration to who should replace him," Elizabeth said. They were having a candlelit supper in her sitting room, in preference to the formal dining room downstairs.

She was simply dressed in a white voile gown embroidered with peonies at the hem and along the deeply cut bodice. Her hair was loosely swept up, secured by a handful of diamond-studded pins. Drake thought she looked very young and utterly enchanting.

"The children should get out more often," he murmured as he raised his glass in a toast to her.

Her cheeks darkened slightly, but she met his eyes with characteristic boldness. "Now that they're older, they will. In fact, we'll probably be hard-pressed to have any time with them at all."

"I hope not," Drake said sincerely. He loved his children and enjoyed being with them, but he also found it very pleasant to be alone with his lovely wife.

He was, however, slightly concerned by the hint of regret that entered her soft gray eyes. "Jimmy is away at school almost all the time. Cat would be, too, if she had decided to go to college."

"She may yet. More and more young women are doing so."

"She says she's too frivolous for so serious a pursuit," Elizabeth said with a smile. "As though she were any such thing."

"Is it my imagination," Drake asked, "or has there been something on her mind lately?"

"I've had the same thought, but whenever I've attempted to draw her out, she assures me that everything is fine."

"It probably is. After all, what could possibly concern her?"

Elizabeth gave her husband a chiding look. "She's at a difficult age, not quite fish nor fowl. Once she's married and settled, things will be easier."

"Married?" Drake broke in. "Surely we needn't think of that for several years."

Elizabeth took a sip of her wine. "I wouldn't be so sure of that. Cat is a very beautiful young girl. She has her choice of suitors."

"But that doesn't mean she need become serious about anyone prematurely."

"Of course not," Elizabeth soothed. She could not resist adding, "However, I remember another young girl, barely introduced to society, who got snapped up rather suddenly."

"That was different," Drake insisted. "There was a rather...intense attraction between us."

"True," she said, blushing only slightly at the memory of the passion he had inspired in her from the beginning, even before there had been love. "But that isn't to say that the same thing can't happen to Cat. In fact, to tell you the truth, I hope that it will. I can't imagine her in a tepid, polite marriage. She needs someone fiery, challenging, a match for her in every way."

"She needs to grow up a bit first," Drake insisted. "You'd had a very different upbringing, without many of the privileges Cat takes for granted. I realize that conditions improved steadily as your father got Calvert Oaks back on its feet following the war, but the experiences of your early years made you far more mature than Cat is right now."

"Still, she is head and shoulders above most of the young women of her class," Elizabeth insisted. "And I'm not just saying that because I'm her mother. She has a vitality and intelligence that make me very proud."

Drake reached across the table and took her hand. He turned it over, letting his thumb graze back and forth over her palm.

"I am proud, too, but has it occurred to you that when we finally have a chance to be alone, we spend it talking about the children?"

"Do you mind terribly?"

"No, actually I don't. They will go their own ways and make their own lives, but they will also always be the living proof of the love we've shared. Which reminds me..." He lifted her hand and placed his lips against the sensitive inner skin.

Elizabeth cupped his face, her fingers brushing over the lean, hard line of his jaw. His skin was faintly roughened from a day's growth of whiskers. He raised his eyebrows inquiringly. "Shall I shave?"

"Oh, no," she protested. "You know I love the way you feel against my skin."

The rest of dinner was forgotten as they adjourned to the bedroom next door. Drake undressed her with lingering slowness. She moaned softly when he dropped soft kisses from the curves of her eyelids across her brow to the soft, sensitive lobe of her ear. When his teeth closed lightly on her, she gripped his shoulders fiercely.

"Drake, tonight I don't want to wait."

He smiled down at her with a purely male light in his eyes. "And here I was looking forward to a slow, voluptuous seduction."

"Later," she promised him as she took hold of the sides of his shirt and very deliberately pulled. Buttons popped, landing on the bed.

She pushed the fabric apart, revealing the smooth expanse of his lightly haired chest, still as hard and heavily muscled as in his youth. A soft sound of pleasure escaped her as she burrowed her face against him.

Drake laughed, delighted by her aggressiveness. In all their years together, their lovemaking had never become predictable. It retained the special spice of the new and beguiling. Yet they also had the familiarity of old lovers who understood best how to please each other.

In the last moments before he lost himself in her, he thought of what an extremely fortunate man Elizabeth had made him. Without her, he would never have known love. With her, he roamed across its vast and ever-varied landscape with the assurance of an explorer who has journeyed the same way countless times but never fails to make fresh discoveries.

He cherished her body with his own, finding in her the fulfillment of his dreams. When they slept at last, it was entwined in each other's arms, in the haven of their own making that held all the world at bay.

Chapter Ten

"MR. BENNINGTON wishes to see you," Jacob told Evan. "However, he is not in the office. He left word that you are to join him on his yacht, *Elizabeth*, which is presently moored in the boat basin."

Evan suppressed his annoyance. He had plans of his own for that afternoon, involving a meeting with the merchant who was interested in using his warehouse. He had hoped to conclude his appointment with Drake quickly. Now it appeared that wouldn't be possible.

"Do you know what he wants to discuss?"

Jacob shrugged. "Another assignment for you, I imagine. By the way, as long as you'll be seeing him, would you give him these files? I've finished updating them and he needs to look over the changes as soon as possible."

Evan tucked the thick envelope under his arm. "The *Elizabeth*, you said?"

"That's right. At the boat basin. You really can't miss her."

A short time later, Evan saw what he meant. The boat basin, situated in Back Bay convenient to both Beacon Hill and Cambridge, was home to some of the finest yachts in the world.

But none equaled the *Elizabeth*. She rode at anchor just within the basin, more than three hundred feet of exquisitely crafted beauty. Rumor had it that she had cost

in excess of two hundred thousand dollars. Even looking at her from a distance, Evan could believe it.

He rode out to the yacht on a launch. Once on board,
he was directed to the bow. The Benningtons were gathered there beneath a wide awning that shaded them from
the sun.

Cat and Jimmy were playing backgammon. He was
dressed in a blue-and-white striped jacket, white linen
trousers and a white shirt. She wore a billowing dress of
white voile cinched at the waist, with soft puffy sleeves to
the elbow and a sailor collar.

Both looked up as he arrived. Cat, who had just made
a winning move, was smiling, but that faded as soon as
he appeared.

Not because she wasn't glad to see him. On the contrary, the instant their eyes met she felt a start of pure
pleasure. Sensibly she strove to conceal it as best she
could.

Jimmy, on the other hand, was delighted to see Evan
and made no secret of it. "Mr. O'Connell, great that you
could join us."

"I just came to drop these papers off," Evan said. He
handed them to Drake, doing his best not to glance in
Catherine's direction.

The sunlight bouncing off the water turned her hair to
scorched gold. Her eyes were wide and luminous, her
mouth softly full. With the slightest encouragement, he
could have forgotten everything except his desire for her.

Nothing could be greater folly. Drake Bennington
might be a cordial, even easygoing, man. Certainly he
welcomed Evan, going so far as to invite him to have a
drink. But his hospitality most certainly did not extend
to his daughter.

As Evan sat down, he reflected that if Drake had the slightest idea of what was going through his mind, he would have personally escorted him off the yacht without recourse to any gangway.

"We won't be leaving for another hour or so," Drake said. "In the meantime, I want to get through as much of this as I can so I don't have to take it with me.

"Here," he said, handing half the stack back to Evan. "Look through these and tell me what you think of Jacob's recommendations."

With an inner sigh, Evan did as he was bid. Rather to his surprise, he was quickly immersed in the files, to the extent of forgetting the drink a steward had placed at his elbow.

He did not, however, lose his awareness of Catherine, who had returned with some reluctance to the backgammon board.

The files Jacob had sent along consisted of a series of reports on possible investments. There were balance sheets as well as descriptions of each. To these, Jacob had added his own thoughts.

Evan found them to be invariably clear and insightful, but on one or two items, he thought the older man was being unduly cautious.

When he said as much, Drake nodded and made a few penciled jottings, but otherwise did not comment. Evan had gotten through the last of the files when the launch returned. On board were a sandy-haired man in his middle years who wore a cleric's collar, and an elderly lady.

"I hope Mari will be all right," Elizabeth said anxiously as she hurried to the deck to watch.

A basket chair had been lowered over the side toward the launch that bobbed up and down on the tide. The elderly woman was helped into the basket, then hoisted on board. The gentleman followed, using the rope stairs.

"My heavens," Mari said when she stepped from the chair into Elizabeth's eager embrace. "That was exhilarating."

Her eyes gleamed behind wire-rimmed glasses as she stood on tiptoe to hug Drake as well. "It made me feel like a girl again."

"I'm so glad you could come with us," Elizabeth said. She took the elderly woman's arm and led her to a chaise beneath the awning, where Cat and Jimmy took their turns hugging her.

Listening to them, Evan gathered that the woman was Mrs. Bennington's aunt, but it wasn't until he put the face and name together that he realized who he was looking at.

Mari Mackenzie was something of a legend in Boston. She had started out as a mill girl in Lowell, married widower Josiah Mackenzie and, upon his death, become heir to almost all his millions. For years she had been involved in a bitter battle with his eldest son, Gideon, who, though now in his sixties, had never given up his hope of reclaiming what he believed should be his.

The man with her was Nathan Mackenzie, Elizabeth's uncle and Gideon's younger brother, also his opposite in every way imaginable. Nathan had been a member of the clergy for more than twenty years. He lived simply, giving most of his money to charity, and appeared completely content.

He smiled and nodded to Evan as they were introduced. "Mr. O'Connell is on my staff," Drake said by way of explanation.

"I believe I heard something to that effect," Mari said. For all that her back was stooped and her face lined, she appeared to miss nothing as she glanced at Evan. "You used to work for Carmody, didn't you?"

Evan stiffened. He was surprised that she even knew of Carmody's existence, although, upon reflection, he realized that he shouldn't be. From what he had heard about Mari Mackenzie, she had her finger in more pies than just about anyone else in Boston.

"That's right," he said cautiously. "He took me on shortly after I arrived."

"Off the boat, were you?"

"In a manner of speaking."

"Nothing wrong with that. We were all off the boat at one time or another. Isn't that right, Drake?"

To Evan's surprise, his employer laughed. "You know perfectly well, Mari, that my ancestors were a rapacious bunch who came here one step ahead of the hangman. They were hardly alone. I think that explains the great American preoccupation with respectability. Most of us have at least one or two skeletons we'd like to live down."

"Today's upstart is tomorrow's aristocrat, is that what you're saying, Drake?" Nathan asked with a smile.

"That's as good a way of putting it as any. Now, if you'll excuse me a moment, I want to get Evan off with these papers."

He put an arm around the younger man's shoulders as they walked toward the gangway. "Tell Jacob I'd like him to get moving on these as quickly as possible. Where you disagreed with him, I'll be taking your recommendations. Jacob may want to discuss that with you, but don't be concerned. He has the best of motives."

Evan had no chance to ask what those might be before Drake added, "I'll be in Newport for the next several months, but it's important that I have a means of staying in close touch with the office. I'd like you to report to Jacob whenever it's necessary, pick up the papers he has ready, and bring them to me. You'll stay a few days, as proves necessary, and we'll go over them together. At the least, the job will get you out of Boston, but I also think you may find it interesting.

Evan wasn't so sure. He disliked the idea of being Drake's messenger boy, but he recognized that he could learn a great deal by being in on decisions as they were made.

That redeemed the assignment, though he was still far from pleased by it. For one thing, it would interfere with his own plans. For another, it would throw him into repeated contact with Catherine.

Every instinct he possessed warned him to be wary of her. She had an effect on him that he could understand well enough even as he recognized its dangers.

She was the last woman he should desire, yet he couldn't seem to help himself. He had only to see her to be reminded of how much he wanted her.

Evan stood on the wharf and watched as the *Elizabeth* set sail. She moved out of the harbor under power, but once beyond the levees, her great canvas wings were opened to catch the wind. The breath caught in his throat.

He had grown up on the edge of the sea and had an innate love of beautiful ships. Never had he seen one more lovely. Not until her sleek, swift hull had at last disappeared from sight did he turn away.

THE OFFICE OUTSIDE Drake's was empty, but Jacob had left a note asking him to drop by on Monday. He deposited the files on the center of the desk and left.

An hour later he was at his warehouse to show a merchant around. William Chisom was a sea captain turned trader with almost four decades' experience plying the route between America and Europe. He had made his first independent deal recently and was due to bring in a cargo of French brandies and silks early the following month.

"I'll be direct with you, Mr. O'Connell," the straight-backed, square-jawed man said, "since I find that saves time."

He took a deep breath. "I'm strapped for cash worse than I've ever been in my life. I put every penny I had into my cargo, and I've got nothing left to pay you with."

There he paused, looking at Evan, whose only reaction was to wait for him to continue. After a few moments, Chisom laughed. "Well, by God, if you haven't already thrown me out of here, maybe we've got something to talk about. This is the third warehouse I've been to, and you're the first owner who's still been listening after I've said I'm broke."

"You aren't broke, Mr. Chisom," Evan said quietly. Inside he was dismayed, having been counting on the deposit for the rent to meet his own obligations in the next few months.

Apparently it wasn't going to work out that way. He had two choices: kick Chisom out, as the others had done, and hope somebody better would come along fast, or make the situation work for himself.

"You merely have expectations in lieu of cash, isn't that correct?"

Chisom laughed dryly. "Aye, you could say that. In fact, feel free to. It sounds a whole lot better than the way I put it."

Evan grinned. He led the way into his office at the back of the warehouse and pulled a bottle out of the drawer of the battered desk he had picked up secondhand. That, two chairs and a file cabinet were his sole furnishings. Hardly fancy, but the place was his, and he liked it.

"Drink, Mr. Chisom?"

The man hesitated a split second, looking thirsty. "The missus doesn't approve, won't have it in the house. But I wouldn't say no to a drop."

They had rather more than that before Evan put forth his proposal. "This brandy and silk you're bringing in from France, I take it you expect to do well on the markup?"

Chisom nodded emphatically. "Three to one, for certain, even taking into account the overhead."

"What if I told you that you could get five to one?"

"Not possible. Not in Boston or New York. Not even in Chicago, for that matter. If there's one thing I know, it's the market for luxury goods and I'm telling you five to one can't be had."

"It can in Texas."

Chisom stared at him blankly. "Texas?"

Evan leaned back in his chair. He was enjoying himself. "Ever been there?"

He might as well have asked if Chisom had visited the moon. "Of course not. What's in Texas?"

"Money, for one thing. And more coming. There's a boom under way down there. Some very smart people are expecting to strike oil soon. Money's been pouring into the state because of it. The money's created a market for luxury goods that almost no one is even trying to fill."

The older man rubbed his chin and looked at him thoughtfully. "You've got contacts there?"

Evan nodded. "Good ones. Here's my offer. You bring in the cargo, store it here rent free, and we work the deal with my friends in Texas. If I get you five to one, I take a quarter of your profit. Otherwise, I get nothing."

Chisom leaned forward, looking at him narrowly. "Let me make sure I've got this straight. I get the warehouse rent free and you take a quarter of a five-to-one deal. Otherwise nothing?"

"That's it."

"You must be damn sure of what you're saying or you'd never make me an offer like that."

"Then you agree?" Evan asked.

Chisom stood up and offered his hand. "I'd have to be a fool not to. The risk is yours, Mr. O'Connell. I'm sure you realize that."

"I do. But, like you, I'm of the opinion that money—real money—can't be made without taking risks."

"Isn't that the truth," Chisom said ruefully. "I've been lying awake at night reminding myself of it."

"I'll send a telegram to my contacts in Texas," Evan said as the two men walked to the door. "There are also one or two people on the railroads who I'll get in touch with. The brandy in particular will need special handling."

Chisom turned to leave. "I like the way you do business, Mr. O'Connell. If this works out, you'll have plenty more from me."

Which was something to look forward to, Evan thought after Chisom had left and he was locking up. Provided he could survive long enough to enjoy it.

Nonetheless he was in the mood to celebrate and went in search of Carmody, thinking that the older man might like to join him. But when he got to the grocery he found only Maude, locking up for the night.

"He's at the ward meeting," she said as she cranked the awning in. "Won't be back until late."

On an impulse Evan said, "Come out to supper with me, then?"

Maude hesitated. She gave the crank a final turn, let go of it and looked at him cautiously. "What would I be wanting to do that for?"

Evan laughed. "I declare, you keep talking like that and a fellow's liable to get a swelled head."

"You know perfectly well what I mean, Evan O'Connell. I'm a respectable girl, and I can't be going around hooley-hacking without stirring up talk."

"Come on now, Maude. I'm not asking you to run away with me. Only to have a bit of supper."

She hesitated, clearly tempted by the idea, but still cautious. "I'd have to be home in time to get the little ones into bed."

"We'll do it together. I'll even read them a story if you like."

She couldn't help but smile at the thought of that. "I wouldn't have thought you knew anything about children," she said as she led the way inside to get her hat and gloves.

"What did you imagine, then? That I'd been hatched?"

"I didn't imagine anything at all," she informed him with a sniff. "It's not as though I spend my time thinking about you, Evan O'Connell. A girl's got better things to do."

"I should damn—pardon me—darn well hope so," he told her with a grin as he took her arm. "Come along, then. I'll buy you a steak, and you can tell me all about those better things."

They went to a restaurant in the business district, a place he had passed on his way back and forth from Drake's office but had never been in. Maude felt a bit of trepidation about venturing into such foreign territory, but Evan insisted.

"Our money's as good as anyone's," he assured her. "Besides, they should be honored to have the patronage of such an attractive lady."

"Get along with you," she murmured even as she blushed.

In fact, the maître d' didn't seem to find anything out of place about the well-dressed man in the business suit and the pretty young girl at his side. He showed them to a table toward the back, assuming that they would want privacy, and left them to order.

Maude stared after the man's retreating back. "He thinks I'm your fancy."

Evan choked. "What a thing to be saying. I thought you were a respectable girl."

"I am, but that doesn't mean I'm dumb."

Evan hesitated. The odds were that Maude was right; the man probably did think exactly that. Gently he asked, "Do you want to leave?"

She gave him a startled look. "Of course not. I don't give a fig what he thinks. He isn't one of us."

"Then he doesn't exist," Evan agreed, relieved.

They perused the menus in silence for a few minutes. When the waiter had taken their orders and gone again, Maude looked across the table at him. "If you don't mind my saying, you look very much at home here."

Evan shrugged. "Why should I mind? There's nothing wrong with that."

"A year ago you wouldn't have."

"So I've changed. People do."

"Aye, that's the truth. But you've changed more than most. You're . . . harder now than you used to be."

That surprised him. He thought, if anything, that he had become more genteel.

At times he had a speaking face. Maude saw what was in his mind and laughed. "Don't be getting your back up, Evan O'Connell. It's no slur. 'Tis a hard world we live in, and it takes a hard man to make it work to his own ends."

She paused a moment, then added, "That's what you want, isn't it? To get ahead, no matter what?"

"Is there anything else to want?"

"Oh, yes. Take myself, for instance. I've no such ambitions as you. All I want is a decent life."

"You've that already."

"True enough, though I'd like it to be a bit easier for my brothers and sisters, and for the children I hope God will send me someday. Not a lot easier, mind you. Just a bit. I'm not looking to make any great changes in the way of things."

"But you think I am?"

She met his eyes steadily. "I know it. I can feel the ambition churning in you. It was there at the beginning, but it's more directed now. You've got some goal in mind, and I'd wager it goes beyond mere money."

Evan laughed, embarrassed by her perception. Like most men, he wasn't averse to talking about himself with a pretty girl. But he hadn't expected her to be quite so insightful.

" 'Mere' and 'money' are two words that never go together in my mind."

"Oh, I see. All you want is to be as rich as Midas and you'll be happy. Is that it?"

"No," Evan said slowly. "That wouldn't be enough." With a grin he added, "However, it would be a grand start."

Maude laughed. "When you've got all that money, what are you going to spend it on?"

"Oh, dinners with pretty girls, of course. Will you come out with me then, Maude? Will you trip the light fantastic and let down your hair a bit?"

"I doubt it," she said practically. "I'm more for hearth and home than anything else. That's what matters to me, not the grand adventuring you're set on."

"You should spread your wings a bit more. You might enjoy it."

"I might," she agreed. "And I might also get them clipped. No, I'll stick to what I know and be glad of it. But you . . . I admire you, I really do. I even think I may envy you a bit. I hope we'll always be friends."

He raised his eyebrows. "But no more?"

She nodded, as clear in her thinking as he was in his. "You're a man to singe a woman's heart, Evan. I prefer to keep mine safe."

He looked away self-consciously. "You credit me with more than you should."

"Do I? I doubt it. It will take a brave woman to love you, or a foolish one. Perhaps the two go hand in hand."

"So I should look for someone who's bold but brash?" he asked, only half facetiously.

Maude nodded. "Oh, and she should be beautiful, too, of course. Not the fluffy sort of bandbox looks that don't last, but the real thing. She should have style and elegance. I suppose it wouldn't hurt if she was rich herself."

"And where are you going to find this paragon for me, Maude? After all, she's your creation, so you should be the one to discover her."

"If I do, I'll let you know. But I've the feeling it won't be necessary."

"Do you have the sight then, Maude, that you can see the future?" he asked laughingly.

She answered him in perfect seriousness. "My grandma had it. She knew most things that happened before they ever did. She said we all know our own destiny, but most of us are too afraid to recognize it."

Evan was silent. He looked across the table, seeing not the gentle face of Maude Carmody, but the luminous features that belonged to another woman.

A woman whose hold on him was growing more intense by the day, even as he did his best to elude her.

Silently he cursed the fate that denied him the safety and serenity Maude represented. How much better to desire her than Catherine Bennington.

And how impossible.

CAT LOBBED the tennis ball over the net as slowly and gently as she could manage. She watched as Olivia stretched out her racket but otherwise did not move. The ball went sailing past her.

"You missed again," Olivia complained. "Can't you be more careful?"

"I didn't miss. You're supposed to move, to try to return the ball."

Olivia put down her racket and frowned at her. "Really, Catherine, you can't expect me to go darting all over the place like some sort of whirling dervish. I might... well, you know... bead."

Sweat, Cat thought. We both might actually sweat. God forbid. "Let's forget it," she said with a forced smile. "Lemonade on the veranda?"

"I suppose," Olivia said petulantly as they left the court and began walking up the path to the house. "Is Jimmy here?"

Cat shook her head. "He went horseback riding this morning with some friends."

"Oh... I didn't know that."

"He said he'd be back for lunch."

Olivia brightened somewhat, as much as she ever did. She frowned down at her trailing skirt and swished it to knock the dust off. "That's all right, then."

A broad, verdant lawn stretched between the house and the water. The girls strolled across it and walked up the wide marble steps that led to the veranda. It was empty at that hour, the family and guests preferring the shade inside, where ceiling fans turned lazily.

The house Drake and Elizabeth had rented for the season was a short distance from the Breakers—the colossal Renaissance-style palace built for Cornelius Vanderbilt. Their residence was somewhat more modest in scale—a mere forty rooms rather than seventy—the former abode of a railroad magnate who had erred in his investments.

Elizabeth had been hinting for several years that she would like to try a summer at Newport. Drake had put it off as long as he could, but when the possibility of the rental occurred, he had agreed.

"If nothing else," he was saying as Cat and Olivia entered the drawing room through the high French windows, "this ought to be amusing. From what I've heard, some of the entertainments that are planned for the next few weeks will rival the Roman circuses."

"Actually," Elizabeth said, "one of them seems to actually involve a circus. There's also talk that Mrs. Vanderbilt intends to import the cast of a Broadway musical and have them perform on her lawn."

"Mrs. Vanderbilt should find a better use for her time and money," Cat muttered. She flopped down in a white wicker chair and looked glumly at her parents. "We could have gone to Europe, you know."

Olivia gave her an exasperated look. "How could you possibly prefer stuffy old Europe to this? Really, Cat, you should be thanking your parents for bringing you here." She flashed them both a simpering smile. "I'm certainly grateful for being invited along."

Drake's sisters—the less said of whom the better, Cat thought—had seized on the opportunity of having their marriageable children seen at Newport.

Ordinarily Drake would simply have refused. But he was in a more benign mood than usual, and besides, with the house as large as it was, he saw no harm in indulging a few relatives. He had, however, insisted on limiting the visits to two weeks.

"I just wish I could stay longer," Olivia ventured, rather pointedly.

Drake and Elizabeth ignored her, something they were both adept at. "Are you going to the van Rhyses' party tonight?" Elizabeth asked Cat.

"I suppose." Her attitude made it clear that she was hardly looking forward to it.

"Charles has been hanging around here quite a bit, hasn't he?" Drake commented. He spoke absently, having picked up the paper and begun glancing through it.

Cat shrugged. "I can't say I'd noticed."

Olivia wrinkled her nose in what she undoubtedly imagined was a feminine manner. "Don't you think he's just terribly attractive?"

Cat's eyes widened perceptibly. "Charles?"

"Why, yes. He's so tall and self-assured, so..."

"Rich?"

Olivia flushed. "Really, Cat, what a thing to say. As though how much money a man has is of any importance."

"Does that mean you'd marry somebody poor?"

Olivia hesitated, clearly wishing to paint herself in the best possible light, but doubting her audience would swallow a bold-faced lie. "I really couldn't say," she ventured finally. "I've never met anyone like that."

"And you won't," Cat told her. Well aware that both her parents were listening, she added, "Young ladies such as ourselves are carefully sheltered from even the possibility of so improper an attraction. We're steered toward gentlemen from our own social order for the precise purpose of propagating our very exclusive species. In short, my dear Olivia, we are brood mares, albeit thoroughbred ones, and we should never lose sight of that."

As Olivia paled in shock at such bluntness, Drake raised an eyebrow languidly. "May I ask how you came to that conclusion?"

"Isn't it obvious?"

"Not to me. So far as I can tell, you've grown up surrounded by love and comfort, encouraged to develop your interests and talents, and provided with complete freedom from the less pleasant realities of life. How you managed to conclude that your sole purpose is to marry someone of your own kind and have children is beyond me."

"I'm sorry," Cat murmured, abashed by his reminder, however gentle, of all she had to be grateful for. "I didn't mean to suggest that I don't appreciate everything you and Mother have done for me. Of course I do. But it always seems to come out the same in the end. No matter how bright a girl is, or what sort of ideas she has about her future, she invariably winds up a wife and mother."

"The same can be said of men," Elizabeth reminded her softly. "Most of them end up husbands and fathers."

"That's different. Marriage and a family aren't the sole province of a man's life. He can have interests far beyond the home."

"So can women," Drake said. "If you recall, we offered you the chance to continue your education. You could be going to one of the better women's colleges this fall, had you chosen to."

"I did think about it," Cat acknowledged. "But the idea of four more years being shut up in a classroom discussing other people's thoughts and accomplishments doesn't appeal to me."

"It wouldn't to me, either," Olivia said. She gave a little shudder at the mere notion. "Women weren't meant for that sort of thing. Too much study overtaxes the mind and results in a nervous disposition."

Elizabeth rolled her eyes at the frescoed ceiling, then caught herself doing it and was too good-mannered not to look embarrassed. "Yes, I know your mother's opinions on that subject. Anyway, it's a moot point, since Cat has decided not to go to college. Apparently," she added with an indulgent look in her daughter's direction, "she isn't too happy doing nothing, either."

"I have to do something," Cat agreed with a sigh. "I just don't know what."

Olivia shrugged, clearly at a loss to understand the problem. "I don't know how you can complain about not having enough to do. I can't find ten minutes to myself in a day. Why, my fittings alone kept me so busy before I came here that I finally told my mother I absolutely had to have a morning in bed."

"I hate mornings in bed," Cat said, "and I hate fittings." She stood up and eyed her parents ruefully. "I'm also making a pain of myself. I think I'll take the bicycle and go for a ride. All right?"

Drake nodded. "Be careful, though. Don't get your skirts tangled in the wheels."

"I shall pull them up," she informed him over her shoulder, "and thoroughly shock the neighbors. How will that be?"

"Predictable," he called after her tolerantly.

Peddling the bicycle away from the house, Cat mused over her behavior. She certainly had her faults—possibly even more than her share—but it wasn't like her to be self-absorbed and petulant. She truly did love her parents and was hardly unmindful of all they had done for her.

It was only that at the ripe old age of eighteen her life seemed without purpose or direction. Worse yet, the moment she tried to think seriously of how she might give it either, she thought instantly of Evan O'Connell.

Sheer, unmitigated madness. He was the last thing that should be on her mind. Perhaps she should be planning on college, or a grand tour of Europe, anything that would take her out of her present environment and force her to confront her future realistically.

She could follow the current fashion among American heiresses and marry an impecunious aristocrat. Somebody English, for instance, or, if she preferred the more exotic, French.

Failing that, she could become a lady adventurer and travel to faraway places. Africa had become popular among a certain intrepid group; so had the Orient. Or she could bury herself in good works, maybe even study nursing and become a model of selflessness.

None of those possibilities appealed to her. That was the problem. Nothing did, except Evan.

The cacophonous blare of a horn behind her made Cat jump. She brought the bicycle to a halt in the reeds beside the road as a wheezing, clattering contraption passed by, its occupants waving energetically.

Automobiles were becoming the fashion around Newport. It was said that to be truly in the swim one had to have at least four. Fortunately they weren't purchased so much to be driven as simply admired. Unfortunately, there was a handful of hotheads who found it necessary to take them out on the roads.

Cat coughed as this one went by, blowing out an acrid stink that lingered in the previously sweet air. Not until it was well away did she get back on the bicycle and begin pedaling again.

Without having particularly intended to, she was heading toward town. She decided to look around a bit before returning home. At least she would have had some healthful exercise in the process.

She was leaning against a lamppost in a deliberately insouciant pose that drew censorious looks from several passersby, when the afternoon train pulled in. Cat watched idly as the passengers disembarked, until the sight of a tall, ebony-haired man drew her up short. Evan, here?

She straightened, her first instinct being to remove herself immediately. Her second was to hold her ground and face him calmly. Easier said than done. As he strode toward her, not yet aware of her presence, she drank in every detail of his appearance.

He was formally dressed in a three-piece linen suit. His thick hair was neatly trimmed and combed back from his forehead. He carried a leather briefcase in one hand and a small overnight bag in the other as he moved purposefully through the crowd of holiday travelers. When he saw her, he stopped.

"Miss Bennington, how nice."

"Mr. O'Connell, how surprising. What brings you here from Boston?"

"Business." He indicated the briefcase. "I have papers for your father."

"He'll be pleased. Newport is boring him."

Evan laughed. He had been caught off guard by the sudden encounter, but he was recovering quickly.

She was wearing a flowing white dress similar to the one he'd seen her in on the boat. But unlike the other women around them, she hadn't bothered with a hat. Her hair was loosely arranged on top of her head. Several stray strands blew gently around her face, where a hint of freckles could be seen.

Cat saw him looking at them and smiled self-consciously. "I've been lax about the sun. Mother has prescribed cucumber lotion and lemon juice."

"You don't seem particularly concerned."

"I'm not," she admitted. "It seems rather silly to come all this way to enjoy the sun and sea, then swathe oneself in veils."

"Are you enjoying it?" he asked. They were strolling toward the carriage rank outside the station. Cat walked her bicycle, which had earned an amused look from Evan.

"I suppose," she said. "Boston must be unbearable."

He thought of the sweltering heat that had kept him awake long into the night, listening to the cries of weary children and the low, tired voices of their parents, clustered with them on the roofs and the front stoops—anywhere that offered the slightest hope of a breeze.

As always in the summer, there was a sickness in the closely packed tenements of the North End. A child he vaguely knew from the bunch who hung about in front of his building had died of a fever the day before. There were fears that others would follow.

"I don't believe any city is pleasant in the summer," he said quietly.

"Will you be staying long?"

"I don't know. It depends on how much attention your father has to give to these matters."

"Are they terribly important?"

He smiled slightly. "I couldn't say."

"You mean you haven't studied them in advance?"

As a matter of fact, he had. Very carefully. Some of the notes he had made were for the discussions he anticipated having with Drake. Others were strictly for his own benefit.

"I've taken a look at them," he acknowledged.

"I hope so. You do know, of course, that's the whole point of having you bring them."

He paused for a moment and looked at her. "What do you mean?"

Cat shrugged, assuming she was telling him something he already knew. "Father could have a bonded messenger bring the papers and take them back. That's what he's always done before, wherever we happened to be. Why, once he even had a man sent all the way from Boston to Paris and back again just to bring him a letter. But he certainly didn't discuss its contents with him."

"I wouldn't have taken this job if it had been strictly to shuttle papers back and forth," he told her as they started walking again.

"So you do understand that he's thinking about making you his new assistant."

His silence gave her pause. "Evan, did you know that, or have I let the cat out of the bag?"

He gave her a crooked smile. "Meow."

"Uh-oh. I should have known. Father tends to play his cards very close, but I thought for sure he had said something to you. Or, failing that, Mr. Stein had."

"About Mr. Stein..."

"He's retiring at the end of the year. Apparently he recommended you for the job."

"Interesting, considering that no one's mentioned it to me."

"Does that mean you don't want it?"

"Not necessarily." In fact, he had no idea whether he wanted it or not. The idea was so startling that he had yet to come to terms with it. "Why would your father consider somebody like me for such a position?"

"What do you mean, somebody like you?"

"A Mick," he said bluntly. "An Irishman straight out of the peat bog with no education and no—"

"Class?" she suggested helpfully.

His crystalline eyes flared. "Now wait a minute...."

"That's what you meant, isn't it?" Cat challenged. They had stopped again. People were pushing past them. She ignored them, all her attention on him.

"Do you really think you aren't as good as men who were born here, who grew up with all the advantages, who have never had to exert themselves to get anything they wanted in their lives? Do you think because you talk differently and are a little rough around the edges that they're better than you?"

"No," he said, smiling now as he looked down into her slightly flushed face and gleaming eyes. "I don't think that at all. But I do know that plenty of other people would. If your father is seriously considering me for the job, he's got some reason that you don't know about. Me either, for that matter." Though, he added silently, he intended to find out—and quickly.

They had reached the rank of carriages. Evan chose one and tossed his bag up to the driver but kept the briefcase. He turned to Cat. "Ride back with me?"

She looked at the bicycle. "I can't just leave this here."

She had barely spoken before he picked the bicycle up effortlessly, turned it on its side and laid it upright on the facing seat. Two of the wheels stuck up in the air, but otherwise it was secure enough.

With a smile, he offered her a hand up. "Watch your step, now. It will be a bit cramped."

It was, forcing them to sit close together on the back seat. The driver snapped the reins, and the carriage set off down the road Cat had lately pedaled. She leaned back, letting the fresh breeze cool her heated skin.

"Please," she murmured, "don't say anything to Father about what I told you. I'd hate for him to think that I've no better control over my tongue than that."

"I won't," he promised, wondering if he was reading too much into it to think that she had made the slip deliberately. Elizabeth Bennington was reputed to be an extremely circumspect woman when it came to anything involving her husband's business. He was hard-pressed to believe that Cat wouldn't be the same.

Cat. When had he begun thinking of her by the pet name he knew her family used, when he should be thinking of her, if at all, strictly as Miss Bennington? It was virtually impossible to consider her in such terms when he was acutely conscious of her slender body so close to his own.

His leg brushed against hers through the layers of their clothing. He breathed in the sun-warmed scent of her, a musky, powdery combination of violets, silk and pure, healthy woman. For an instant his senses reeled. He had a sudden, acute understanding of why men and women were kept separate in certain cultures, and why their contact was so restricted in his own.

He and Cat were breaking the rules. They both knew that. The only question was how much further they would go.

CHINESE LANTERNS illuminated the gardens behind the van Rhys mansion. Guests clustered on the lawns, listening to the string orchestra and chatting among themselves. Mrs. van Rhys, a tightly-corseted, florid-faced lady, fluttered about, waving her large feathered fan and murmuring about all the things the servants were forgetting to do.

"Why give the damn party," her husband—half a foot shorter but equally stout—demanded, "if it's going to cause you so much aggravation?"

"Oohh," Mrs. van Rhys cried, "you just don't understand. You never even try. It must be perfect or I shall be an absolute laughingstock. Oh, no!" she screeched as she spied a black-garbed waiter emerging with a fresh tray of canapés. "Not the puffs on the silver. The puffs go on the lacquer. They look so much better there. Oh, I must speak with Monsieur Renaud again. Such an impossible man. Thousands of dollars to hire a chef, and now he pretends not to understand a word of English."

She hurried off, murmuring and exclaiming, in the general direction of the kitchen. Jimmy and Cat grinned at each other. "I'd pretend, too," Jimmy said. "She's a terror. Still, I'm sorry she's so upset."

"Don't be silly," his sister said affectionately. "She's in her glory. For a week she'll talk about nothing except what went wrong with her party, which will oblige everyone to reassure her endlessly that it was wonderful."

"What happens after that?" Jimmy asked.

Cat shrugged. "Another party, another dissection. What else ever happens here?"

"Nothing that I can see," her brother agreed. He grinned at his sister affectionately. "However, that's no reason not to have a good time. Do you want me to go on fending off the sharks, or shall I make myself scarce?"

"'Sharks'? What are you talking about?"

"Oh, come on, Cat," he reprimanded her gently. "Take a look around. We're at the center of what amounts to a cordon of eager gentlemen primed and ready to make their move the moment the approach is cleared. At the moment, I'm standing smack in the middle of it, playing the devoted brother. However, if you'd rather I didn't..."

Cat lowered her thick lashes and took a quick, surreptitious glance around. Rather to her surprise, she saw that Jimmy's description was only mildly exaggerated.

There did seem to be a number of young men watching them with more than merely casual interest. She suppressed a sigh as she reflected that she had some idea of how a tethered goat must feel.

"I suppose you have your own quarries to pursue," she said resignedly.

"That's all right," he assured her. "I'll stay if you like."

His loyalty touched her, but she couldn't bring herself to take advantage of it. Especially not when she knew she was being silly. The whole purpose of such affairs, at least so far as the young people were concerned, was to meet one another. She simply had to bury her reservations and join the crowd.

"Never mind," she said. "Just introduce me to a few of your less obnoxious friends and you can be on your way."

"I'm not sure I have any less obnoxious ones," he mused with a smile. "After all, they go to Harvard, to a man, take the same classes, belong to the same clubs. Fact is, it's not always that easy to tell one from another."

"Don't let Father hear you say that," she cautioned lightly. "He'll think you're infected with the same problem I seem to have."

"An inability to take our situation seriously?"

"Exactly. You and I show an unmistakable tendency to be troublemakers."

"There are worse crimes," he said quietly. Their eyes met for a moment in perfect understanding. Both smiled.

"Come along, then," Jimmy said. "There's a fellow from North Carolina, of all places, who isn't half bad. His father's somebody in furniture, but he wants to be a poet. He's shy of Northern girls, says they're too aggressive."

"And you're going to inflict me on him?" Cat murmured in mock horror.

"Mention that Mother came from Virginia. That'll settle him right down."

Perhaps it would have, but Cat never got a chance to find out. Barely had Jimmy taken his leave after introducing her to the sandy-haired boy than Charles suddenly appeared at her side. He made short work of the unfortunate Southerner, who seemed to fade into the woodwork.

Once the other man was gone, Charles smiled boldly. His narrow face beneath carefully brushed brown hair had an almost feral leanness. His eyes, as they raked Cat over, were a shade too familiar.

"I like that dress," he said. "One gets so tired of seeing young ladies always gotten up in white. Yellow becomes you."

In fact the gown was closer in hue to pale gold. It perfectly offset Cat's amber hair and complemented the rich, warm tone of her skin. It was also somewhat more sophisticated than the gowns worn by most of the girls her age. The off-the-shoulder cut revealed more than the usual expanse of alabaster skin, while the elaborately beaded bodice and waist emphasized the perfection of her figure.

Cat liked the dress, enough so that when her father had raised his eyebrows upon seeing her in it, she had felt confident enough to merely laugh. But the expression on Charles's face as he surveyed her made her feel suddenly ill at ease.

She glanced around for Jimmy, only to see him in rapt conversation with not one, but two, young ladies. With a resigned sigh, she decided that she would have to deal with Charles on her own.

"You really mustn't let me monopolize you," she said sweetly. "After all, this is your party."

He raised a hand, forestalling her. "Don't put the blame for that on me. This was strictly Mother's idea. But as long as I have to be here—" he took her arm peremptorily and led her toward the dance floor "—I may as well enjoy it."

Cat went along rather than cause a scene, but she was seething with resentment. She said barely a word as they danced, leaving Charles to carry the conversation, such as it was. He grew tired of her monosyllables quickly enough and scowled at her.

"You might be more pleasant, Cat."

"Don't call me that."

"Why not?"

"Because it's for family, not outsiders."

"You're too touchy," he complained. "Most girls make themselves more agreeable."

He spoke so plaintively that she couldn't help but laugh. "I'm sure they do. You're considered quite a catch."

"But not by you?"

Cat shrugged. She was regretting getting into this with him, but she couldn't see how to back out gracefully. "What does it matter what I think?"

His hand tightened on her waist. "It matters. You must know how beautiful you are."

"Is that all you care about?" she asked, eyeing him dubiously.

"No, of course not."

"It helps that I'm a Bennington, doesn't it?"

"Of course it does," he admitted bluntly. "I could hardly marry just anyone. Only a fool would select a wife who isn't of his own kind."

"I'm not interested in getting married."

He stared down at her for a moment, taken aback. Then he decided that she was teasing and laughed. "That's very good, Cat."

"I mean it, Charles. Marriage doesn't appeal to me."

He chuckled again, a singularly annoying sound. "When did you decide this?"

She was hardly about to admit that it had come to her on the spur of the moment, especially when that wasn't strictly true. The thought that she wanted to do something else with her life had been crystallizing in her mind for some time. Resolutely she told herself that the impossibility of her feelings for Evan had nothing to do with it.

"I've always had the sense that I might not marry," she claimed. "My parents set such an extraordinarily high standard that I can't imagine ever being in a position to live up to it."

He looked down at her wonderingly. "You really do see them as locked in some sort of romantic idyll, don't you?"

His derisive tone stung her, but Cat resolutely ignored it. "It would hardly be appropriate to discuss my parents' relationship with you. Suffice it to say that I've grown up witnessing a great love, and it's spoiled me for anything less."

He was silent for a moment, considering, before he said, "Did you know that your mother ran away from your father shortly after they were married? She went home to Virginia and threatened not to return. Worse yet, she was expecting you and your brother at the time. Your father had to go all the way down there to bring her back. It was quite a scandal."

Cat's mouth had fallen open. She shut it with a snap and glared at him. "How can you possibly have the nerve to make up such a story?" She stopped in the midst of the dance floor, daring him to take another step without answering her.

"I didn't make it up," he said as he pulled her stiff body back against his. "It was common knowledge at the time. I heard my mother talking about it and imagined you always knew."

"That was a long time ago," Cat ventured, hardly aware of what she was saying. She was struggling to come to terms with the sudden image of her parents as opponents rather than as the loving, supportive partners she had always known.

The vision was so distressing that she automatically leaped from it to the comforting reality she knew. "Besides . . . it all worked out in the end."

"Exactly my point," Charles said. "Love, at least the way the shop girls imagine it, doesn't exist. What counts is mutual respect, shared values and objectives, that sort of thing."

"What about—" She broke off, aware that she had been about to mention a word she most certainly would regret. Passion was the last thing she wanted to make Charles think of.

Nonetheless he guessed what was in her mind. A slow, knowing smile spread across his face. "There are certain things you needn't be concerned about, Cat. They can be safely left to your husband."

She affected not to know what he meant, and at length the dance ended. Despite Charles's efforts to persuade her otherwise, she declined to dance with him again.

Instead she slipped away onto the veranda. The fresh salt breeze eased her incipient headache. She had an all-but-irresistible desire to run down the slanting lawn, throw off her slippers and wade in the surf.

With a regretful sigh she turned back in the direction of the party, but she made no effort to rejoin it. She was content to watch through the open doors as couples whirled by. They all seemed so happy and carefree. She wondered why she couldn't be the same. Why she couldn't simply enjoy a life virtually anyone would have envied.

Impatient with her own contrariness yet seemingly unable to do anything about it, she remained on the veranda until several couples emerged to take the air. Only then did she reluctantly return to the party.

Jimmy noticed her enter alone and went over to her, concerned. "Is everything all right?"

"Fine," she assured him. "I was getting a headache and thought it best to be outside for a while."

"If you aren't feeling well, we can leave."

She was tempted, but stalwartly shook her head. "It would be rude. Supper's about to be served."

"Hang supper. We'll go home and raid the icebox. Cook is sure to have left something good."

She smiled at him fondly. "Remember all the times we did that when we were little?"

"Little? I remember when we did it last week." He laid a gentle hand on her arm. "Seriously, Cat, you aren't having a good time. That's obvious. So why don't we just go?"

"I'd like to," she admitted. "But it isn't fair to you. Besides," she went on when he would have objected, "I'm being silly. You shouldn't pay any attention. It's just a mood."

"You don't have moods," he told her quietly. "Or at least you never used to."

"Perhaps it has something to do with being eighteen. I'm finding the transformation from child to adult a bit difficult."

He smiled wryly. "Aren't we all. At least it's easier for a man. Nobody expects us to simply sit around looking appealing until we get married off."

"That's a shame," Cat said. "I wouldn't mind seeing the positions reversed."

"You sound like one of the Pankhursts," he teased.

"As it happens, I agree with a great deal they say. Rights for women are long overdue."

"Tell Charles that," Jimmy said as he glanced over his shoulder. "Here he comes again."

"Oh Lord," she said, looking around for some avenue of escape, "he'll want to take me in to supper."

"Sorry, old chap," Jimmy said as Charles attempted to do precisely that. "Cat's promised to sit with me. We haven't had a chance for a good chat in days. Can't fall out of touch with my little sister, you know."

"The two of you are in each other's back pockets as it is," Charles grumbled.

"Comes from being twins," Jimmy informed him as he bore Cat off. "Special bond and all. Nothing for it."

What Charles thought of that, they didn't linger to find out. Instead Jimmy guided her swiftly to the buffet table, insisted that she heap her plate, then found them seats with a cluster of his school friends who, after their initial bemusement at finding Cat in their midst, turned out to be boisterously congenial.

She ended the evening in high good humor, laughing at their stories, and went home feeling a bit less at odds than she had before.

THE FEELING DIDN'T LAST. When Cat went down to breakfast the following morning and found Evan at the table, in conversation with her father, she was abruptly swept by the same unsettling sensations she had been experiencing since their first encounter. The smile with which she had awakened vanished as she plummeted back into unwelcome reality.

"Good morning," she murmured, forcing herself to act as naturally as she could manage.

"Good morning, dear," her mother said. "Sleep well?"

"Fine," Cat assured her. She shook her head as the butler offered coffee, put her napkin in her lap and accepted a piece of toast.

"How was the party?" her father asked.

She glanced across the table at Jimmy, who answered for her. "About what you'd expect. You and Mother didn't miss anything."

Elizabeth and Drake exchanged a private look, suggesting that indeed they hadn't. "What do you say we go out on the boat today?" Drake suggested, still looking at his wife.

"Olivia?" Elizabeth asked politely. "Would you care for that?"

The sallow girl looked uncertain. "Jimmy, are you going?"

Cat suppressed a grin as she watched her brother squirm. "I have other plans, actually."

Rather pointedly, Olivia waited for him to describe them. Equally pointedly, Jimmy did not. Clearly he wanted to take no risk of her inviting herself along.

At length, when she had run out of alternatives, Olivia said, "If no one would mind, I think I'd rather stay here and rest. This visit is turning out to be rather more enervating than I had expected."

Drake's mouth twitched. "Cat didn't have you out on the tennis court again this morning, did she?"

Olivia shook her head vigorously. "I really don't mind keeping up with the latest fashions, but that's one I simply don't understand." Generously she added, "It's fine for you, of course, Cat. You enjoy that sort of thing."

Cat chewed her toast and didn't comment. She was looking ahead to a day on the water with Evan when it suddenly occurred to her that he might not be coming along. She needn't have feared, however, for her father promptly said, "You'll join us, I hope, Evan. We can use the time to continue going over these papers."

"You can use it to rest," Elizabeth broke in with mock sternness, "and let Mr. O'Connell do the same. He's hardly had a moment's peace since he got here."

"That's all right," Evan said, surprised by her consideration. Elizabeth Bennington wasn't at all what he had expected. She was as beautiful as the portrait in her husband's office indicated, and as she had been on the yacht, but she also had a warmth and directness he did not associate with wealthy, pampered women.

Looking at her, he suspected that Cat's strong character did not come purely from her father. Her mother had more than a little to do with it.

"Nevertheless," Elizabeth said firmly, "you must come along with us. A day on the water has a way of clearing one's head. Everything will look much brighter afterward."

He supposed she was referring to the knotty business problems Drake was expecting him to help sort out, but from his point of view, she might also have meant his thoughts about her daughter. He doubted anything would brighten that dubious picture, but he was willing to give it a try.

"I'VE ALWAYS BEEN CURIOUS about Ireland," Elizabeth said. She was seated on a lounge chair beneath the awning that shaded one end of the deck. Her white dress fluttered in the breeze as she nodded to the steward, who placed a pitcher of lemonade on the wrought-iron table.

They were about two miles out of Newport. The air was brilliantly clear and the sky cloudless, except on the southern horizon, where stray wisps showed. The remnants of lunch had been cleared away, and now there was nothing to do except enjoy the day.

"Most of my mother's people came from Scotland and the Netherlands," Elizabeth went on, "but a few were Irish. I believe there were Irish on my father's side, as well."

Beside her, Evan smiled. He had felt uncomfortable at first to be thrown in among the family on what was turning out to be a purely social occasion, but that was fading as he talked with Elizabeth.

He knew she was going out of her way to make him feel relaxed, and he appreciated it even as he wondered why she bothered. Gradually he was coming to the conclusion that it was simply her way. He was a guest; she would do whatever she could to make sure that he had a pleasant time. That he was also her husband's employee didn't matter.

Her genuineness prompted him to greater candor than would otherwise have been the case. "The Irish have been on the run for generations. It would be surprising if we didn't crop up almost everywhere."

"I suppose..." She glanced at Catherine, who was leaning against the railing chatting with Jimmy. Drake was stretched out on the settee, dozing. They were under sail; there was no sound except the snap of the wind in the canvas and the far-off cries of seabirds.

"Did you leave family in Ireland?" Elizabeth asked softly.

Evan nodded. "Two sisters, both married and with children. The rest—my mother and father, another sister and a brother—were dead by the time I left."

"Is that usual? To lose two siblings as well as your parents?"

Evan shrugged. "It happens. Maeve died trying to birth a baby, her third. She was twenty at the time. Sean was the oldest of us. He was killed in '93."

"Killed by whom?" Catherine asked. She had been listening to the conversation while attempting to appear not to. But curiosity had gotten the better of her. She gave up her pretense of studying the scenery and came over to join them, taking a seat next to Evan.

"That's hard to say. He had gone to Dublin to find work and was coming home one night when some trouble broke out. Gladstone's bill for home rule for Ireland had just been defeated in the House of Lords, you see, and feelings were running high. At any rate, rocks were thrown, the authorities overreacted and several people were killed, including Sean."

"Then you believe the police killed him?" Cat asked.

"Possibly."

The calmness of his admission stunned her. "If I thought the police had killed my brother," she glanced over at Jimmy, still standing by the rail but also listening, "I'd be enraged."

Evan looked at her gravely. "It doesn't pay for an Irishman to give in to his emotions like that, Miss Bennington. All that does is get *him* killed, as well."

Cat was silent for a moment, absorbing his words. Slowly she said, "You aren't an idealist."

He gave a short, hard laugh. "No, that I am not. Oh, there was a time when I might have been. But I've come to the conclusion since then that ideals are pretty well useless. Only wealth and power matter."

"I hope you don't really mean that," Elizabeth said quietly. "Surely without ideals, wealth and power lead inexorably to the worst excesses."

"True enough," Evan agreed, "but that doesn't change the fact that only the rich can afford to believe in something beyond money. They've already got it, so they're safe. For the rest of us, it's the scramble to survive that comes first."

"You paint a bleak picture, Mr. O'Connell," Elizabeth murmured.

"But an accurate one." Drake spoke as he sat up, running a hand through his rumpled hair. "Like it or not, the world is a hard place. Money makes an enormous difference."

"Too much of one," Cat protested.

Before he could stop himself, Evan shot her an amused look. "Does that mean you'd be willing to give it up?"

"I certainly think I could live without all the frills I've been used to," she informed him.

Jimmy laughed. "I'd like to see you try."

"I could," Cat repeated. When no one leaped to agree with her, she flushed. "How difficult could it be? Look at all the people who do it."

"Please, Cat," her brother said with a sigh, "don't sound any dumber than you have to."

"That wasn't nice, Jimmy," Elizabeth intervened. "I'm sure Catherine means well."

"Why should you live any other way?" Evan asked softly. The family turned to look at him, but it was on Catherine that his attention was focused.

She looked as always, remarkably beautiful. But beyond that, he was struck yet again by how perfectly she reflected his dreams.

"I know how the rest of the world lives," he said, speaking directly to her. "Far better than you will ever know. And why should you? This is where you belong. You should enjoy the life you have, not be embarrassed by it in any way."

"I'm not embarrassed . . . exactly."

"But you feel uncomfortable?" When she nodded, he said, "You shouldn't. The world needs people like you."

"For what?"

"To exemplify the best. To show how good we can be."

"What a lovely thing to say, Mr. O'Connell," Elizabeth murmured.

"Lovely," Drake repeated. He gave Evan a single, searching look and changed the subject. For the rest of the day's sail, they talked about impersonal things.

Evan was relieved by that; he fully understood that he had been skating on thin ice by speaking to Cat so frankly. But he was also glad he had done so. It made him feel closer to her, however tenuous and futile that connection might be.

By the time they returned to shore late in the afternoon, the sky was clouding over. The wind had shifted and was blowing briskly out of the southeast. With it came a faintly tropical scent that caused Evan some concern.

"There's bad weather coming," he commented as they walked up the dock toward the broad lawn and the house.

"Oh, no," Cat protested. "It's lovely."

"The wind's changed."

"It does that all the time," she assured him. "It doesn't mean anything."

He was unconvinced, but said nothing more. When they got back inside, Drake asked him to come to the library to go over the papers before the family went out that evening to a party.

EVAN WORKED LATE, taking his supper on a tray in the library. He went up to bed before they had returned, but woke when he heard the murmur of voices going past his door.

For a time he lay with his hands folded beneath his head, thinking about Cat, until he realized that he was envisioning her getting ready for bed. With a murmur of disgust at his own weakness, he turned on his side and resolutely courted sleep.

It came at last, but uneasily. He drifted between dreams in which a golden-haired girl held out her arms to him, only to recede from him faster and faster as he tried to reach her.

In the morning the sun was shining and there was still only a faint line of clouds on the horizon, more than on the previous day, but hardly anything to be concerned about.

"What are your plans for today?" Elizabeth asked her children when the family, along with Olivia and Evan, were gathered at the breakfast table.

"I thought I'd take *The Snail* out," Jimmy said. "Try a run along the coast. The yacht's great, but sometimes I like the feel of a smaller boat."

"Be careful if you do," Drake said as he put down the newspaper he'd been glancing at. "There's a stiff wind."

"All the better," Cat said. "May I come, too?"

"Sure," Jimmy agreed. At a chiding look from his mother, he sighed and said, "Olivia, you'd be welcome, too."

The sallow girl looked taken aback. Clearly the idea of going with Jimmy tempted her. But not for a sail on a small boat lacking even the most basic comforts.

"Unless," Elizabeth said, stepping in adroitly, "you'd prefer to come shopping with me. A rather clever couturier has opened up in town. I thought I'd take a look at what she's offering."

"Oh, yes," Olivia agreed with an almost audible sigh of relief. "I would like that."

Jimmy shot his mother a look of pure gratitude, then turned to his sister. "I'll put you in charge of lunch. That's women's work."

"Fine," she told him saucily, "and I'll put you in charge of rowing, should the wind fail."

"It won't," Jimmy said confidently. "It's going to be a great day."

Evan spent it working in the library with Drake. There was a complication involving a real-estate deal that took several hours to straighten out.

They broke for lunch, then went back to work. By midafternoon they were still at it when there was a knock at the door.

Elizabeth looked in, saw the two of them in their shirt-sleeves and the desk littered with papers, and shook her head. "Don't you think it's time you called it a day?"

"What time is it?" Drake asked. Before she could reply, he glanced toward the windows. "Later than I'd thought. It's already dark."

"It's barely 4:00 p.m." Elizabeth said. "The storm has been coming on for hours, and the rain hasn't even started yet."

"Storm?" Evan said, frowning. He got up and walked over to the windows. Outside the sky was a leaden, yellowish color, with great roiling banks of clouds hanging so low as to seem to touch the treetops. He opened the French door slightly and felt the sudden rush of wet, cold air.

"Cat and Jimmy are back, aren't they?" he asked Elizabeth, not caring if anyone noticed his familiarity.

"Oh, of course. They must be..." Her voice trailed off, becoming doubtful. She and Drake barely glanced at each other before hurrying from the room.

Cat and Jimmy were not back. That was quickly determined by looking in their rooms and questioning the servants. No one had seen them since shortly after breakfast, when they had set out, picnic basket in hand, toward the jetty where *The Snail* was kept.

"I'm going to take a look," Drake said as he headed for the door, not bothering to put on a raincoat.

Evan followed him. "I'll come with you."

"Be careful," Elizabeth called after them. She stood in the open door, her hands clasped, struggling to remain calm but with a rising sense of dread that would not be denied.

They were back within a few minutes, returning to the house just as the skies opened. Lashing rain pelted the veranda. A finger of lightning starkly illuminated the scene for an instant before vanishing, to be followed by thunder.

"There's no sign of them," Drake said grimly. "I'm calling the lifeboat patrol."

"Do you really think that's necessary?" Elizabeth murmured.

"Chances are they've holed up someplace and are fine," Evan said. He glanced from one to the other, seeing the terrible fear etched on their faces and knowing that his own mirrored it. "But it would still be best to take every precaution."

Drake nodded. He strode swiftly to the back of the house, where the telephone was kept, and made the call. While he was gone, Evan took Elizabeth's elbow and led her gently into the library.

She went unresistingly. He had the impression that she had no idea of anything beyond her worry for her children. When he placed a brandy snifter in her hands, she looked startled.

"Go on," he said gently. "It will do you good."

She nodded and took a long swallow before attempting to speak. "I'm sure you're right. They've undoubtedly found shelter somewhere. Jimmy is a very good sailor, and so is Cat. They wouldn't do anything foolish."

"Of course not," he agreed, sounding more confident than he felt.

Drake had returned. Beneath his tanned skin, his face was gray. "The lifeboat patrol has had several calls already about other boats, but they'll do their best."

"Did they say anything about where they might be?" Elizabeth asked in a low, agonized tone.

"They seem to feel it's best to presume they're still at sea and proceed accordingly."

"Oh, God," Elizabeth murmured. She dropped her head, tears sliding down her pale cheeks.

Drake sat down on the couch beside her and put an arm around her shoulders. He said nothing, but his whole attitude bespoke his love, and his own fear.

Evan felt that he should look away, knowing that he was witnessing an acutely private moment, but he could not wrench his eyes from the pair. Behind them, as though almost in the room, he could see the children for whom they were so afraid—bright, courageous Jimmy, and Cat, beautiful, perfect Cat.

He cleared his throat. "Mr. Bennington, have you got another boat. Something small and fast?"

Drake looked up at him blankly for a moment before his words registered. "Another boat? Yes, we have several. But..."

Before he could finish, Evan went on. "In the West Country of Ireland, where I grew up, a lad learns to sail at the same time he learns to walk. I haven't forgotten any of that. Let me take one of those boats and go out after them."

Drake stared at him. "You'd be risking your life."

"Not at all," Evan said. "Why, in Ireland this kind of weather is thought perfect for sailing. I'll have a fine old time and find them to boot."

Elizabeth gave him a soft, if damp smile. "Mr. O'Connell, we both know that's a load of blarney."

"Maybe," he admitted. "But it's still better than waiting around for the lifeboat patrol."

"It is that," Drake agreed. He touched his wife's face tenderly and stood up, looking at Evan. "I've got two small, fast sloops down at the docks. You take one, I'll take the other."

"Drake..." Elizabeth protested.

He turned to her, his face hard and unrelenting. "Surely you don't expect me to stay here?"

For a moment their eyes remained locked. Hers were wide and pleading, yet behind them was the knowledge that he was right. No matter how it tortured her to think of her husband in danger as well as her children, he had to go.

But that was easier decided than done. Barely had Drake and Evan left the house than the wind picked up even further. It battered them as they ran, heads bent, across the lawn toward the dock.

"You're sure you want to do this?" Drake shouted above the scream of the wind. They had paused long enough to put on rain slickers, waterproof pants and boots, as well as to hastily assemble first-aid kits.

The kits were strapped to their chests under the slickers, where at least they would stay dry. Anything exposed to the driving rain was already soaked through. Their hair clung to their heads as rivulets of water washed down their faces.

At the end of the dock the boats bobbed wildly, their hulls battered by the force of the storm. Farther out, the *Elizabeth* rode safely at anchor, close enough to shore to be protected, yet not so close that she might run aground.

In the open sea, where they had to go, she would be useless. Even under power, she was too heavy to make any appreciable headway. But more than that, both men could see that the troughs between the waves were deep enough to capsize her.

"Let's not waste time," Evan shouted back. He jumped into one of the boats and quickly unlashed it. Within minutes he had the sail raised and was relieved to see that it held, despite the rushing wind. Swiftly, he moved astern and took his place by the rudder.

Drake had done the same. He lifted a hand to Evan as his small boat turned toward the sea. Almost instantly, he disappeared into the driving rain. Evan paused a moment longer, sitting motionless and alert.

Deliberately, in the way he had been taught, he opened his mind and absorbed the signals nature was sending him. He felt the power and direction of the wind as well as the rhythm of its fury.

He caught the motion of the water and let it sink into him, telling him when the waves would crest, when they would fall. None of this occurred to him consciously. Rather, he knew at a much deeper level, where instinct and reflex dwelled. When that knowledge was in him, he was ready.

Even so, the moment he left the sheltered cove, he was almost overturned. He had to fight desperately to keep the boat upright. There was no sign of Drake; he could only hope that the older man was managing. Blanking Drake and everything else out of his mind, Evan turned the boat southward, directly into the teeth of the storm.

For an hour, perhaps more, he fought the fury of the howling wind and surging water. His body was strained to its limit by the elemental force of nature against which his own will, however desperate, seemed puny.

Yet he held on. Vainly his eyes scanned the water again and again, searching for some sign of the missing boat.

He refused to give up or even to allow himself the slightest twinge of doubt, although he knew that the chances of anyone surviving such a terrible storm were slim.

His own life hung in the balance again and again as he battled to stay upright. Water sloshed several inches deep in the hull. He had no time to bail it out; all he could do was cling to the rudder, trying to hold the boat steady as it plunged ahead into the next trough, and the next, and the next.

Time became meaningless, the storm endless. He had always been in this boat, on this sea, in peril for his life. The other reality he had known—land, warmth, safety— had been no more than an illusion.

He was completely caught up in the elemental struggle he was waging. Yet the moment he glimpsed the huddled shape on the point he was rapidly approaching, he knew what he was seeing.

In the end it proved impossible to bring the boat in to shore. The little vessel had proved indomitable through what had been a nearly impossible voyage, but its spirit was not equal to the final demands placed on it. As Evan relentlessly pointed the prow toward the beach, he knew the boat would not make it.

At the last moment, he threw himself into the water, fighting the surging current that threatened to pull him under. With the final remnants of his strength, he dragged himself up on to the beach even as the boat struck an outcropping of rocks and was broken apart by the impact.

CAT MOANED SOFTLY. Her eyes were closed, and she was sure that she was dreaming, or, more correctly, that she was in the throes of a nightmare.

Her entire body throbbed with pain. Not an inch of her felt unbruised. Her lungs and throat were swollen and burning, her head pounded, and when she tried to open her eyes, the lids seemed glued shut.

That sensation, more than anything else, terrified her. She cried out.

"Easy," a deep, soft voice said. Something cool and wet touched her face, wiping away the gritty stickiness from around her eyes. "Try now."

She did so and almost instantly regretted it. The light that entered through the crack between her lids was so bright as to be blinding. Immediately, she shut her eyes and turned her head away.

"It's all right," the voice murmured again. "Don't push yourself too hard. You're safe now."

Evan. The realization that he was there, with her, banished every other consideration. She opened her eyes fully, heedless of the discomfort, and stared at him.

"You..."

Surely that wasn't her voice? That weak, cracked sound that caused her such pain to utter? Her hand went to her throat in shock.

His face swam before her, the eyes tender but watchful. "You swallowed a lot of salt water. That's bound to hurt."

Then she remembered. The storm, their frantic efforts to reach shore, the moment when the enormous wave had seized the boat, flipping it over as effortlessly as a summer breeze flips a feather. Jimmy.

Terror filled her. She sat up abruptly, a scream rising in her tortured throat.

Instantly Evan caught her. He held her firmly against his broad chest, feeling the tremors sweeping through her. Her slender body quaked as she relived the horror she had passed through.

He smoothed her hair gently, murmuring soft words of comfort and reassurance, wishing all the while that he could take her pain and fear into himself.

The thought of such a beautiful and delicate woman in such torment ate at him. Yet he was helpless to do anything but hold her as she confronted her memories.

"Jimmy...?"

Evan's face tightened. He had hoped she wouldn't think of her brother for another few minutes at least, until she'd had a little more chance to adjust to what had happened.

Reluctantly he held her slightly away from him and looked down into her wide, apprehensive eyes. "I couldn't find him, or the boat," he said quietly. "You were on the beach. I have no idea how you got there."

Cat squeezed her eyes shut. She knew she was going to cry and despised herself for it, but she was far too weak to prevent it. Evan continued to hold her tenderly as she wept, her sobs shaking him as much as they shook her.

"Why?" she whispered brokenly when she had at last regained some measure of control. "Why in the name of God would this happen?"

Evan had no answer for her. He had seen too much of the vagaries of fate ever to be surprised by it, but that made this no easier to accept. He did, however, have a small word of hope.

Tilting her chin back, he said firmly, "Jimmy might have made it. We can't know for sure that he didn't."

Of her father and his peril, he said nothing. She had more than enough to deal with as it was.

It was not in Cat's nature to despair. She seized the hope he offered and clung to it even as she clung to him. They remained close together until her growing awareness of her surroundings caused her to raise her head.

"Where are we?" she asked softly.

Reassured by her returning strength, he smiled down at her gently. "In a hut a short distance above the beach. I was lucky to find it."

Cat glanced around, seeing at once how right he was. The hut was small and rudely furnished, but it also provided shelter from the storm that continued to batter them.

A small oil lamp provided the light that had seemed so blinding earlier but now appeared pale and weak. She was sitting on a wood plank floor, wrapped in a blanket, beneath which she was . . .

She looked up at Evan in shock. He read her thoughts and flushed slightly. "Your clothes were soaking wet. I had to take them off."

He had also removed most of his own clothes for the same reason, though he had kept on his trousers. His chest was bare, bronze in the lamplight.

She stared, fascinated at the play of muscles beneath his smooth skin, until she realized the direction of her thoughts and looked hastily away.

"It's cold," she murmured, holding the blanket more securely around herself.

"There's a fireplace. I'll see if it works."

He stood up with an almost palpable sense of relief. She was going to be all right. Moreover, she was dealing with the situation sensibly. Which was more than he could say for himself. It took all his willpower to walk away from her.

With her golden hair tumbling around her bare shoulders, her eyes wide and luminous, her lips full and soft, she was an enticement to his senses that he could barely resist.

Moreover his desire for her went far beyond the physical. His yearning to cherish her was a need he had never before experienced. He wanted to protect and care for her every bit as much as he longed to make love to her.

No two desires could have been more contradictory. The gentlemanly side of his nature demanded that he act with the utmost propriety and do nothing that could even remotely be construed as taking advantage of the situation.

But there was also another side, far more basic and far less restricted by any such elevated concerns. That was the side that urged him to take full advantage, to compromise her in every possible way for the precise purpose of making her his. Certainly he would never have another chance.

He gritted his teeth as he checked the flue before shoving kindling in around the wood and putting a match to it. The wood was aged and dry; it caught instantly. Within minutes a cheerful blaze was warming the hut.

"Is that better?" he asked when he returned to her.

Cat nodded, though she kept her eyes averted. She had been staring at him while he laid the fire, fascinated by his body's every movement. Warmth stirred in her that had nothing whatsoever to do with the dancing flames.

"Evan."

He sat down beside her, looking at her with some concern. "Yes."

"Thank you for saving me."

He smiled ruefully. "You're welcome."

"You were out looking for us, weren't you?"

When he nodded, she said, "That was very brave."

He shifted self-consciously. Her gratitude unnerved him, though he wasn't sure why. Perhaps it had something to do with not wanting her to feel indebted to him in any way. He preferred to have no sense of obligation shadow whatever happened between them.

"It was damn stupid, too," he said gruffly. "That boat I was in was destroyed."

She looked at him, her eyes the color of slate. "How will we get back, then?"

He shrugged and stared into the fire. "We'll have to wait until morning, then hike back. There will be search teams out. With luck we'll find someone to give us a ride."

Cat nodded, clearly unenthused by the prospect. Returning to the world meant confronting what might very well be tragic news. She shied away from it, wondering if she was cowardly to want to postpone the time of reckoning for as long as she could.

"I wish..." she murmured hesitantly.

"What?"

She raised her head and looked at him directly. Her fear for Jimmy was so great that she desperately needed to deny even the thought of death. "I wish that there was nothing except this place . . . and us. Isn't that silly?"

He stared at her for a long moment, watching the play of light and shadow over her delicate features. Slowly he became aware of the rapid beat of his heart and the hardening of his body.

At the same time he saw the outline of her nipples pressing against the thin blanket and knew that he was not alone in his arousal. He was, however, alone in understanding where it could lead.

"I'll see about bringing in more wood," he said and stood up abruptly.

While he was gone, Cat managed to stand up and walk over to the fire. Her legs were very shaky, and at first she was afraid that they wouldn't hold her. But after a moment or two she felt steadier.

Her hair was still damp. Either Evan had undone the pins holding it or the sea had washed them away. At any rate, it fell partway down her back in a sodden mass.

With some effort she began to separate the strands and hold them closer to the heat to dry. While she was doing that, she noted a livid bruise on her upper arm and was reminded of how battered she felt.

She glanced toward the door, wondering when Evan would return. He had already been gone several minutes, but it took time to load up a pile of logs and carry them back. Standing up quickly, she dropped the blanket and surveyed herself.

Her small, white teeth bit into her lower lip as she took in the extent of the damage. Several other large bruises dotted her hips and thighs. In addition, her slender calves were scratched and scraped.

She dimly remembered feeling the pain as she crawled up onto the beach. Hardly a pretty sight, she thought with a rueful smile. But far better than she had any right to expect under the circumstances.

She was reaching for the blanket to wrap herself up again when the door to the hut opened. Evan stood against the backdrop of the storm, his arms full of wood, his thick ebony hair blowing wildly. There was a light in his eyes that she understood instantly, even though she had never seen it before.

"What are you doing?" he demanded, his voice low and hard.

At once she scrambled for the blanket, yanking it up in front of her. "I wanted to see why I hurt so much." The excuse sounded lame, yet it was the truth. She had not had any other motive, at least not that she could admit.

"You hurt because you damn near got killed," he said as he came into the room, slamming the door behind him. He did not look at her again as he dropped the wood on the floor and threw several more logs on the fire. "How did you expect to feel?"

"I don't know," she whispered, suddenly miserable at the thought of how she must seem to him—stupid, thoughtless, immodest. She tried to pull the blanket more securely around herself, but her fingers were stiff, and after a moment he frowned impatiently at her fumblings.

"Can't you do anything for yourself?" Before she could reply, he stood up, took the blanket from her and wrapped it under her arms, tucking one end between her breasts.

Cat stood frozen, immobilized by his touch. She was acutely conscious of the tiny distance separating them, no more than a few inches. The heat of his body seemed to reach out to envelop her, banishing the cold specter of death, affirming life in all its radiant joy.

Focused straight ahead, her gaze was on a line with his thick, muscular neck and the square frame of his jaw. As she watched, fascinated, a pulse leaped to life in the hollow between his collarbone.

"Evan..."

He stared down into her eyes that were open and revealing in their innocence. For a moment he closed his own, fighting against the impulse he was desperate to deny. When he opened them again, she was still looking at him.

"Cat, don't."

"Don't what?"

"You know...you must know what you're doing to me."

She did, though the experience was completely new to her. It filled her with a heady sense of her own power as a woman, hitherto only dimly suspected.

Her mouth lifted at the corners as she said, "I think I do, but I'm not sure. Perhaps you should tell me."

He stared at her, his gaze hard and glittering. "I have better things to do than indulge a spoiled little rich girl who doesn't have enough sense to keep her fingers out of the fire."

Cat jerked away, stung. Once again she felt humiliated, but this time a wiser voice in the back of her mind told her that the emotion was misplaced. Gathering her courage, she faced him directly.

"What are you afraid of, Evan? That you might have to admit to something that doesn't fit into your tidy plans? That you might actually have to own up to being human, even to the extent of desiring a woman you don't like?"

It was his turn to smile, though he tried to suppress it. "What makes you think I don't like you?"

Whatever she had expected him to say, it wasn't that. Flustered, she murmured, "I just thought...I mean, you've made it obvious, haven't you?"

He shook his head. "Not to me. In fact, I thought I was making something of a jackass of myself over you."

Her eyes widened. "You what?"

"You heard me. I've wanted you from the first moment I saw you, Cat Bennington. Steering clear of you has become a major occupation with me. Which makes this present situation just a wee bit humorous."

He let his gaze wander over her gently. "But then, Mother Nature always has liked a joke now and again."

"I had no idea..." she whispered, stunned.

His eyebrows rose. "Didn't you?"

"No, truly, I didn't. I thought you considered me spoiled and silly. In fact, I've been afraid that you'd suddenly realize how I felt and be amused by it."

"Look at me, Cat," he said quietly. "I'm not laughing, am I?"

On the contrary, she had never seen him look more serious. His features were set in taut, unrelenting lines. His crystalline eyes blazed. Inexperienced as she was, she knew instinctively that he was in the grip of a force that would not be denied.

For a moment fear darted through her. She was uncertain, not so much about what she had set in motion as about her ability to deal with it. She had been raised according to a strict code of morality that dictated a woman remained a virgin until her wedding night, that she did not share her body with any man other than her husband. She was not, ideally, even supposed to be aware of the possibility of doing so.

Yet beneath all that was a softer, more humane strand of teaching given to her by her mother and, to a certain degree, subtly reinforced by her father—the teaching that love was both the ultimate source and expression of the best in human beings. And beside it other considerations were, if not inconsequential, at least not as important.

She loved Evan. That truth, which eased so gently into her mind, exploded with the force of the most profound revelation. She loved him. Not merely the outer man, however compelling, but the man she sensed within. A man who had doubts, who was vulnerable, who was, in short, human. As she was.

"Evan," she said softly, looking at him, "I could have died a few hours ago. My life would have ended. Maybe in some way it did." Daring greatly, she placed her hands on his chest, her fingers twining in the soft whorls of glistening black hair she found there.

"I never realized before how tenuous life is. It can be gone in an instant. Knowing that, I don't want to waste any more time."

Beneath her smooth palms, his muscles tightened. The weight and pressure in his loins were all but irresistible. He had to clench his hand at his sides to keep from seizing her.

Desperately he said, "You're overreacting to what happened, Cat. You don't want to do something you'll regret forever after."

"How do you know I'll regret it?"

"You'd have to."

"Are you such a poor lover?"

He stared at her with such shock that she laughed. "Have I offended you?" she asked. "Are you one of those men who believe women shouldn't think of such things?''

"No, I'm not. But—"

"I've heard the Irish were rather repressed in certain areas."

A light flared deep in his eyes. Had she been wiser, it might have sent her reeling. As it was, she merely stared at him, fascinated, as he murmured, "Oh, really. Who told you that?''

"I can't remember." She was hardly aware of speaking. The shape of his mouth enthralled her. His lips were firm, perfectly shaped, slightly parted. His hand slid up her bare arms, making her tingle with warmth. He carefully lifted her hair from the back of her neck, touching her nape lightly before twining his fingers in the silken strands.

Without warning, he pulled her head back. The motion was gentle, but she was taken by surprise. Her lips parted and were instantly covered by his.

Evan made no concessions to her innocence. Later, when he had satisfied his hunger, at least to some small extent, he would be able to, but not now.

His mouth closed over hers, drinking in the taste of her. The inward thrust of his tongue wrung a gasp of shock from her that gave way almost instantly to a moan of pleasure.

She had never so much as suspected that she could feel as she did now. That such a capacity had slumbered within her, all unknown, stunned her almost as much as the pleasure itself.

Instinctively she raised her arms, wrapping them around Evan's broad, muscled shoulders. Through the rough cloth of the blanket she felt his powerful chest pressing against her breasts. The abrasive sensation sent a tremor reverberating through her.

The effort to hold her head upright was suddenly too much. She let it fall fully back, exposing the slender line of her throat to him.

Evan groaned with the force of his need. He had not expected her to be so overwhelmingly responsive. That she was delighted him, but it also made a mockery of his efforts to regain his self-control.

To ignore her innocence when he kissed her was acceptable to him. To overlook it any further was not.

He had no remaining qualms about what was going to happen between them. Later he might, but just then, doubts were impossible. There was an elemental rightness above their lovemaking that would not be denied.

It reinforced his determination to make the experience perfect for her even as he fought the urge to simply lay her down and thrust his way between her legs without any consideration beyond his own satisfaction.

His hair-roughened chest rose and fell with a labored breath as he fought for control. Cat was not helping matters. Instinctively, she arched against him, moving back and forth in a rhythm that was maddening to them both.

Through a red mist of passion Evan stared at her. She was still Cat—beautiful, ethereal, the woman he had always thought of as being above the ordinary, tawdry reality of human existence.

But she was something else as well—a woman awakening to her own capacity for passion; perhaps a little afraid of it, but still courageous enough to confront it head-on.

There was an earthiness to her that he hadn't expected. Beneath his hands and mouth pale marble and gold turned to warm, pulsating flesh that compelled his possession.

With a swift, fluid movement, he bent and lifted her high in his arms. She gasped softly as he strode across the room and laid her on a pile of blankets. For a moment he towered over her, half naked, all male, unstoppable in his intentions.

A last curl of hesitation fluttered within her, vanishing as though it had never been. She smiled and lifted her arms.

Chapter Fifteen

CAT TURNED on her side, brushing the fall of hair away from her face. She propped herself up on her elbow and looked down musingly at the man asleep next to her.

He looked younger than when he was awake, closer to his true age and far less guarded. It gave her a glimpse of the way he might have been had his life been different.

Tenderness welled up in her. She reached out and lightly, so as not to wake him, traced the line of his mouth.

Those lips that had tormented her so delightfully over the past few hours were cool and smooth to her touch. She sighed softly as she withdrew her hand, but continued to watch him.

She understood now why people made such a mystery of sex. It was an elemental force, overwhelming in its effect. To pretend otherwise was to trivialize the basis of life itself.

No wonder society surrounded it with all sorts of taboos and sanctions. And no wonder such stringent punishments were reserved for those who violated them.

They—she especially—had violated the most deeply held tenets of their world. In a society where the double standard not only existed but flourished, she had placed herself completely outside the bounds of propriety.

Should her behavior become known, she could expect to be virtually shunned. Not by her family, though. She knew they would always love her no matter what she did.

That knowledge humbled her even as she wished fervently that she might somehow be able to be true to herself without hurting them. But as for the rest of the people she knew, she didn't care what they thought or said of her. That was inconsequential compared to what she and Evan shared.

The memory of it made her flush. Never in her wildest dreams would she have thought herself capable of the sort of behavior he had inspired. He had known exactly how to arouse her to such a fever pitch of excitement that the most daring caresses seemed right and desirable.

Warmth curled through her, making her stir beneath the blanket he had thrown over them both. Her breasts felt full, the nipples as tight as when he had sucked them into his mouth.

The lingering soreness between her thighs did not distress her. So brief had the pain been that it was already forgotten. The pleasure, however, was not.

She reached out again, this time touching the thin white scar that ran across his brow near one eye. He moved slightly, and his thick dark lashes fluttered.

"Cat . . ."

Her name, said in that soft, slightly groggy male voice, was irresistible. Hardly aware that she did so, she leaned closer to him.

"Is something wrong?" he murmured, coming more fully awake.

Wrong? How could anything possibly be wrong? Smiling, she shook her head.

Evan, however, was not convinced. With the return of consciousness had come memory. His cheeks darkened. Passion flared within him as he reached for her.

She was all silky smoothness in his arms, warm and unresisting. He ducked her head into the hollow of his shoulder as he stroked her back gently. "Are you all right?" he asked.

She nodded against him. "Fine, wonderful, perfect. How about you?"

He smiled with relief at her obvious contentment. A pardonable hint of male arrogance and satisfaction showed in his eyes as he turned slightly to gaze down at her. "No regrets?"

She shook her head firmly. "You?"

"Only that we didn't do this sooner." He leaned back, drawing her with him, and laughed. "You nearly drove me crazy, woman. Stark raving mad. Anything has to be better than what I was going through."

As he spoke, he knew he was right, despite his lingering qualms. It was true that he had no regrets, but that didn't mean he had no concerns. Obviously something had to be worked out between them. Possessing her had only strengthened his resolve never to let her go.

But all that could wait. For the moment, it was enough that they were together.

The storm continued to rage outside. It would be hours yet before they could even think of leaving. A slow smile lifted the corner of his mouth.

"Are you very sore?"

Cat blushed fiercely. She was unaccustomed as yet to his bluntness, or to the extent of his knowledge about women.

His familiarity with her body dismayed her at the same time that she had the sense to appreciate the joy his knowledge had brought her. Mutely she shook her head.

He pulled the blanket back slowly, revealing her body by stages. Cat shivered under his gaze. His features were harshly intent, his eyes narrowed with concentration as he studied her. Beneath his gaze, she felt her nipples hardening and instinctively glanced down at herself.

Her breasts were high and firm, the crests tinged a delicate pink that deepened to rose at the peaks. Beneath them, her body narrowed smoothly to a slender waist before spreading out gently at her hips.

Her belly was not quite flat; there was a slight softness that flowed into faintly bluish shadows near her hipbones. Between her thighs golden hair tangled in soft curls. Her legs were long and slim, tapering to slender feet.

She gasped softly as Evan moved over her, gently urging her legs apart. He caressed her mouth lightly with his as he settled between her thighs. She had discovered scant hours before that she loved the feel of him like that. Far from making her feel in any way trapped, his weight and power only quickened her own intense excitement.

She ran her hands down his back, savoring the feel of his rippling muscles. He was so strong that he could hurt her easily, but she knew without the slightest doubt that he would never do so.

His every touch was tempered by gentleness and what she instinctively understood was his innate regard for women. He was not a man who would ever seek to use the physical advantage nature had given him in order to take what he wanted. On the contrary, he saw his magnificent body as a finely tuned instrument for the giving of joy.

"I love you," she whispered into his mouth as he kissed her long and deeply. He raised his head for a moment, staring straight into her eyes. She waited for him to say the words, too.

Instead he began to caress her, stroking her from her breasts to her thighs so that she quivered helplessly. His teeth grazed her nipple as he positioned her under him. She was already ready, moist and soft from his earlier possession and fully aroused once again.

He entered her slowly, mindful of how new this still was to her. As he moved, he watched her face intently for the slightest sign of discomfort. But there was none, only the slow spreading of wonder and joy over her features.

"Beautiful," she murmured against his throat. "So beautiful."

Evan could not speak; the effort was beyond him. But he agreed completely with her. Never in his life had he experienced anything at once so exalting and so humbling. Being with her, in her, made him feel reborn in the most elemental way.

The glittering intensity of his eyes might have frightened her had she not understood its source. He was clinging to the last remnants of his self-control in his effort to go carefully with her. Much as she appreciated such consideration, she did not want it.

Her hips arched, drawing him deeper into her tight, pulsating depths. His iron-hard thighs and arms gripped her more closely.

"Sweet, Cat," he murmured, his voice like rough velvet around the edges. He moved again, wringing a soft cry from her. His hands slid beneath her firm, rounded buttocks as he locked her tightly against him.

The awareness of themselves as separate individuals began to blur, then dissolve entirely. They moved as one, felt as one, loved as one. And when their union was complete, their joy total, they were one.

For a single, blinding moment, Cat felt what it was to be Evan. She knew him to the essence of his being, as he knew her.

The moment passed; in the slow, drifting aftermath of love they slipped back into consciousness. But the memory of what they had shared lingered in the secret recesses of their spirits where it could never be forgotten or denied.

"I MUST SPEAK with your father," Evan said several hours later. They were lying in front of the fire. The storm continued, but they could both tell that it was finally beginning to abate. Soon this interlude out of time would end. The real world would inexorably draw them back.

She ran a hand down his bare chest, feeling the muscles tense beneath her touch. Their time together had been so perfect, so beyond anything she could ever have dreamed, that she was hard-pressed to accept that it was ending. Yet it was, and somehow she and Evan had to go on.

She shut her eyes for a moment, struggling against her own desperate fears. So overpowering were they that she could not bring herself to speak Jimmy's name. All she could say was, "We don't know...what the situation will be."

He drew her closer, wishing there was something he could say to ease her dread, but knowing that there was not. There was no point in pretending that they might not walk into tragedy when they left the hut. If the worst had happened, Cat would have to use all her strength to deal with her own grief and to help her mother. There would be no time to think of what had happened between her and Evan.

That did not, of course, mean that he wouldn't bend heaven and earth to help her, no matter what the cost to himself. He didn't discount the possibility that if the night and the storm had brought death, in its aftermath she might draw away from him.

Deep in his soul he understood the link between random disaster and personal guilt. It wasn't impossible that she would somehow hold herself responsible for her brother's and father's fates.

His arms tightened around her. He smoothed the silken fall of her hair absently as he stared up at the ceiling. On the other hand, it was perfectly possible that both Jimmy and Drake had survived.

The elder Bennington had an intrinsic toughness Evan instinctively recognized. It was not yet so evident in his son, but he sensed that Jimmy had it, too. He had the sudden, strong conviction that they had not succumbed to the tempest.

Which meant that they—and especially Drake—would have to be dealt with.

A slight, bemused smile lifted the corners of his mouth. He had always thought somewhere in the back of his mind that he would one day have problems with the men in the New World who were, to him, like the English in Ireland.

The men with the money and the power, and the iron will to hold on to both. He'd escaped them once through the simple exigency of emigrating. But he wasn't about to escape them again, nor did he want to.

The time for running was over. The time to stand and hold his ground, to fight for what he believed in, had come.

He said nothing more to Cat, knowing how desperately she was trying to hold at bay her fear for her brother. He would make no mention of Jimmy while his fate was uncertain.

Instead, he held her while she slept fitfully. The fire burned low, eventually going out, but the air in the hut remained warm. Toward dawn, Evan also slept, his arms firm around Cat, her head on his chest and their legs entwined.

A sound—a high-pitched creaking—woke him. He opened his eyes and glanced around for a moment, trying to place what he was hearing. His eyes fell on the shuttered window. Narrow shafts of sunlight streamed through it.

He moved carefully, laying Cat on her back and covering her with the blankets before he rose. Once on his feet, he quickly pulled on his clothes and left the hut.

Outside, in the brightness of morning, he blinked to clear his head. The sky was more than clear; it had the pure, gleaming quality of having been washed clean that follows a violent storm.

Off to the side, below the hill, he could see the waves continuing to pound against what was left of the beach. But farther up, where he stood, there was virtually no sign of what had passed. Only the flattened salt grass was a lingering reminder of nature's fury.

He became aware that he was not alone. A boy was watching him from the narrow road that ran past the hut. It had been the creaking of his bicycle wheels that had awakened Evan.

"Hello, there," the boy called. "You come through all right?"

Evan nodded and walked toward him. "Do you have any news? Any idea of how bad it was?"

The boy shrugged. He was about thirteen, sandy haired and pug-nosed, but serious in his manner. Quietly he said, "Bad. I heard some people were killed." He glanced toward the beach. "Out there, on the water."

"Do you know who?"

The boy shook his head. "There's a village about half a mile from here. That's where I'm from. You could get news there." When Evan hesitated, he added, "You can ride if you want. I'll walk alongside."

Despite himself, Evan smiled. Surely he didn't look quite so decrepit as to be incapable of a half-mile stroll.

"There's a lady with me," he explained. "She was in the water last night." At the boy's quick look of concern, he added, "She'll be all right, but she may need a carriage."

"I can get one. I'll ride back now and see to it."

Evan nodded. "When you get there, tell somebody responsible what's happened. The postmaster, if you have one. Ask him to telegraph to Newport to tell her family she's safe."

When he told the boy Cat's name, his eyes widened. "She's one of the Benningtons?" he asked, making no effort to hide his awe.

Evan suppressed a sigh. He needed no reminders of Cat's special distinction, but it seemed he was going to get them anyway. "Just tell the postmaster," he instructed the boy.

When he was gone, pedaling furiously up the road on his bicycle, Evan went back into the hut. Cat was still asleep. He knelt down beside her, studying her features with the intensity of a man driven to memorize them.

Realizing what he was doing, he broke off abruptly. He refused to believe that they would be parted, come what might.

She stirred, her lashes fluttering, and opened slumberous eyes. The moment they focused on him, she smiled. "Evan..."

The utter sweetness of her tone and expression, the complete, unfeigned welcome in her eyes, tore through him. It was all he could do not to press her back down onto the blankets and love her again. Only the knowledge that time was slipping past stopped him.

"The storm is over," he said.

She stared at him for a moment, then tore herself from his grasp and jumped up. In an instant she was at the window, pulling the shutter away. "It is!" she exclaimed.

He smiled faintly. She had tugged the blanket along with her, but it covered only her front, giving him an unrestricted view of her long legs, her rounded bottom and her long, slender back.

"A boy came by from the village near here. He's getting a carriage for you."

When she merely glanced over her shoulder and nodded, he said, "You'd better get dressed."

Abruptly aware of her dishabille, she flushed. He had spread her clothes out near the fire when he had taken them off her. They were stiff and wrinkled, but dry. She gathered them up but made no effort to put them on until, with a muttered exclamation, he turned his back.

"Did he say anything else?" she asked as she dropped her camisole over her head.

Evan hesitated. He had hardly forgotten that the boy had said there had been deaths, but he didn't want to mention that to Cat. She would naturally fear the worst.

"We didn't talk very long. Once he understood the situation, he offered to go for help."

"Thank heaven," she breathed fervently. "Mother and Father must be worried sick, and Jimmy—" She broke off, biting her lower lip as she struggled with the buttons of her dress.

Evan was no more anxious to tell her that her father had also gone in search of her than he was to admit that the storm had exacted a mortal toll. Instead he remained silent while she finished dressing.

When she was ready, they straightened up the hut together. Cat folded the blankets and put them back in the chest where Evan had found them, while he made sure the fire was out and brought in more wood to replace what they had used.

As they worked side by side, they glanced at each other. Both knew that they were unlikely ever to see the hut again, or to forget what had transpired there.

They were standing outside in the sunshine, still not speaking, when a carriage came along the road. The man driving it pulled up at the sight of them. He introduced himself as the local doctor, confirmed that they were both all right, then stood by as Evan helped Cat into her seat.

"Word has been sent to your family, miss," the doctor told her respectfully. "A telegram was being dispatched as I left to get you."

"Thank you," Cat murmured. She sat back against the leather seat, feeling suddenly exhausted. Evan looked at her with concern. She was very pale, and there were violet shadows beneath her eyes.

Silently he cursed himself for having been so profligate with her strength the night before. Heedless of what the doctor might think, he put his arm around her shoulders. She nestled against him instinctively and remained that way throughout the trip to the village.

They were greeted there by curious stares from the residents who had learned Cat's identity. The doctor offered them the hospitality of his home, where she was able to rest while Evan arranged for transportation back to Newport.

The storm had blown them fifty miles southwest. The railroad tracks had been blocked by falling trees, so no trains were running. By carriage or even by automobile, had one been available, the journey would have taken the remainder of the day.

They were discussing what to do when the boy who had found them came pelting up the walk to the doctor's house.

"Telegram, sir," he said importantly when Evan met him on the porch. The boy thrust the yellow envelope into his hands. Before Evan could open it, he went on ingenuously, "It's from Mr. Drake Bennington in Newport. It says, 'All are well here. *Elizabeth* coming for you top speed. Profound gratitude for your safety.' Do you want to reply, sir?"

Evan shook his head. He fished in his pocket for a quarter, that had somehow survived being washed away by the storm and tossed it to the boy, who grinned and caught it in midair.

With the telegram in his hand, Evan went back into the house. Cat was in the parlor. She looked up as he returned, her gaze going from his face to the paper he held. For a moment, what little color remained in her cheeks disappeared.

"It's all right," he said swiftly as he crossed the room to her side. "Everybody's fine. Your father is sending the *Elizabeth* to pick us up."

She gave a little cry and clung to him, her slender body trembling with the force of her relief. He held her gently, staring off over her head at the wall and wondering what he was going to say to convince Drake Bennington to give him his daughter.

_____ *Part Two*

New York, Spring 1905

CAT STEPPED OFF the curb gingerly, looking up and down the street before she ventured to cross. At noon the area around Wall Street was jammed with a motley collection of carriages and automobiles, all competing with each other for space in the narrow, twisting byways. Horses shied at the belching, banging engines, drivers raised their fists at each other, and pedestrians went in peril.

She had left her hotel only a few hours before and had spent most of the intervening time inside, yet her ivory linen suit already showed several smudges of dust.

She shook her head as she glanced down at it. New York was no dirtier than Boston, only larger and noisier. Despite the inconvenience, she liked the city.

Inwardly she could admit that her affection might have something to do with the fact that this was her first trip alone. She had come down at the beginning of the week and had spent several days taking care of various matters. Moving about the city independently pleased her.

In the evenings she dined by herself in the hotel restaurant, where she knew she was the subject of speculative glances from other, mostly male, guests. No one spoke to her, though, perhaps because of the cool reserve she cultivated. She had developed the ability to look straight through a man without seeing him to a degree that sometimes surprised even herself.

When she had made it safely to the other side of the street, she breathed a sigh of relief and let her skirt drop. Lifting it had not really been necessary; the new styles cleared the ground, if only by a scant inch or two. But habits lingered, often to her amusement when she considered how much of her life had changed.

Mari was waiting for her in the restaurant. The elderly woman sat erect and serene at a table near a window. Sunlight filtering through the white lace curtains illuminated her features, still beautiful despite the markings of time.

An attentive waiter hovered at her elbow. The maître d' who had escorted Cat gave a low, respectful bow before taking himself off.

"I'm so glad to see you," Cat said as she bent and kissed the soft, papery cheek. "Was the trip comfortable?"

"Oh, perfectly," Mari assured her with a smile. "These new trains are a wonder. Sit down, dear. Are you hungry?"

"Starved," Cat admitted as she took her place. "I spent the morning talking with a gentleman at the stock exchange, as you suggested. He seemed a bit taken aback by some of my questions, but he did answer them."

"I should hope so," Mari said. "He was seeing you as a favor to me, and I made it clear that I expected him to do more than merely go through the motions."

The two women exchanged an understanding smile across the table. From the beginning, Mari had been frank in explaining to Cat the problems she would face as a woman in the business world.

Even with the Mackenzie fortune behind her, she would not find the going easy. Men would either treat her as an amusing anomaly, not to be taken seriously, or they would ignore her altogether. At least, they would try.

"The Blakiston deal seems to be in good shape," Cat said as she removed her gloves. "You should be able to sign the contracts next week."

"Good. You did a very nice job."

Cat flushed slightly at the praise. Compliments from Mari were not precisely rare, but they were no less appreciated for that. In the almost five years that she had been the older woman's assistant, Cat had made more mistakes than she cared to think about.

Mari never commented beyond saying that success never came without taking risks, and that whenever there was risk there was bound to be occasional failure. That was simply, as she put it, the cost of doing business.

"Is there anything in particular you'd like to do this evening?" Mari asked. "It isn't too late to get theater tickets, if that appeals to you."

Cat was tempted; there were several plays currently on Broadway that she would enjoy seeing. But she was concerned about Mari overtasking herself. Though she was in her early seventies, she kept to a schedule that would have exhausted many women half her age.

Cat knew that there were times when Mari was weary to the point of actually feeling ill, but her indomitable pride prevented her from ever admitting it.

"Actually," Cat said, "I was thinking of making it an early night. We have a long trip ahead of us yet."

"Not so long," Mari said. "Each time I visit Calvert Oaks, the journey seems shorter. Of course," she added, softly, "that's because I'm always so eager to get there that I imagine I've arrived practically before I've left."

"I can't wait," Cat admitted. "It's been more than a year since my last visit. Far too long."

"Sarah and Philip adore seeing you," Mari told her. "It's given them such joy to watch you grow up."

Cat made a rueful face. "They must love me, they've never said a word these past few years about the course I've chosen."

Mari's bright eyes surveyed her carefully. "You think they disapprove?"

Cat shrugged. "My parents do. Why shouldn't they?"

"Your parents don't so much disapprove as simply fail to understand," Mari corrected her gently.

"I'm not sure there's much of a difference." She fell silent, thinking that she would shortly be seeing her parents again for the first time in several weeks.

Her meetings with them were always difficult, and had been so since she had moved out of the Louisburg Square house to stay with Mari. "That summer," as she still thought of it, had changed all their lives to some degree or other, though it had been almost five years before. Her own life had been turned upside down. She was still trying to right it.

"At any rate," Mari said soothingly, "Virginia will be lovely at this time of year. It's perfect for a wedding."

Cat nodded. Her cousin, Helena, was to be married the following week. That occasion was the reason for the upcoming trip. Virtually the entire Calvert family would be on hand. As a granddaughter, Cat could not have stayed away.

Not, she told herself, that she would have wanted to. She liked her cousin, though she hadn't seen much of her in recent years, and she was happy for her.

But the wedding was an inevitable reminder of her own solitary state, not precisely unheard-of for a woman of twenty-four, but certainly unusual, given her background.

At the very least she should have had a suitor in the wings, perhaps even been engaged. Instead she had virtually no social life, apart from her family and business.

Certainly there was no man who remotely interested her. She went through her days oblivious to them.

Mari picked up her menu. "You look pale, dear Let's order."

They were silent for several minutes, until the waiter arrived. Then they placed their orders and waited until he had departed again. Once he was gone, Mari settled back in her chair and looked at Cat closely.

"You know," she said quietly, "I always wanted to have children. When I discovered that I wasn't able to, I was deeply saddened. But as I've grown older, I've become convinced that all things happen for a purpose."

She smiled as she reached across the table and touched Cat's hand. "If I'd had a daughter, I would have wanted her to be like you—bright, brave, beautiful. You have everything in the world to be proud of, Catherine, but sometimes I sense such a sadness in you that it frightens me."

Cat swallowed hard. She had been unprepared for Mari's frankness, or for the depth of the older woman's feelings. Quickly she shook her head. "I'm not sad. Truly. Why should I be?"

Mari gave her a measured look. "Five years can be a very long time. It can also be no time at all. That depends on the person and the feelings involved."

Cat's gaze veered off toward the middle distance. She could not meet Mari's eyes and think of Evan at the same time. Too much would be revealed in her own.

"In my case, five years is an eternity. I have a completely new life now." She forced herself to smile. "Would anyone have believed, when I was eighteen, that I'd turn into at least a middling businesswoman? As I remember, I was something of a dreamer."

"You had a great enthusiasm for life," Mari corrected gently. "Somewhere along the line, that seems to have gotten buried."

"I grew up," Cat insisted. "There's nothing wrong with that."

Mari didn't contradict her, but Cat could tell that the older woman was dissatisfied. She was also too wise to pursue the matter. Mari had gotten where she was in life by combining patience with wisdom. She knew how to wait.

They enjoyed a companionable dinner and walked back to the hotel arm in arm. With Mari's arrival, the connecting door in Cat's room had been opened to give them a comfortable suite. Mari's maid had unpacked for the night and was waiting to help her mistress prepare for bed.

"I feel guilty about this," Mari said with a slight smile. "You've been working hard and should have a chance to enjoy yourself."

"I will," Cat promised her, "when we get to Calvert Oaks. But in the meantime, I'm looking forward to a bath and bed."

But when she had gone back into her own room, shutting the door between them to give Mari her privacy, she found that the prospect of rest was not so pleasing.

The day's events, particularly the hours she had spent at the stock exchange watching the trading floor, had left her charged with energy. She knew that if she went to bed now, she would do nothing but toss and turn.

It was still somewhat light outside. Full darkness would not descend for another hour or so. Even then it would be muted by the gas lamps that lined every street. There was no reason for her not to take a little stroll.

She left the hotel a few minutes later, after scribbling a note for Mari in case the older woman came looking for her for any reason. The lobby was full of people coming and going, to late dinners and to the theater, or to rendezvous of a different nature.

For all her efforts, Cat had not managed to make herself oblivious to that part of life. She saw the tender looks some couples exchanged and felt pain deep in her heart.

The evening was pleasantly cool. She walked south along Broadway, enjoying the rhythm of the city that never seemed to sleep. Boston, at least, shut down for a few hours each night. New York showed no such inclination.

She had paused to look in a store window when out of the corner of her eye she happened to notice a tall man getting out of a carriage. The light from the nearby gas lamp struck his ebony hair. She stiffened for an instant before what had become her habitual self-control took over.

How many times in the past five years had she imagined that she saw Evan? For a time every tall, dark-haired man had drawn her attention. She had felt the same sudden spurt of shock and hope, followed swiftly by disappointment and self-derision.

Finally she had adopted the habit of seeing nothing and no one that did not suit her purpose. It was a strange way to go through life, but at least it let her maintain the illusion of stability.

Except on occasions such as this, when a sudden glimpse of a stranger caused her to forget herself. She shook her head impatiently. As she did so, the stranger turned, and she found herself staring straight at Evan.

This time there was no mistake. He was exactly as he appeared in her most vivid dreams, only more so. He seemed larger, stronger, harder in his features and his manner. He was a man who had come into his own and was now at the full height of his powers.

For a moment her heart stopped. When it began to beat again, its rhythm was ragged.

Her lips shaped his name, but she had no breath to say it. That was hardly necessary. He had seen her a scant moment after she saw him. The same shock she was experiencing roared through him.

He had not set foot in Boston in almost five years, not since the night when he had crawled away, beaten and bloodied, made bitter by defeat, but also determined to rise above it.

But not, he was realistic enough to know, in the city where Drake Bennington had such power. His victories, when they did come, had been elsewhere.

Many times he had imagined walking the streets around Beacon Hill and the Public Garden, envisioning Cat there and thinking about meeting her again—how she would look and act, what they would say to each other, how she would inevitably try to excuse her part in what had happened to him.

But never had he thought that he might meet her in New York, especially not alone in the evening on a busy street corner. Yet there she was, looking as coolly beautiful, as self-possessed and composed, as always.

No, he corrected himself, not always. He remembered a night when she had been anything but cool and composed, and when he had been the one to possess her very soul.

He inclined his head very slightly. "Catherine."

At last she managed to speak. "Evan...what a surprise."

He smiled without humor. It was a baring of teeth that sent a tremor through her. "Yes, I imagine it is."

"What are you...that is, what brings you to New York?"

"Business." His eyes raked over her, taking in the elegance of her dress, the proud tilt of her head beneath her wide-brimmed hat, above all, the absence of a man at her side. "You're alone?"

"Is there something wrong with that?" His tone stung her, reminding her as it did of the derision she had once felt from him. Provoked, she did not try to resist the urge to challenge him.

"It's unusual," he said bluntly.

Cat couldn't help herself. She laughed. If there was one word that summed up her situation, that was it. "Yes," she said, "it is. I realize women don't usually go promenading about on their own, but as there's no actual law against it, I felt like a breath of air, so I decided to take it."

Evan looked at her for what seemed like a long time. Slowly he said, "Yes, you were always like that, taking what you wanted without thought of the consequences."

Cat stiffened in shock. Anger tore through her, for the moment burning away all the tender feelings she had nurtured over the years.

"How dare you?" she demanded, her fists clenching. "How dare you say such a thing to me when you were the one who—" She broke off, unable to even speak of it, and turned away.

Evan's hand lashed out. He had not meant to touch her; in fact, he had barely seen her before he had sworn to himself that he wouldn't. But the thought that she might try to leave overcame every other consideration. His fingers closed around her arm, drawing her to him. "I was the one who what?"

She ignored the question, trying instead to jerk free. His grip was relentless, but, oddly, she felt no pain. He held her only hard enough to prevent her from shaking loose. After a few seconds she realized that she was caught and stood quietly.

"You know perfectly well what you did," she said, pride keeping her voice steady. "There is certainly no reason to go into it."

"On the contrary." Evan's light blue eyes had narrowed as he grasped the sincerity in her tone. She believed what she was saying, for all that it made no sense.

"Tell me, what did I do?"

Cat stared at him. Her throat had closed so tightly that she could not speak again. She could only express with the shining glitter of her eyes the rage and contempt she felt that he should even ask.

"Tell me," he demanded again, baffled by her anger and contempt. He took hold of her by both arms and shook her slightly. "Tell me."

"You . . ." She choked on the word but forced herself to go on. "You betrayed me. You used me, and then you abandoned me. Is it any wonder that I hate you?"

That last part was a lie; she could no more hate him than she could hate herself. But she prayed he would not realize that. She wanted nothing so much as for him to go away, to leave her now, on this street corner, in the rapidly gathering darkness.

Somehow she would make her way back to the hotel; somehow she would survive. But first he had to leave. As he had before.

"Betrayed?" he repeated, staring down at her as though he had never heard the word before. "I betrayed you? Is that really what you think?"

"What else? One moment you were there, acting as if we had a future together. The next you were gone, never to be seen again." Her lips curled contemptuously. "I suppose I should have expected it. Seduced and abandoned. It's a cliché, and a particularly trite one at that."

Her eyes burned. Rather than have him see the sheen of tears in them, she looked away. The silence drew out between them. If she waited long enough, held on to the remnants of her self-control long enough, eventually he would have to let her go.

But the moments passed, and Evan's resolve only strengthened. Something was terribly wrong. He still wasn't sure what, but he was certain that he had to at least try to set it right.

"We can't talk here," he said quietly. "Come with me. There's a hotel nearby. We'll have a cup of coffee—"

"We can't." She turned back to him, looking directly into his eyes. It did not occur to her to reject what he was proposing, only the details of it. "I'm staying there, with Mari."

Evan hesitated a moment. It was growing steadily later. Already the street was less busy than when they had first seen each other. They could not stay there much longer without drawing unwelcome attention. Besides, he wanted her to himself.

"I've borrowed a friend's house," he said at length. "We won't be disturbed there."

Cat knew she should refuse. What he was suggesting was not only improper, but given his capacity to hurt her, it was downright foolhardy. Not that she felt in any way physically threatened by him. It was her heart she feared for.

Yet she did not seriously think of refusing, and her silence was her acceptance. A moment later they were walking down the street together into the darkness.

_____ *Chapter Seventeen*

THE HOUSE EVAN HAD BORROWED was situated three blocks from Broadway, toward the East River. It was on a quiet, tree-lined street of similar houses, all of red brick, three stories high, with stone stoops in front. The sense of peace and solidity that always lingered in such family neighborhoods reassured Cat.

This was hardly the sort of place where assignations occurred. She would simply spend a short time with Evan, clear up whatever misunderstanding existed between them, and take her leave. Perhaps by the time she did so, they would even be friends again.

Only someone who was supremely adept at lying to herself would have believed any of that. Cat did not. As she entered the house she did her best to hide both her nervousness and her excitement.

The entry hall was cluttered with pots of ferns in brass containers. There was a mahogany highboy against one wall, and a marble-topped table against the other. Several paintings of English country scenes were hung in gilt frames from the ceiling molding. A bowl of tired-looking roses sat on the table.

"There's a maid," Evan said as he relocked the door behind them, "but she's away at the moment. I hope you won't mind if we fend for ourselves."

Cat shook her head. She followed him down a corridor to a short flight of steps that led to a cheery kitchen looking out over a backyard garden. When he opened the windows to let out the stale air, she caught the scent of honeysuckle.

"Sit down," he said as he struck a match to a gas lamp on the wide, plank table that occupied the center of the room. "My friend keeps meaning to put in electricity, but he hasn't gotten around to it."

"Who is he?" Cat asked as she took one of the wooden-rail chairs.

"A fellow I met in Texas. He's from New York originally, but he isn't anxious to return here. When he heard I was going to be visiting, he offered me the house."

"So that's where you've been," she said, as much to herself as to him. All the years, all her wonderings, had never included any place so strange as Texas. "What took you there?"

He shot her a quick look that actually held a glimmer of humor. "A desire to stay alive. Shall I make some coffee?"

Absently Cat shook her head. "I don't understand. What were you afraid of?"

Evan sat down across from her. He stretched out his long legs and leaned back in the chair, looking perfectly relaxed. Inside, he was anything but. He could still hardly believe that she was actually there with him, let alone that she truly seemed not to know what had happened, or at least not the part her father had played in it.

That was too much to accept, at least on its face. He had spent so many years nurturing his anger against her, even as he had nurtured the love that refused to die, that he couldn't suddenly give it up.

Some of the derision she had heard before was back in his voice when he said, "Your father can be quite intimidating when he chooses."

Cat shook her head. "I don't believe you. Aside from the fact that he's the fairest of men, you could never be afraid of him."

The mere idea was ridiculous to her. For all her differences with her father, she could not think for a moment that he would have given Evan any reason to feel that he meant him harm.

"It wasn't him so much as the goons he sent against me." At her startled look, Evan smiled. "I don't mind a fair fight, but four against one is hardly even. I was lucky to escape with my life."

The breath left Cat in a rush. On a thin reed of sound, she said, "My father would never do such a thing."

Evan shrugged. He had hardly expected her to agree, but her refusal to believe him stoked his anger. Had she ever felt a moment's loyalty to him? A moment's love?

"Then how do you explain what happened?" he demanded. "We came back to Boston a few days after the storm. I had resolved to wait until then to speak to your father. Remember, we had discussed that?"

Cat nodded slowly. They had talked about it in the few private moments they had been able to steal after they returned to Newport.

Both had agreed that it would be better to wait until the trauma of her own and Jimmy's near death had passed. But neither could bear to delay very long. Evan had agreed to speak with Drake before the week was out.

"I met with him in his office on Friday afternoon," Evan said, unable to hide the bitterness that crept into his voice as he remembered what had transpired.

"Naturally I didn't tell him what had happened between us, although I think it's possible he suspected. All I said was that I had come to care for you deeply, that I had reason to believe you felt the same, and that I was asking his permission to marry you.''

Cat swallowed hard. She had never known that the conversation between Evan and her father had reached that point. Drake had refused to discuss it with her. ''What did he say?'' she asked in little more than a whisper.

''He was angry. That was very clear. He accused me of taking advantage of your youth and inexperience, and of being a fortune hunter.''

''Oh, no! It wasn't like that at all.''

''I couldn't blame him,'' Evan said, surprising her. ''That must have been what it looked like. But I kept insisting that I truly loved you, and that if he would only give us a chance, I would do everything possible to make you happy.''

''What did he say?''

Evan hesitated. This was the part he had never understood, since such deceit was unlike the Drake Bennington he had known. Nonetheless it had happened.

''Actually he seemed to calm down, even to begin to consider what I was telling him. He said several times that he only wanted you to have a good life with the right man.'' With a rueful laugh he added, ''I believed him.''

''What changed?'' Cat asked softly. ''Why did you stop?''

The smile he gave her was cold and hard, embodying memories that would have been better left alone.

''I stopped when I was lying face down in a gutter in the North End, watching my blood seep away in the rain and thinking that I was going to die. The goons thought so, too, or they would never have left me.''

He leaned closer, his long fingers closing around her wrist. ''Your father, the father you love and trust so much, meant me to die. I know it, he knows it, and now you know it. The only question, dear Catherine, is what are we going to do about it?''

''You're crazy,'' she whispered from between clenched teeth. ''Anyone could have jumped you. It happens all the time, especially in the North End. You have no reason to think my father was responsible.''

''Oh, but I do. While the goons were taking turns using me as a punching bag, I heard them talking about the fine gentleman who had paid them for the night's sport. They were speculating as to what I'd done to get on his bad side. Not that they much cared. It was all the same to them, so long as they collected their money.''

Cat wavered. For the first time she was forced to consider the possibility that what he was telling her was true. The mere idea sickened her, but she could find no other explanation.

Watching the play of emotions across her expressive features, Evan felt a moment's twinge of guilt. Not that he had misled her in any way. He had told her exactly what had happened.

Still, he was sorry to disillusion her about the father she loved so much. Sorry and glad all at the same time. Drake Bennington had robbed him of love. It seemed only right to do the same to him.

''Look,'' he said as he eased his hold on her wrist, though he did not let go altogether, ''your father was simply doing what he thought was right. He's always handled his problems quietly and forcefully. I know, because I did a lot of that for him.'' His laugh was hollow. ''I just never expected to be on the receiving end of it.''

Cat, her eyes wide and luminous, stared at him in dismay. ''You can't mean that you beat up people for him?''

"No, of course not. But I did find out who was crossing him from time to time. He took care of the rest himself. I convinced myself that he let the offenders' own fears do the job for him, but in my case that wouldn't have worked. He must have realized that and decided on more direct action."

Cat stared down at the table. The wood shimmered before her eyes. A tear ran down her pale cheek, followed swiftly by another.

"When you didn't come back," she said thickly, "I thought you had changed your mind."

Evan frowned. "You knew perfectly well that I hadn't."

"I knew nothing of the sort! What are you talking about?"

The lines on his forehead deepened. "The note I sent, asking you to come to me, and the response I received."

"Note?" Cat repeated blankly. "I never saw any note from you."

Evan stared at her, searching her face for some sign that she was lying. Instead he found only what gave every appearance of being genuine bafflement.

Slowly he said, "I got Carmody to send you a note on my behalf. I didn't say anything in it about the beating, because I didn't want to worry you, but I did say that I was indisposed and asked you to come to see me. Instead you replied that you had decided it would be best if we didn't have any further contact."

"There was no note! If there had been, I would never have replied in such a fashion!" Indeed, wild horses couldn't have kept her from his side, but she wasn't about to say so. Already she had the sense of having gone too far out on a limb.

If she was telling the truth, Evan thought with a surge of hope, then someone had intercepted the note and sent the false response. For a moment he entertained the possibility that Carmody himself was behind it, but he dismissed that out of hand.

The old ward leader might have his own ideas about how things should be, but he granted others the right to make their own mistakes. He would not have interfered so underhandedly.

Which left someone in her family. "I assumed," he said slowly, "that your father had talked with you and convinced you not to see me again."

"We did speak of you," Cat murmured, thinking back to that conversation, "but only when I became puzzled as to why you didn't call again. I finally nerved myself to mention you to Father."

"What did he say?"

She swallowed hard, forcing the words from her throat. "That you hadn't been at the office, either, and that he had no idea where you had gone. He seemed genuinely surprised himself. At least, I thought he was. Now it appears that I was wrong."

Her sorrow was so strong that she pulled free of him and buried her face in her hands. Her slender shoulders shook with the force of her grief as she wept. Her crushing disillusionment had blasted the very foundations of her life.

"My father is a good man," she said between her sobs. "How could he do such a terrible thing?"

Evan hesitated. This was his opportunity to tear her away from Drake completely. All he needed to do was speak a few well-chosen words and the job would be done.

But he could not bring himself to utter them. Until that moment his anger had been directed at both her and Drake. He had not separated them, but had seen her merely as an extension of her father, a possession that he coveted for himself.

Now, in a blinding instant, he realized the folly of that, and the unfairness. Drake had wronged him and deserved his rage, but Cat did not.

"He loves you," Evan said quietly, "and he was trying to protect you. He believed that I wasn't the right man for you. Perhaps, somewhere deep inside, I believed it, too."

She looked up, uncomprehending. "What did you say?"

"You heard me. If I had truly believed in us, I would have found some way to get to you regardless of what had happened. But that would have meant pressing you to make a choice. On the one side was the world you had grown up in, where I knew you belonged. On the other side was me and—to say the least—an extremely uncertain future."

He paused for a moment, his eyes scanning her face. "I was afraid, Cat. Given the intensity of your father's opposition, there seemed no way you would agree to come with me. Your response appeared to confirm that. Rather than have salt rubbed into the wound, I simply left."

"You could have stayed," she said, unable to hide her bitterness at his lack of faith in her. "At least you could have remained in Boston. Perhaps in time you would have seen things differently and given me another chance."

"No," he said firmly, "I couldn't have. There was no purpose in my remaining in Boston so long as your father was so firmly set against me. No matter how much I wanted to fight him, I knew I could not." He paused a moment, then added, "At least, not then."

"What does that mean?" She wasn't sure she wanted to hear the answer, but she felt compelled to ask all the same.

Evan didn't answer her at once. He stood up and walked a little away from the table. For several moments he stared out the windows at the night. When he turned back to her, his expression was closed. She knew that she was looking into the face he showed to the world—resolute and unyielding.

"I've grown rich in Texas," he said quietly. "And elsewhere. Rich enough to stand against any man foolish enough to cross me, including your father. This time, when we meet again, it will be on far more equal footing."

Dread filled Cat. It seemed that the two men she loved most in all the world were bound for a confrontation that could bring only pain and grief. Moreover she had no idea what she could do to prevent it.

"You plan to challenge him?" she asked through stiff lips.

"I suppose you could put it like that."

"How?"

"Very simply." He walked toward her, smiling. "I've found his daughter again, and this time I'm not going to let her go."

Cat needed a moment to absorb that. When she did, her eyes narrowed. Very distinctly she said, "You are being presumptuous."

He put his head back and laughed. "And you're still every inch a lady, able to express the greatest disdain in the fewest possible words." His manner sobered as he looked down at her. "I've never even claimed to be a gentleman, so I won't make the mistake of trying to match you on that level. But you can't deny that there's something very powerful between us. It cuts through all the barriers, Cat. It's going to bring us together again, whether you want it to or not.''

''No,'' she said as firmly as she could manage. His hands were on her shoulders again, firm, but with a certain overpowering tenderness that undermined her resistance far more than force ever could. Gently he lifted her from the chair and drew her to him.

As his arms closed around her, she recovered herself sufficiently to press her hands against his broad chest. That was a mistake. The moment she touched him, common sense fled. The hurt and bewilderment that had festered in her for so long counted for nothing against the clamoring demand of her body and her heart.

God help her, she wanted him. More even than that night in the hut when she had been a novice to pleasure. More than in all the dreams that had haunted her down through the years. More than she would ever have imagined possible.

Sweet, hot fire ran through her veins. It burned away all else, even the most basic instincts for self-protection and survival. Her hands trembled as she raised them to cup his face, but the tremors were not caused by fear. She was beyond that. Only desire existed.

It was the same for Evan. He had forgotten his anger, forgotten the man who had caused it, forgotten everything except the woman in his arms. Once she had been everything he dreamed of. Then, for a brief instant, she had been real. He had discovered that he preferred reality to dreams.

Without a word he bent and lifted her into his arms. She nestled against him naturally, as though they were lovers of long experience who had never been separated.

His stride was long and purposeful as he carried her from the kitchen, up the steps to the main floor. There he paused for a moment, gazing into her silver eyes.

"Are you sure?"

She wasn't certain if he had actually spoken the words or if she had merely heard them in her mind. It made no difference. Without hesitation, she nodded.

Upstairs it was dark and quiet. No lamps had been lit, but sufficient light filtered in through the curtains to illuminate their way. Evan carried her down the carpeted hallway to a room at the back of the house. He pushed open the door to reveal a large four-poster bed covered in red velvet that matched the brocade on the walls.

"My friend," he said with a smile, "has somewhat gaudy taste." In fact the place bore a certain resemblance to the better class of brothel, something he was glad she could not realize.

What was about to happen between them bore no relationship to the sort of encounter that went on in such establishments. He cherished Catherine as he had never cherished any woman, and he intended to express that in the fullest way possible.

Though the raging hunger of his body urged him to be quick, he was determined to savor every moment. When her hands rose to remove her hat, he caught them and placed them gently at her sides. "Let me."

She stood, docile but watchful, as he drew out the pin that held the broad-brimmed hat in place, then laid both hat and pin on the dresser near the bed. When that was done, he carefully sought out and unfastened the single tortoiseshell clip that held her chignon in place.

When it was removed, her honey-hued hair tumbled around her shoulders. He combed his fingers through it, releasing the perfume that clung to the silken strands.

A nerve leaped in his clenched jaw. She watched it, fascinated, as he reluctantly withdrew his hands and began to undo the first of the buttons that held her jacket closed. There were four in all, and they yielded grudgingly. By the time the last was open, she was eager to make an end to it all.

But Evan would not let her. He took off the jacket and placed it carefully on a chair, then studied her as she stood before him. Her high-boned cheeks were flushed, and her eyes glittered with a wild life of their own. He took satisfaction in that even as he admired the straight, proud carriage of her shoulders and the steadiness with which she met his gaze.

Beneath the suit jacket, she wore a high-collared blouse of ivory silk that looked so delicate he feared it would rip apart at his slightest touch. It proved more resilient than that, however, if more difficult than the jacket. By the time he had unfastened each of the dozen or so small pearl buttons, his breath was labored and his heart hammered painfully against his rib cage.

Her skirt, at least, was easier. That had only a handful of large buttons below the waist in the back. He made short work of them, and the fabric pooled at her feet. She stepped out of it gracefully, a soft, utterly feminine smile curving her lips.

Beneath the blouse and skirt she wore a beribboned camisole and petticoat. A corselet narrowed her waist slightly, but she wondered why she bothered with it at all. Some women were dispensing with them as unhealthy. Cat thought she might, too.

Certainly Evan made it clear that the contraption would not be missed. He cursed softly under his breath as he undid the hooks at the back. There was an audible sigh of relief from them both when he at last tossed the offending object aside.

"Sit down," he said huskily.

She obeyed without thought, perching on the edge of the bed. Her breath caught in her throat as he knelt before her and drew off her shoes. Her stockings followed as his callused palms stroked over her soft calves and beyond.

"Evan," she whispered, "please . . ."

He looked up and gave her a brilliant, slashing smile. "I intend to. You'll be pleased beyond belief, Cat. But first you have to be patient and let me be the same."

Instinctively she understood his need to control the pace of their lovemaking. For the present she was content to yield the initiative to him. Later, though, she looked forward to turning the tables.

He drew her up again and slowly, with studied concentration, slipped the straps of the camisole from her shoulders. The swell of her breasts above the fragile lace drew his gaze. He brushed a hand over her, tracing a spasm of pleasure across her skin.

Her nipples hardened beneath his gaze, prompting him to drop his head and let his mouth close lingeringly over one of them. She moaned deep in her throat. His midnight-dark hair was rough silk in her fingers as she grasped his head and drew him closer.

"Evan," she whispered haltingly, "you're driving me mad."

"It's only fair," he murmured against her. "You've been doing that to me for years. Every night in my memories, my dreams, you were there."

She wanted to tell him that it had been the same for her, but she could not manage the words. Instead she tried to express all that she had felt with her body, straining against him until the pressure of their need became intolerable and he all but flung her down on the bed.

Even then she was not afraid. As he stood before her in the shadowy light and rapidly stripped off his clothes, she watched with unabashed fascination.

In the hut she had been a virgin, burdened with a certain measure of timidity. Since that time, she had thought little of men and desired none. But she had not lost the capacity to yearn. On the contrary, her yearning for Evan was a living presence within her.

She watched as his elegantly tailored jacket of soft dark wool fell away, followed by his crisp linen shirt, its whiteness a sharp contrast to the bronze darkness of his chest.

He had been large and heavily muscled before, but the intervening years had made him even more so. She wondered at the sort of life he had endured, even as she knew that she did not have the courage to ask him. Not now, at least.

He held her eyes as he unfastened the leather belt around his waist and swiftly undid the buttons beneath it. When he had removed his trousers, she swallowed hard, suddenly acutely conscious of the extent of his arousal.

In deference to the hint of concern that flitted across her face, he left his last garment on. Placing a knee on the bed, he bent over her and slowly ran his hands from her breasts down to the shadowed cleft between her legs. As she trembled beneath his touch, he smiled.

"Still so eager, Cat?"

"Yes," she admitted, ashamed, yet proud at the same time. Let him think what he would of her need for him. This was a part of her that only he had touched, whether he knew it or not, and she would not deny it.

His smile deepened as his hands returned to her breasts, slipping beneath the camisole to cup and fondle them. He watched as her eyes grew languorous and smoldering. When her nipples were hard little points against his palms, he pushed the camisole down farther to expose her completely.

"Lovely," he murmured as he touched his mouth to her again, suckling first one breast and then the other until she moaned with pleasure.

The sound seemed to break through some final barrier within him. Swiftly, he stood back and reached for the waistband of her petticoat. Beneath it she wore a pair of muslin drawers. He grasped both at once and pulled them off in a single motion.

Cat had to stifle a cry of surprise. She was completely naked now except for the camisole wrapped around her waist. He took hold of it, intending, she thought, to pull it off as well.

But instead, as their eyes met, he deliberately ripped the delicate fabric. It gave way with a shrill sound that seemed to linger in the air long after the camisole itself was gone.

HE MOVED within and above her. He was all the world and beyond. The very rhythm of her breath was his. Her heart beat to the pace he set; her hips rose and fell at his urging. There was nothing except Evan and the joy they were sharing.

The sheets had been pushed down to the foot of the bed. There was nothing to impede the glistening, twisting entanglement of their bodies. The room was hushed, and outside there was only silence.

Cat cried out. Her head was thrown back against the pillows. Her hair streamed out around her, gleaming like stolen sunlight in the darkness. Her breasts were swollen, the nipples aching in their fullness.

Deep within, at the very core of her being, she felt him hard and demanding, moving ever more powerfully with each stroke until she thought she could not possibly bear anything more.

"Enough," she sobbed, trying to wrench free of him. If she did not, the pleasure would surely kill her. Each time they had melded their bodies together throughout the long night she had believed that she had found the ultimate in fulfillment.

Each time she had been wrong. He had taken her from peak to peak, always higher, until she believed that she would perish somewhere out there, hurtling into the heart of a splintering sun.

Her pleas went unheeded. He drove her further and further, until at last he felt the tremors seize her so powerfully that she would have been shaken from his hands had he not grasped her so firmly. He waited until they had only just begun to subside, then moved again, driving her remorselessly up again.

"Say it," he rasped against her mouth. "Say you are mine."

Her head lashed back and forth in denial. Each time he had demanded this of her, and each time she had managed to refuse it. But the boundaries of her strength to deny him were close at hand.

She could not hold out much longer. His strength and will appeared inexhaustible. Hers were not. Still, she tried.

He smiled when he saw that she continued to resist. It was the excuse he needed to grasp her sleek flanks and arch her even more tightly against him.

He had been concerned in the fury of his desire that he might hurt her, which above all he did not want. But he had discovered that she was stronger than he had thought, a match for him in every way.

This time, when he felt the deep inner pull within her, he did not resist but surrendered to it, finding a completion so perfect as to shatter his senses and send him tumbling into deepest sleep.

HE WOKE AS the first gray light of dawn was pushing away night's curtain. Cat was standing at the foot of the bed. She had put on her petticoat and was reaching for her skirt.

"Where are you going?" he asked.

She turned, seeing him propped up on his elbows, watching her. For a moment her face flushed with memories of what had passed between them. Then the self-discipline she had painfully learned over the years slipped into place and she was able to smile.

"Back to the hotel. Mari is very open-minded, but I don't want to see how much I can shock her."

Evan frowned. She seemed perfectly serene, almost untouched by the events that had left him feeling reborn. That worried him. "No," he said, "I suppose you can't do that. When will you be back?"

She hesitated, torn between her own contradictory feelings. In silence, she reached for her blouse and drew it on. As she buttoned it, she said, "Evan, I need some time to think about what's happened, to get used to the idea of you suddenly being back in my life."

He rose from the bed and came toward her, unconcerned at his nudity. Her mouth went suddenly dry as she stared at him. Never had she seen anything more beautiful. He embodied the primal power at the center of life, tempered with an intelligence and strength that drew her overwhelmingly.

Her resolve wavered. She wanted nothing so much as to go into his arms, to find there the oblivion of blinding pleasure and to let nothing intrude on the world they could make together.

All that stopped her was a deeply rooted belief that in her present state of mind, she would lose herself in him. All the hard-won independence and confidence she had wrenched from the recent difficult years would be gone. She would be back where she had started, a young girl vulnerable to the most terrible hurt and helpless to prevent it.

"Why?" he demanded, facing her with his hands on his hips and his feet planted firmly apart. His unyielding

stance told her more eloquently than words that he would
stop her if he could.

She determined not to give him any opportunity to do
so. Swiftly she reached for her jacket and put it on. "Tell
me something, have you forgotten about what you believe my father did to you? Did last night wipe that out?"

He looked at her in shock, astounded that she should
even connect the two. Did she imagine that what had
passed between them had been some sort of retribution
on his part?

But when he asked her, she smiled at the mere notion.
"Hardly. If that's how you take vengeance, people—
women, at least—would be lining up to do you harm."

Her bluntness astounded him even more. She laughed
as she watched him struggle to compose himself.

"I've changed, Evan," she said softly. "Above all, you
have to realize that. Five years ago I was still very much
a child. I thought of little beyond my own happiness, and
I imagined I could have it simply for the asking, if I only
knew what to ask for. Now I know none of that is true.
Life is a good deal more complicated."

"Yes," he agreed, "it is. But neither one of us is sim-
pleminded. We can work things out."

"You haven't answered my question. Do you still
blame my father?"

It would have been so easy to deny it and have her in
his arms. But he could not bring himself to do so. The
anger and resentment had been with him for too long.
They had taken on a life of their own.

"People can change," he said at length, "but not the
past. What happened, happened."

"Then you understand why I need some time away to
think things through for myself." When he remained silent, she let him see a glimmer of her resolve in the proud

tilt of her head and the steadiness with which she faced him. Yet there was no denying that her voice shook as she said, "Do you imagine it's easy for me to be involved with a man who thinks my father is guilty of a terrible crime? Our relationship would have been difficult enough under any circumstances, but this magnifies the problem enormously. I have to be very sure before I make any decision."

"Can you be so methodical in your emotions?" he challenged. "Can you simply choose not to love?"

"No," she replied softly. "But I can choose not to act on that love. I'm not saying I would enjoy doing so, but it is possible."

The distinction was lost on Evan. For him, the existence of love automatically demanded its expression. For five years he had poured his love for Cat into the building of his business empire. It shook him to realize how much that empire was a monument to his refusal to give her up.

For a brief time she had once more been within his grasp. Now she was slipping away again, this time of her own volition. He felt driven to stop her at all costs, but he knew that if he made any attempt, she would flee all the faster. He was forced to stand back and do nothing as she touched a gentle hand to his cheek and left the room.

Outside in the gathering dawn, Cat stood for a moment, breathless and shaking. The effort it had taken to walk away from Evan had left her feeling drained. She leaned against the wrought-iron fence that surrounded the small garden in front of the house.

Her eyes were closed, and she felt the coolness of the damp morning air against her lids. Several blocks away, on the river, a boat whistle sounded. The long, haunting sound made her tremble.

What on earth was she to do? After the night they had spent together, her love for Evan was stronger than ever. He was as firmly entrenched in her soul as he had been in her body, perhaps more so, for while the body erodes, the soul is immortal.

Yet she also loved her father. What had been a child's adoration had matured into a steady, deeply imbued mingling of respect and care that their present difficulties did not truly touch.

Yes, there were problems between them because of the life she had chosen to lead. But she did not doubt for a moment that her father loved her as much as she loved him.

Evan hated him. He had not said so out loud, but she was certain of it nonetheless. And how could he be blamed? If he was right—and she was sickened by the mere thought—her father had committed a terrible crime against him.

Everything in her cried out against that. Her father must be innocent, yet the evidence said otherwise. She shook her head wearily as she straightened and began walking.

A milk wagon passed her, the horse's harness jangling in the stillness. As she neared Broadway, she saw a cluster of newsboys gathered at the corner where bundles of papers had been dropped off. They glanced at her as she passed, making her aware of how incongruous it was to see a woman of her sort wandering about at such an hour.

She received a similar look from the sleepy clerk at the hotel desk as she went by on her way up to her room. As quietly as she could, she let herself in, shut the door behind her and breathed a soft sigh of relief.

Not that she could truly afford to relax. There was too much to think about, added to which was the pressing need to keep her thoughts concealed. She was not ashamed of what she had done, but she was wise enough not to want it to become known.

She listened for a moment at the connecting door, long enough to determine that Mari was still asleep. In the bathroom she turned the taps on full force as she stripped off her clothes.

For half an hour she soaked in the tub, letting the warm, jasmine-scented water wash away the unaccustomed aches and twinges she was feeling. A small price for such joy, but also a reminder that her situation was far from simple.

She glanced around the pleasant room with the most modern accoutrements—the claw-footed bathtub in which she reclined, a sink enclosed in a wooden cabinet, a commode placed discreetly off to one side behind a screen.

Above the sink was a mirror in which she could see herself. For a time she watched the woman in the tub, staring at her as though she were a stranger.

In a way, she was. Her behavior of the night before was inexplicable by any standard except that of love. At least in the hut she had had the excuse of a near brush with death to explain her actions.

Last night there had been no such excuse, nor had she felt the need for one. She had gone with him as naturally as though she had done the same every day of her life. Moreover, she was without regrets.

At least, she was without regrets as far as those few hours went. Toward the past and, more important, the future, she felt differently. As Evan had said, the past could not be changed, so there was no point in thinking about it. The future was another matter.

She leaned her head back against the rim of the tub and stared up at the ceiling. Though she searched her mind and heart, she could find no clear course to follow.

She was caught between her love for Evan and her love not only for her father, but for her entire family, all of whom would surely be hurt if she chose Evan. Already she had worried and baffled them by her actions. She could not bring herself to do more.

Yet neither could she face the possibility of turning away from Evan. He was too intrinsically a part of her, as she suspected she was of him. They were bound together in a way she couldn't understand, but which was undeniable nonetheless.

A deep sigh escaped her as she finally rose from the tub. Water sluiced off her body, which glowed with remembered passion. She hastily wrapped a large towel around herself and padded back into the bedroom.

Mari was waiting for her, in a wing chair near the bed. Cat looked from her to the undisturbed covers and flushed.

"I hope I'm not intruding," Mari said gently. "I put my head in to see if you were awake, and when I noticed..." She made a vague gesture in the direction of the bed. "I became a bit concerned. Of course, when I heard the water running I presumed you were all right."

Still she had stayed, waiting for Cat to emerge. Acknowledging that, Mari said, "I thought about leaving and pretending I hadn't seen anything, but that struck me as rather hypocritical. Still, if you'd rather I did, dear, just tell me so."

Slowly, Cat shook her head. "There's no point, is there? Obviously, I wasn't here last night."

Mari looked at her for a long moment, clearly fighting a battle with herself. At length, she said, "You're a grown woman, Cat. I really don't think you would have done anything foolish. Still, I admit to a certain concern. It would grieve me a great deal to see you hurt."

"I'm hoping I won't be," Cat said. She went over to the closet and withdrew the clothes she planned to wear that day, a comfortable skirt and blouse suitable for traveling.

"I'll leave you to get dressed," Mari said, standing up. "Let me know when you're ready."

A short while later they were seated in the hotel dining room, having breakfast. Cat was amused by her own appetite. Normally she had little more than coffee and toast, but when it came time to order she had decided that wouldn't be enough.

Certain novels that she had surreptitiously read made allusions to the need for sustenance after lovemaking. She felt as though she were living out a cliché as she dug into a plate of fried eggs, sausage and hash browns.

"It's a long trip," Mari said with a smile when Cat shrugged apologetically. "You don't want to get hungry."

"No danger of that after all this." She put down her fork, took another sip of coffee. Quietly, aware of the impact her words would have, she said, "Evan O'Connell is back."

Mari's eyes widened noticeably, but apart from that she controlled herself very well. "I see. And how is he? Still the same?"

Cat laughed ruefully. "If by that you mean maddening, attractive and impossible to resist, then yes, he hasn't changed."

"What about apart from all that?"

Cat thought for a moment. Softly she said, "I think he's become the man he would inevitably have become, only a bit sooner, perhaps."

"How is that?"

"Confident...hard...successful. He's made a fortune, it seems, in Texas, of all places."

Mari's face grew thoughtful. "Texas, eh? A good place to do it, what with all that oil they've found there recently."

Cat shrugged. She wasn't particularly interested in Evan's wealth or how he had made it, only that he was back. "He thinks Father tried to have him killed."

"God in heaven..." Mari stared at her, dumbstruck. Her very astonishment comforted Cat. Clearly she wasn't the only one who thought such a thing unlikely.

But after a moment Mari's shock faded, and her eyes narrowed as she murmured, "It's often difficult to know what a man is capable of doing."

"Surely you don't believe..."

Mari held up a hand, forestalling her. "I'm not saying he did it, Cat, or that he didn't. Only that I think Drake certainly possesses the capacity for violence, as does Evan. They're both men who will fight to protect what's theirs."

"Evan says my father hired goons who beat him and left him for dead."

Mari jerked as though she had been struck. Instantly she shook her head. "Now that doesn't sound like Drake at all. If there was any retribution to be meted out, he'd do it personally."

"Nonetheless, that's what Evan believes. I can't convince him otherwise, so either I have to resolve this in my own mind, or I have to refuse to see him again."

Mari was silent for several minutes. Her eyes were full of understanding and compassion, but when she spoke it was with the ring of practicality.

"I believe you could make the decision not to have any further dealings with Evan. I even think you could stick to it. But it would only be at a terrible cost to both of you. Is that what you want?"

"Of course not." Cat spoke more loudly than she had intended, and with a note of desperation that caused a waiter to turn and look at them. She lowered her head, staring at the food she realized she wouldn't be able to finish.

"Of course not," she repeated softly. She looked directly at Mari and managed a smile.

"I want everything. The career I've been building with your help, the love and respect of my family, a wonderful husband, children. Everything. The only problem is that I'm afraid it isn't possible."

Mari refilled her teacup from the pot at her side, her motions graceful and sure despite the weight of her years. Over the rising steam she said, "I won't try to dismiss your fears, Cat. They're real, and in the end they may prove insurmountable. But it isn't in you to give up before you've even begun. You won't be able to see Evan for a while anyway, since you're going to be at Calvert Oaks. Take that time to think about what you want to do. But remember, life is very much an ongoing business. Nothing is ever really solved or settled. One lives from day to day, year to year, making the best of it all. That isn't a bad thing. On the contrary, it can be very good. It is, however, a bit frightening to contemplate."

"A bit," Cat agreed wryly. She was feeling better already, simply for having talked with Mari. But she didn't underestimate the problems ahead. She had a difficult decision to make, one that would shape the entire course of her life.

It seemed right and proper that she was going to make it at Calvert Oaks. That was where the women of her family had laid the foundations for their own lives, each generation adding to what the past had built and reaching forward into the future.

The time had come for her to do the same.

CALVERT OAKS shimmered in the late-spring sun. It had rained the night before, cleansing the air so that the white walls of the main house appeared to possess an inner light of their own.

The three-story building was in the Greek-revival tradition that had flourished in the South during the previous century. Graceful white columns fronted a portico protected by an overhanging roof. Twin brick chimneys were set on either side of the wide, tiled roof. Shutters painted sky blue were open to admit a soft breeze off the nearby James River.

Cat leaned out the car window, drinking in the first sight of her birthplace. Though her parents had already owned the Louisburg Square house, her mother had stayed at Calvert Oaks during her pregnancy. That had been a difficult time in her marriage, when she had needed the security of home and family.

It was there that the twins had seen the first light of day, ushered into the world by their grandmother, who had been trained in midwifery by an old black woman, now long dead.

"Nothing's changed," Mari said with an audible note of pleasure. "Oh, I know they've modernized, even put in electricity, and Philip's developed this fascination with cars. But really, it's still the same."

Cat had to agree. Calvert Oaks was immutable. The house and everything it represented had stood through the turmoil of the Civil War and the vast changes that followed it, when much of the rest of the South had crumbled.

Now it was under assault of another kind, from the new century and its rush to modernize. Cat had no doubt that Calvert Oaks would, like the great trees for which it was named, bend to the new wind but never break.

As the car came to a stop, she spied an elderly man waiting on the veranda. Despite his years—he was in his mid-seventies—Philip Calvert retained the erect bearing of his youth. He was dressed in the simple trousers and open-necked shirt he had always favored and which were the most practical wear for a working plantation owner.

That he still took an active role in the management of his land was evident from the mud splattered over his boots. He had spent the morning inspecting the new waterworks, but he had made a point of returning to the house in time to greet his granddaughter and Mari.

He was smiling broadly as he came down the steps. His once-blond hair, now silver, gleamed above his blue eyes that had lost none of their keenness. His face was narrow, his skin weathered by decades of exposure to the elements.

One of his shirt sleeves hung empty at his side, the cuff neatly pinned up. It had been so since long before Cat's birth, the arm having been lost at Antietam. Both she and Mari were too accustomed to its absence to take any notice.

"My dear," Philip said as he took Mari's hand and raised it to his lips in a gesture that for him was perfectly natural. "It's so good to have you here again."

"Thank you, Philip," she said with a soft smile. She had always liked him, going back to the distant time of their youth when she had come with Sarah on a visit to Calvert Oaks. Over the years that first fondness had ripened into sisterly love.

"Grandfather, you look wonderful," Cat said, unable to restrain herself any longer. "It's so good to see you again."

She blinked back tears as she hugged him. His body was still strong and hard by virtue of the rigorous life he led. The arm that grasped her was a solid reminder of the times during her childhood when she had run to him to be boosted up onto his shoulder and carried around as he pointed out those things he thought she would find interesting. She was a child no longer, but there was still an ineffable comfort to be found in being with him.

"You look as beautiful as always, Cat," Philip said gently when he stepped a little distance away to study her. His eyes were tender as they swept over her.

He looked at her through the filter of memory, seeing her not only as she was now, but remembering the child and then the young girl she had once been. Remembering also the daughter who had borne her and the woman who was that daughter's mother.

The door opened behind them and Sarah stepped out onto the porch. "Cat, Mari, you're here at last." She came down the steps quickly and embraced them both.

In her late sixties, Sarah had fulfilled her husband's prediction of so many years before by becoming a woman who grew old with grace and beauty. Her superb bone structure and the perfection of her skin were only partially responsible; intelligence and animation had the most to do with the riveting quality of her expression.

Wherever she was, whatever she was doing, people tended to look at Sarah Calvert and to enjoy it, but no one more so than her husband, whose steady adoration had only grown with the years.

She was simply dressed in an elegant gray dress that matched the pewter sheen of her eyes. A collar of lace framed her throat. Her hair, which, like her husband's, had long since turned silver, was swept up in a soft chignon.

She wore pearls at her ears and a bracelet of gold on her wrist. The gold glinted in the sunlight as she raised her hand to gently touch Cat's cheek.

For a moment their eyes, so similar in shape and color, met. Sarah frowned. She saw something in her granddaughter that worried her. When Cat glanced away uneasily, her concern was confirmed.

But Sarah said nothing. Over the years she had developed a wisdom that went beyond mere intelligence. She knew how to wait for the proper time and place. "Let's not stand about in the sun," she said softly as she led the way inside.

As Cat stepped into the marble entry hall, she took a deep breath. For a moment she had felt as though her grandmother had looked directly into her soul. Sarah had always seemed to have that ability, but it had never particularly disturbed Cat before. Only now, when she had something to conceal, did it strike her as upsetting.

Familiar aromas—lemon polish, lilacs, honeysuckle and the warm scent of baking bread—soothed her. An instant later she had forgotten her apprehension as she spotted Jimmy coming down the central staircase.

"How was New York?" he asked as he gave her a hug. "Have you conquered the stock market yet?"

"Not quite," she told him dryly, "but it's beginning to make a little sense, at least."

"That's all it will ever do. Last time Father sent me down there to look around I come home with my head spinning." Quietly he added, "Sometimes I think I'm not cut out for a career in business. Trouble is, I can't think of anything else I'd rather do."

"You'll sort it out," Cat said, certain that she was right. Jimmy had graduated from Harvard the year before and since then had been working as their father's assistant.

The man who had filled the post after Jacob Stein's retirement had been moved on to other things, ceding to Jimmy a position that was the perfect place from which to learn about the complex business empire he would one day be expected to run.

But a year was not long enough to endow a young man of privileged upbringing with the toughness needed for the task ahead of him. Much more time and patience were required. Their father accepted that and didn't press Jimmy to take on more than he was ready for. For his son, however, the days were sometimes very long and frustrating.

"Mother and Father are here," Jimmy said as he took Cat's arm. "We weren't sure exactly when you and Mari would get in, so they went for a ride. I'd like to talk with you before they get back."

"What about?" Cat asked. They left the entry hall and walked out into the garden, which stretched for a considerable distance on either side of the house.

The warm, moist weather of recent days had prompted the roses planted almost a century ago to bud early. Their perfume drifted on the air as the twins strolled along one of the gravel paths that twined through the garden.

"They're worried about you," Jimmy said quietly. "My guess is that our cousin's impending wedding has made them think about your own future. They're concerned by the way it seems to be unfolding."

"I appreciate that," Cat murmured, "and I'm sorry that I can't make their minds easier."

"Can't or won't?"

"Put it however you like." As soon as the words were out, she looked contrite. "I don't mean to sound so hard, Jimmy, really I don't. But I don't know what else to say, either. After all, it's not as though I was doing anything so terrible."

"No," he agreed, "you aren't, at least not so far as I'm concerned." He sat down on a stone bench beside a small fountain. Cat joined him there.

"Do you think they really believe there's something wrong with my life?" she asked.

"Only that you seem very much alone. I know you spend a lot of time with Mari, which is fine. But that's not the same as beginning to create your own family."

"What about you?" Cat asked with a slight smile. "I don't hear wedding bells ringing over your head."

"And you won't for a while," he said with such vehemence that she had to laugh.

"I know," Cat said. "You're going to tell me it's different for women."

"I wouldn't have the nerve. You'd probably clobber me, like you did when we were little."

"I seem to remember you giving as good as you got."

"Probably, but the point is that no matter how we squabbled between ourselves, we always stuck together. Right?"

Cat nodded. "One for all, and all for one."

"I still feel that way," he told her gently. "You're my sister, I love you, and there's nothing I wouldn't do for you. But I also love our parents and I hate to see them so worried."

So did Cat. When they returned to the house, she went upstairs to her room to wash and change. She came back down again just as Elizabeth and Drake were coming in from their ride.

Her parents had their arms around each other. Elizabeth's head rested on her husband's shoulder, and she was looking up at him with a rather dreamy expression that Cat suddenly recognized.

She was torn between surprise and understanding as she considered that Calvert Oaks still contained many secluded places where couples could be alone. That her parents had availed themselves of one was hardly shocking. It did, however, remind her of their extraordinary closeness and make her wonder if she would ever experience anything similar for herself.

Elizabeth saw her and smiled. Cat thought she saw a glimmer of concern flit across her mother's face, but she couldn't be sure.

"You look very elegant, darling," she said as she gave Cat her cheek to kiss. "That color is quite becoming."

"Thank you, Mother." Since she felt compelled to dress in a very businesslike manner most of the time, Cat had been glad of an excuse to slip into something more feminine.

Her rose silk dress was trimmed with black velvet at the sleeves and waist. With it she wore a cameo brooch on a ribbon around her throat. Her golden hair was swept up, but loosely enough to leave soft wisps at her brow and the nape of her neck.

"How is Mari?" Drake asked after he had greeted his daughter.

"Fine. She's resting at the moment, but I suspect that's only because she brought a stack of reading with her and needs a bit of quiet time to start getting through it."

"And what about you?" Drake asked with a smile. "Is this a working trip for you, too?"

"There are a few things I have to sort out," Cat admitted. She was leery of discussing her work with her father, knowing as she did that he wasn't comfortable with it. But she was also reluctant to pretend that it didn't exist. "The new acquisition is going through," she told him. "Mackenzie Industries will be bigger and more profitable than ever."

"And Gideon Mackenzie knows it," Drake murmured. He exchanged a glance with his wife, who nodded almost imperceptibly.

"Great-uncle Gideon?" Cat said, surprised to hear him mentioned. His name hardly came up from one year to the next. She was barely conscious of his existence.

Yet she hadn't forgotten completely about him. Shortly after she had gone to work for Mari, the older woman had explained the nature of her long battle with her eldest stepson.

"He feels cheated," she had said, "because Josiah left the bulk of his estate to me. You might think that after all these years Gideon would have gotten over it. Heaven knows, he's been successful enough on his own. But he lacks the capacity to forget even an imagined injury. It's festered inside him."

"I ran into him the other day," Drake explained, "quite by accident, since I certainly don't make a practice of being in his company. He made some comment about the acquisition. I got the impression that he's been keeping a fairly close eye on your progress at Mackenzie."

"Why should he do that?" Cat asked, puzzled.

Elizabeth and Drake looked at each other again. This time it was she who spoke. "Darling, we really didn't intend to bring this up right now. We hoped to wait for a quieter moment. But since it has come up, I suppose we'd better just go ahead and tell you that we're concerned about Gideon. He's always been a rather nasty man. I remember him frightening me when I was a child, and I know your grandmother feels only loathing for him. Even though he's hardly young anymore—seventy this year, I believe—he's still capable of being a threat. We simply want you to be careful."

"Mari seems to feel more than capable of handling him," Cat reminded them. "After all, she's been doing it for years."

"That's true," Drake acknowledged, "and in all that time, Gideon has believed that he would ultimately wrest control of Mackenzie from her. He's well aware that she has no children of her own, and he imagines that when she dies, he can take over."

"But he's almost as old as she is," Cat protested. "What makes him think that he'll survive her?"

"Who knows?" Elizabeth said. "I truly don't believe that Gideon is quite rational. Although Mari has never formally indicated that she intends for you to follow her, it's clear that the opportunity will be yours should you want it. We're concerned that Gideon won't stand still for that."

Cat's eyes gleamed. Both her parents had stubborn natures, and she had inherited a full measure from each of them. "Then he's welcome to try to prevent it."

"Does that mean," Drake asked evenly, "that you want to become Mari's heir?"

"I don't know," Cat admitted. "I love her far too much to want to think about a time when she won't be here. But I also enjoy being involved in the business. Of course, everything I've done has been under Mari's guidance. I may not be good enough to take over for her."

"You might also develop other interests," her mother suggested.

Cat laughed self-consciously. "Is that a hint?"

"No," Elizabeth said matter-of-factly. "I'm less concerned than your father is about your being involved with business, particularly since there was a time in my life when I had similar interests. But I also think it can be a very arid life unless you have a family to care for, and to care for you."

"Your mother is right," Drake said quietly. "We want what is best for you, nothing more...or less. Surely there's nothing wrong with that?"

"No," Cat murmured, still surprised by what her mother had revealed about herself. She'd had no idea that Elizabeth had ever wanted to be anything other than what she was.

Absently she said, "I can't imagine your being truly concerned about Gideon. There's nothing he can do to harm me."

Her parents appeared unconvinced, but they didn't bring the subject up again.

After Drake and Elizabeth had changed out of their riding clothes, the family gathered on the veranda for a cool drink before going over to Quail Run.

The bride-to-be's parents were hosting a dinner party in their daughter's honor. As they came up the circular

drive, the house—smaller but no less elegant than Calvert Oaks—was ablaze with lights.

Cat's uncle, William, and his half-Cherokee wife,
Sunbird, greeted them on the steps. He was a tall, sol-
idly built man of middle years who strongly resembled
Philip, except for his darker hair. Sunbird was a ra-
diantly beautiful woman, tall and still slender, despite
having borne five children.

The party was already in full swing when they arrived.
Cat and Jimmy were urged to join the young people,
which they promptly did. Sunbird and William's daughter, Helena, was at the center of a group of friends, but
she broke away when she saw them.

"Oh, Lord!" she exclaimed as she looked at Cat.
"You're absolutely gorgeous, as always. Is Olivia still
eaten up with envy? Has she given up on Jimmy yet?"

"Yes and no," he said with a laugh as the cousins embraced. Helena was as tall as, or perhaps slightly taller
than her mother, with the same ebony hair, which provided a sharp contrast to her ivory skin. Her eyes were
slightly slanted, and she moved with a feline grace that
never failed to draw appreciative male glances, chief
among them those of her fiancé.

"Come and meet Daniel," she said. "He's from
Charleston, but he went to Harvard, so you should like
him."

Jimmy grinned at her presumption; he could think of
more than a few Harvard men to whom he wouldn't give
the time of day. But Daniel Lancashire proved not to be
one of them.

He was an attractive, pleasant young man with an un-
dertone of strength that would undoubtedly serve him
well. Helena hung on his arm, clearly enraptured, and he
seemed to more than return the sentiment.

Later in the evening, when supper was over and the dancing had not yet begun, Cat stole a private moment outside. She stood on the veranda, staring out into the night, thinking of the man she had left behind in New York.

By this time Evan would have received the note she had sent to him in which she explained that she was going to Virginia but would be back shortly and hoped to have come to some resolution before then. As she stood listening to the soft whisper of the breeze against her cheeks, she wondered if there was any chance of that hope being fulfilled.

Certainly she was feeling very far from resolved just then. The confusion born of her encounter with Evan had in no way diminished. On the contrary, seeing her father again had only brought home to her the utter incongruity of Evan's accusation.

As Mari had said, she didn't doubt that her father was capable of violence. What she rejected was the idea that he would hire other people to do his dirty work.

Yet Evan believed that he had, and she doubted very much that there was anything she could say to convince him otherwise.

She smiled ruefully as she considered that there was one positive aspect to the whole mess, namely that her parents clearly wanted her to marry. The improbability of their considering Evan O'Connell as a prospective husband didn't change the fact that they might be persuaded to accept a fait accompli if they were convinced that it made her happy.

But that was getting ahead of herself. She wasn't sure that she wanted to marry Evan, or anyone else. She liked being independent, helping to run a business, meeting men on equal terms and occasionally even besting them.

That gave her a confidence in herself that she had never felt before. She was loath to give those things up.

But perhaps, she thought as she looked in through the high windows at her cousin and Daniel, dancing together blissfully, she wouldn't have to. Evan could hardly expect her to sit home knitting.

He, above all, would understand her need to be out in the world, meeting its challenges, because he felt the same way. They were both rebels of a sort, he against the still-entrenched class structure, and she against the restrictions placed on her sex. They both broke the rules and undoubtedly would go on doing so, separately or together.

Something stirred deep within her, an emotion she had done her best to ignore throughout the past five years. In the midst of her family, surrounded by those who loved her, she was undeniably lonely.

It had come on her slowly, creeping up little by little until finally it became a looming presence in her life. No matter how hard she tried to repress it, the loneliness was always there.

Or at least it had been until she saw Evan again. With him, the hollow feeling of purposelessness that too often plagued her was gone. He filled her with an overpowering sense that the world, for all its caprice, was not without reason. It held meaning and design, provided she could grasp them.

A soft sigh escaped her. She was tired, worn out by the confusion in her own mind, and she didn't want to think any more that night. All she cared to do was go back inside, enjoy the party and forget about everything else.

Rather to her surprise, she managed to do so. It wasn't until much later, when she was lying in bed at Calvert Oaks, that the reason occurred to her. She had been able to put aside her worry because her decision was already made. She rather suspected it had been made the moment she had turned around on that dark street corner and seen him again.

_____ *Chapter Twenty*

EVAN PUSHED the curtain aside and glanced out the window. It had been raining when he left New York, and it was still raining. The weather matched his mood.

Behind him, Carmody gave a deep, heartfelt sigh. Reminded of the other man's presence, Evan turned around. His hands were thrust deep into the trouser pockets of his impeccably tailored dark suit, pushing the jacket sides apart to reveal a vest that accentuated the broad line of his chest. His square jaw was firmly set, his lean cheeks smoothly shaven. His eyes were all but impenetrable as he looked at the older man.

"So you think I'm a fool, do you?"

"I didn't say that," Carmody replied. "I only pointed out that you've got a damn good life going for yourself and I don't see why you want to mess it up."

Evan couldn't resist a wry smile. "What makes you think marrying Cat will do that?"

Carmody pushed himself out of the overstuffed chair and lumbered his way over to the cabinet that held his whiskey stock. He had put on weight in the past few years and was now completely white-haired. His shoulders were stooped, and he affected a shuffle, as though the news of the impending nuptials weighed him down.

Despite all that, Evan didn't doubt that his faculties were as sharp as ever. Carmody might look like a crotchety old bear, but he was in fact a wily old fox.

"It wouldn't if she were Catherine Malone or one of that sort. But Catherine Bennington's a whole different world, boyo, and if you're smart, you'll admit it."

"I do," Evan assured him. "Believe me, I do." He sat down in the chair across from the one Carmody laboriously reoccupied and swirled the glass the older man handed him. The amber liquid gleamed in the soft gaslight. Carmody still disdained electricity, though he'd acquired another telephone.

Evan took a sip of his drink, enough to catch the taste of it, no more. He'd never been one to drink to excess, but these days he thought it prudent to keep as clear a head as possible.

God knew Cat made that difficult enough. Since their reunion in New York, when she had calmly informed him that she was willing to see him again, he had been torn between elation at having rediscovered her and wariness about where their relationship would lead.

It had taken him very little time to decide that an affair with her would never be fully satisfactory because it allowed her too much freedom. He was frank in admitting that, if only to himself. Marriage would tie her to him far more tightly.

Not, of course, if she had any inkling of how little he trusted her. He still didn't know whether or not to believe her about the note and her response, but beyond that was his instinctive wariness of anyone who made him feel as she did—taken out of himself, spun around several times and hung out to dry.

No, it wouldn't do at all for her to know the effect she had on him, or how cautious he was as a result.

Rather to his surprise, she had agreed readily when he proposed. He imagined that was because of the strong conventional streak in her nature, ever at odds with the spark of rebellion he couldn't help but appreciate.

At any rate, he was losing no time firming up plans for their marriage. Cat would have the smallest possible opportunity to change her mind.

None of which prevented Carmody from trying to change his. "If you're thinking this will get you accepted by the Brahmans, you're crazy. Even if Drake Bennington does agree to have you as a son-in-law, he sure as hell won't be bending over backward to do you any favors."

"That's fine with me," Evan said. "He's the last man I'd take help from."

"Doesn't seem to me that you need it," Carmody said with a grin. "Not from what I've heard."

"I've done all right," Evan acknowledged. "And I'll do better. Cat won't want for anything."

"She's got a job of her own, hasn't she?"

"Oh, that. She just helped Mari out from time to time. It's nothing serious."

Carmody gave him a skeptical look but dropped the subject. The talk turned to events in the ward and from there to politics in general. About an hour later, they were interrupted by the squeal of children.

"That'll be the wee ones," Carmody said with an anticipatory smile. A moment later two small boys and a girl tumbled through the door. The eldest was about four, the youngest looked as though he'd only recently found his feet. Maude came in close behind them.

"Hello, Da," she said with a smile. "Evan, how have you been keeping?"

"I declare, Maude," he said, laughing, "I might as well have been away for a week if that's all the reception I get."

"Sorry," she replied. "I tend to be a bit distracted these days. *Brendan*, let go of your sister's hair this instant!"

The eldest boy obeyed, but gave the little girl a look that suggested he'd be back to give her more of the same. Maude sighed and sat down on the couch, lifting the littlest one onto her lap.

"At least I can keep him out of the line of fire for a while yet. He'll get into his share of mischief soon enough."

"You have a lovely family," Evan said sincerely. The children were all attractive and well dressed. Maude herself looked beautiful. She was no longer quite so slender, and her eyes had a slightly harried gleam, but apart from that she appeared unchanged.

"Thank you," she said softly as their glances met. "Marriage and motherhood agree with me."

"You know she married Michael Shaugnessy from the next ward," Carmody said. "A nice enough lad for all that he's not really Irish."

"Not that again, Da," Maude protested. "Having a single Scots grandfather doesn't wipe out all the rest of a man's ancestry, does it?"

Carmody shrugged. "I said he's nice enough, didn't I? Besides," he added with a grin for Evan, "he lets me win at chess."

"What brings you back to Boston?" Maude asked.

Briefly Evan explained to her that he was to marry and to whom. When he mentioned Cat's name, Maude's eyebrows rose. "It sounds as though you took my advice," she said.

"What's that?" Carmody demanded.

"I told him to marry somebody beautiful and rich," Maude said with a laugh. "I've got to admit, though, I wasn't quite thinking of Catherine Bennington. My imagination didn't go that far."

"It seems his did," Carmody grumbled. "I've told him he's heading for trouble, but he doesn't believe me."

"And why should he?" Maude replied. "I've never met Catherine Bennington, but I'll wager she's a woman like any other. If they care for each other, they should be happy together."

"Exactly what I think," Evan said, feeling he ought to at least get a word in edgewise. The children had broken off their play and were listening to the conversation in earnest, their heads swiveling back and forth.

They continued to stare at Evan as he went on. "After all, people are basically the same, aren't they?"

Carmody snorted derisively. "If the Benningtons are the same as everybody else, then how come you're so hotfoot to become one of them?"

"I'm not," Evan insisted. "It's Cat I want, not her whole bloody family."

"Most particularly not her father," Carmody said. "You're not a wee bit fond of himself, are you?"

"I dare say he feels the same," Evan admitted. "Or at least he will, once he hears about Cat and me."

"You mean he doesn't know yet?" Maude exclaimed. "But the way you talked, I thought it was all settled between you."

"It is, between Cat and me, which is all that counts. I'm doing Drake Bennington the courtesy of informing him, nothing more."

Carmody whistled softly. "If I were you, lad, I'd find some other way to phrase that before I sat down with the man. Otherwise things might get just a touch rough, if you take my meaning."

"I've tried courtesy with Bennington. It doesn't work. He only takes it for weakness."

Carmody frowned. "He's got a better reputation than that."

"In business. This is personal."

"True enough, lad. It's hard to imagine getting more personal. Anyway, I wish you luck."

"So do I," Maude said softly. "I hope it all works out for the very best." She couldn't quite conceal the note of doubt in her voice, but Evan pretended not to hear it.

HE WALKED THE DISTANCE from the North End to Beacon Hill. He needed the exercise, and besides, the walk gave him a chance to think. The rain had stopped, and the air, despite the occasional whiff of exhaust fumes from the passing cars, was relatively clear. He strolled along briskly, oblivious to the glances he drew.

He was clearly too well dressed to belong amid the rough-and-tumble of the tenements. Yet there was a toughness about him that set him apart from the usual denizens of the business district. Though he looked like them superficially, he gave off an aura of physical power and will they lacked.

The women were hardly oblivious to that. Their gazes lingered appreciatively on the tall, broad-shouldered man with the thick ebony hair and chiseled features. More than a few had difficulty recollecting that it was impolite to stare.

Only once did Evan's step falter. It was as he was leaving the North End, when he passed a particular corner he remembered all too well. The last time he had been there it had been dark and raining. Now it was day, and the sun was shining, but the difference was insignificant so far as he was concerned.

He paused, glancing at the place where the goons had come at him. The intervening five years might not have existed, so acute was the memory.

He had been tired, but elated by his talk with Drake, and anxious to see Cat again. If he hadn't been thinking about her so much, he might have had some warning. As it was, he had sensed nothing until a man suddenly stepped in front of him and demanded his name.

"O'Connell, is it?"

Foolishly, he had nodded. The man had smiled and struck the palm of his own hand with his fist. Evan had heard a noise and glanced down in time to see that the man was wearing brass knuckles.

As were the man who had come up behind him and the two others who appeared seemingly from nowhere. Thanks to his size and strength, and the fact that he was not without experience in street brawls, he had been able to hold them off for a short time.

But the outcome had never been seriously in question. It had taken all four of them to do it, but eventually they had gotten him onto the ground, where they proceeded to pummel him senseless.

His last conscious memory of that night was of looking up at one of the men, seeing the gleaming knife in his hand and knowing he was going to die.

In fact, of course, he hadn't. Something about the angle at which he had fallen, or a trick of the light that made the assailant miscalculate, or some other factor he didn't care to dwell on, had caused the knife thrust to go awry. Instead of penetrating his heart as it was intended to, it had lodged between two ribs until it was deftly removed several hours later.

The doctor who cared for him had marveled at his survival, commenting that he hadn't seen many men who could lose that much blood and still manage to crawl for help.

His astonishment had turned to anger when Evan insisted on leaving the dispensary before dawn. The comment he had overheard from one of the goons had convinced him that Drake Bennington wanted him dead. He wasn't going to hang around long enough to oblige him.

Simple rage had kept him going during the days when he rested at Carmody's. After his failed attempt to communicate with Cat, he had resolved to get out of Boston as quickly as possible. It had taken little time to convince William Chisom to buy the warehouse instead of renting it, particularly when he offered to let him pay in installments.

That done, he'd set himself to thinking where he might go. His options had been limited, to say the least. He had realized quickly that his best chance still lay with the cargo that Chisom was bringing in from Europe. It had been a quick step from there to deciding to go to Texas himself to arrange for its sale.

On his last day at Carmody's, less than a week after the attack, he had sat down to try to write another note to Cat to let her know where he was going. Not because he truly believed she would reconsider her decision, but because he didn't like the idea of simply disappearing into thin air, no matter how she felt about him.

The effort had proved futile. His feelings had been too profoundly confused. He hadn't directly blamed her for the beating, but her refusal to come to him certainly hadn't helped matters. At that moment, he had truly wanted nothing more to do with her.

But the feeling had changed. He hadn't been in Texas long before he realized that he wanted her as much as he ever had, perhaps more. He had almost returned then, intending to tell her what her father had done and give her the choice: her family or him.

Gradually, as his reason reasserted itself, he had realized the senselessness of that. What could he offer her that she should risk everything to be with him?

At that time, the answer had been nothing, at least by the standard to which she was accustomed. But times had changed. He was a rich man now, and growing richer by the day.

It was not inconceivable that his fortune would soon rival that of Drake Bennington himself. He could then give Cat all the comforts and protection which her father had always provided. He could even go through the motions of being cordial to her family.

But he had not forgotten what had happened, and he intended to be extremely careful that it would not be repeated. Drake wouldn't catch him unawares again.

The butler who answered the door of the Louisburg Square house gave Evan his first indication that all was not well within. The elderly man's face was stiff, his expression faintly condemning.

Clearly he either did not feel the usual restraints common to servants or he was waiving them in Evan's case.

"If you will wait here...sir," the butler said, "I will inform Mr. and Mrs. Bennington of your arrival."

He left Evan standing in the entry hall, having neglected to offer him the comfort of the sitting room, where callers were usually accommodated. Evan merely smiled wryly at the slight. He was willing to bet that he would encounter far worse before the afternoon was done.

Cat joined him a moment later. She came up to him with a smile and stood on tiptoe to kiss him. "I'm glad you're here," she murmured softly.

"So am I." The taste of her lingered on his mouth. She was simply dressed in an apricot silk dress that rustled faintly as she moved against him.

When they drew apart moments later, Cat tilted her head toward the doorway at the far end of the hall. "They're not in the best of moods," she warned.

"Do I take it that I'm a less-than-welcome guest?"

"I'm afraid so. Oh, Evan, I wish everything were different."

"It's all right," he assured her gently. "You have to look at this from your parents' point of view. I'm undoubtedly a great shock to them."

"Perhaps I should have waited to say anything until you were here, rather than just blurting it out."

"I'm sure you did nothing of the sort. Besides, how would it have looked if I'd shown up today with no explanation?"

"Odd," she admitted. "At any rate, they're, shall we say, anxious to see you."

"I'll bet," Evan murmured under his breath. As she took his arm, he touched her hand gently. "It will be all right, Cat. We'll make it that way."

She managed a weak smile before they entered the parlor together.

Drake was standing next to the couch where Elizabeth was seated. They had been speaking quietly between themselves, but broke off at Cat and Evan's arrival.

"O'Connell," Drake said with the briefest acknowledgment.

Evan smiled coldly as he faced the man who had once plotted to kill him. "Mr. Bennington."

They stared at each other for a long moment until Drake made an impatient gesture. "Sit down."

Elizabeth looked at them anxiously as they took their places on the couch opposite her. Cat was as tense as her mother, while the two men were doing their best to appear imperturbable.

Drake even managed to look faintly amused as he said, "I've been given to understand that you two have become reacquainted."

"We're going to be married," Evan said bluntly. He heard Elizabeth's sharp intake of breath and for an instant regretted being quite so direct. But there was nothing to be gained by dancing around something they already knew. Besides, he thought, the sooner it was out in the open, the better.

Drake eyed him steadily. "You indicated that such was your intention five years ago. It didn't happen then, so why should I believe it will do so now?"

"Because," Evan said with equal calm, "I'm a good deal wiser than I was five years ago."

Cat had flinched the moment her father mentioned the events of that summer. The last thing she wanted was for Evan's suspicions to be aired.

Either Drake would be outraged and deny them, which would only perpetuate the conflict, or he would give some indication that he was actually guilty of what Evan believed, something she could not bear to face. It was so much easier to leave the issue alone, allowing her to bury it, unexplained and unexplainable in the deepest recesses of her mind.

"Let's not talk about the past," she said quickly. "It really isn't important. What counts now are the present and the future."

Her father gave her a gently chiding look. "Very philosophical, my dear, but hardly realistic. There was a time when I was quite impressed by Evan's intelligence and ability. Not, I admit, to the extent of considering him a prospective son-in-law. But there was at least a measure of respect between us. I don't think I'm wrong to say that is absent now."

"Does that really matter?" Evan inquired, almost lazily, as though the issue were of no great importance to him. "It's Cat's and my feelings for each other that count."

"Only if you intend to live in isolation," Elizabeth interjected softly. She looked from Evan to her daughter as she asked, "Do you?"

"Of course not," Cat said. "What Evan is trying to say is that we would certainly like to have your blessing. However, our plans don't depend on it."

"I see," Drake murmured. He looked at his daughter steadily, as though something in her appearance might reveal how she had come to this point, poised on the brink of a decision that he was afraid would separate her forever from her family.

His chest tightened painfully at that thought. He held pride and honor to be essential, but not at the expense of love. For Cat, he would tolerate a great deal, so long as she would be happy in the end.

Evan was thinking much the same. He saw how pale she was, and how bleak, yet defiant, her eyes were. Forgetting for a moment his own reasons for hating Drake, he said quietly, "I realize that it can't be an easy thing to give up a daughter to a man you don't trust. This is very difficult for all of us."

Drake shot him a quick, penetrating glance. He hadn't expected Evan to grant any concessions, let alone show such understanding of his own position. His eyes narrowed.

He sensed a certain confusion in the younger man. It was as though there were two contradictory forces at work within Evan, one that made him want to protect Cat, and the other that drove him to rip her from her family.

"You're right," Drake said quietly. "It is difficult, particularly because this has come as such a surprise to both Elizabeth and myself. We are concerned that you may be acting precipitously." Cat started to protest, but before she could do so, her father added, "I don't think we're out of bounds to ask you to wait. Take some time to get to know each other better. Surely you have nothing to lose by that?"

Evan couldn't repress a flicker of admiration for the way Drake was handling the situation. Rather than attempting to forbid them to marry, which would only have had the effect of driving Cat into Evan's arms, he was being the soul of patience.

None of which meant that Evan's suspicions weren't aroused. If he and Cat did agree to wait, the way would be opened for her parents to arrange any number of excuses for separating them.

Her love and loyalty were so strong that she would be hard-pressed to endure their blandishments. Travel, other men, even business opportunities she otherwise wouldn't have had, could all be dangled before her. He was not about to risk that.

"My business interests are such that I'll be spending most of my time in New York," he said. "If Cat is still here in Boston, it will be difficult for us to be together very often."

"There are trains," Drake reminded him with an edge of sarcasm. "Not to mention telephones. You need hardly be out of touch."

"Of course not," Cat interjected quietly. Her hands were folded in her lap, her features carefully composed, as though what she was about to suggest was perfectly ordinary and acceptable. "It looks as though the work I've been doing for Mari will take me to New York more and more often. Why, I wouldn't be surprised if I ended up moving there myself in the next few months."

Drake and Elizabeth exchanged a glance, while Evan did his utmost not to laugh. While he and her father argued back and forth in a kind of verbal duel, Cat had deftly maneuvered the situation to her own liking.

No parent, however doubtful they might be about their daughter's prospective husband, would want the two of them living in a separate city far from family supervision. That would, almost inevitably, lead to certain irregularities that would be best avoided at all costs.

Evan made a mental note to remember that she had more than a little skill at manipulation as he sat back to await Drake's response.

In the end it was not Drake but Elizabeth who yielded. "All right," she said softly. "I think we can see that we aren't going to be able to change your minds, even temporarily. When do you want to be married?"

Cat expelled a long breath as her anxiety dropped away. She chose to believe that her parents had been converted and would now share her enthusiasm for the great event.

Whatever doubts about that lingered she firmly brushed away. "As soon as possible," she said. "There's no reason for us to wait."

"Actually," Elizabeth replied, "you'll need a gown, bridesmaids and so on. The church must be reserved, the reception planned, invitations sent out. All those things take time."

"But I don't want that sort of wedding. Something simple would be far more to my liking."

"What about Evan's preferences?" Drake inquired with studied mildness. "Will a simple, hole-in-the-corner affair satisfy you, or would you rather make it an event all of Boston will remember?"

"Much as I appreciate your concern," Evan said dryly, "I couldn't care less how it's done, so long as it's soon." With a slight smile, he added, "As for Boston remembering, I dare say they'll do that under any circumstances."

Drake suppressed a sigh. He hadn't really thought there was much of a chance of setting Evan and Cat at odds over the wedding plans, but he'd still figured it was worth a try.

He was more than half convinced that his daughter was being used as a stepping-stone to respectability and had therefore thought it likely that Evan would want to flaunt their wedding to the world. But either the other man genuinely didn't feel that way, or he was too smart to fall into the trap Drake had tried to set. In either case, it seemed that there wasn't going to be any dissension.

"A small wedding, then," Elizabeth said. A fond look flitted across her face. "That's practically a family tradition, so no one should really be surprised."

"How's that?" Evan asked. He was curious about this family he was set to join, but didn't want to make that too plain. It seemed wiser to maintain a certain aloofness.

Elizabeth looked at her husband and smiled. "Drake and I had a large wedding planned at Calvert Oaks, but there was some trouble a short time before, and we ended up with a small affair. At the time I was a bit disappointed, but looking back, I realized that I'm glad it was that way. A wedding is such a private, even intimate, moment, that it seems almost inappropriate to share it with too many people."

Drake nodded, his eyes very tender as he gazed at his wife. Evan was struck by the unabashedness of their love for each other. He was hard put to reconcile the evidence of the older man's fundamental integrity with what Drake had tried to do to him.

But he told himself that wasn't important. Cat was his and, for the moment, at least, nothing else mattered.

CATHERINE PAUSED outside the main entrance to the bank she had just left and took a deep, reviving breath. The business meeting that had occupied most of her morning and part of the afternoon was finally over.

All things considered, it hadn't gone too badly. She estimated that it had taken her only the first hour or so to convince the three bankers she was meeting with that they should take her seriously. After that, they had actually made some headway. Mari would be pleased by her report.

Deciding that the day—what was left of it—was too pleasant for her to stay stuck inside a moment longer, she opted to walk back to Louisburg Square. Perhaps the fresh spring air would clear her head.

The meeting's success was particularly fortunate in light of the trouble she'd had keeping her mind on business. But then, she rather thought that a young woman four days from her wedding could be pardoned a bit of absentmindedness.

Four days. She laughed softly to herself and allowed the smallest bit of a skip to enter her step. When she and Evan had decided that they wanted to be married only ten days after their meeting with her parents, she had thought for sure that Drake and Elizabeth would protest. Even a small, informal wedding, they would say, couldn't be arranged in so short a time.

To her everlasting gratitude, no objections had been raised. Elizabeth had immediately set about making all the necessary arrangements. Cat wasn't sure how she had done it, but she was organizing what promised to be an elegant affair in record time.

Which left Cat with virtually nothing to do except be fitted for her dress and enjoy being with Evan, at least when she wasn't working. She frowned slightly as she remembered the discussion they'd had that evening.

Evan had no pressing business of his own to attend to and therefore had wanted to spend the morning selecting their rings. Cat had explained that she was due at the bank.

"Can't you put that off?" he'd asked.

She'd shaken her head. "It was arranged several weeks ago. Besides, if I did ask for a delay just because I happened to be getting married, the men I'm meeting with would think me frivolous."

"Just because," he repeated. "I'd say it's rather more than that."

His chagrined look prompted her to reach out to him. "Please, Evan," she'd murmured as she'd laid her hand on his muscled arm, "don't be angry. Of course our wedding is important. But it's so difficult for a woman to be taken seriously in the business world. I can't risk doing anything that would weigh against me."

She was tempted to ask him what he would do if their positions were reversed—if he had an important meeting with financial backers, would he cancel it to go look at wedding rings?—but she stopped herself in time. He was already annoyed; there was no point in adding fuel to the fire.

The incident had been smoothed over, but the memory of it still rankled. Surely Evan understood how important her work was to her? Granted, they hadn't talked about it directly, but he, above all, should know the deep sense of satisfaction that came from pitting oneself against a challenge that others said would be too great.

If an immigrant Irishman from the wilds of Connemara could become a tycoon, then so could an upper-class Boston female who refused to be content with what society said was proper.

She enjoyed her work, she was becoming good at it, and she had no intention of giving it up for anyone. Happily she was confident Evan would never ask her to do so.

Four days. In four days she would be Mrs. Evan O'Connell. She rolled the name over in her mind, savoring each syllable of it.

Evan hadn't yet told her where they would be honeymooning; he was keeping that a surprise. But once they got back, they would be moving to New York. He had mentioned something about buying a place there, but he was holding off until she had a chance to see it. So long as it was convenient to the financial district, Cat thought it would be fine.

She had relatively little interest in their living arrangements provided they had plenty of privacy. It was almost a month since they had made love, and the time was weighing heavily on her. She lay awake at night imagining the feel of his hands and mouth on her body until the longing became all but intolerable.

Sometimes she wondered if there wasn't something wrong with her that she could feel such passion. But then she remembered the other women in her family who had known great love and decided that she was merely following a well-established tradition.

She paused for a few moments on the curb as several cars and carriages passed. It hadn't escaped her notice that every week there seemed to be fewer horse-drawn conveyances and more of the motor-driven variety. Despite the stink of the engines, she couldn't say that was really a turn for the worse. After all, the horses left behind their own particular kind of pollution, which was none too pleasing to the nose.

When the traffic cleared sufficiently, she crossed the street and started along the next block, only to stop abruptly when she noticed a familiar figure leaving a nearby building. She hadn't seen Charles van Rhys since his departure for Europe four years before but he had changed very little, and she had no difficulty recognizing him.

"What a fortunate coincidence," he said stiffly when they had greeted each other. "I was planning to call on you next week when I'd settled in a bit." His mouth beneath the thin mustache he had cultivated lifted in a slight smile. "I've missed you," he murmured. "Four years is a long time."

Catherine sighed inwardly. Their last meeting had been difficult, coming as it did after Charles had spent a year attempting to lay siege to her affections. He had gone so far as to actually propose marriage. Her refusal had infuriated him, snapping his always tenuous control on his temper. Had they not been in at least a semi-public place at the time—attending a social event—she suspected he might have gone so far as to strike her.

"You aren't in a hurry, are you?" he asked, taking her arm. "Perhaps we could have a cup of tea together and talk. My club is only around the corner."

Gently but firmly, Cat disengaged herself. She had no intention of going anywhere with him. The sooner he understood that, the better. "That would be nice, Charles, but I'm due at home. You see. I'm getting married on Saturday, and my dress still has to be fitted."

"M-married?" He stared at her in blank surprise. Slowly his face darkened. "I heard nothing about an engagement."

"It was rather sudden," she acknowledged.

"Who are you marrying in such a great rush?"

Cat hesitated. She was reluctant to tell him anything, but simple courtesy demanded that she respond. "His name is Evan O'Connell. He used to live in Boston, but he's been in Texas the last few years."

Charles's face had gone blank. Only a nerve twitching in his right eyelid revealed his shock. "O'Connell? The Irishman?"

Surprised, Cat asked, "You know him?"

"I . . . no, I don't. We've never met. After all, he was only your father's employee. There was no reason for us to have any contact. But I've heard of him."

His tone suggested that what he had heard was not pleasant. Cat stiffened. "I suppose it does put some people off to learn of his success, but I think it's to be commended. He overcame tremendous odds to get where he is today."

"And where is that?"

"Why, when you said you'd heard of him, I thought you knew. He was in on the beginning of the oil boom in Texas. His leases are quite extensive, but he's begun to branch out now into other businesses."

Evan had mentioned that to her only in passing, saying that he preferred not to keep all his eggs in one basket. She intended to find out later where he had his money invested. It wasn't impossible that she had picked up a thing or two that would be of help to him, or vice versa.

"Texas," Charles said with a sneer. "I might have known. Some of the lowest of the low are making their fortunes there. Your Mr. O'Connell must have fit right in."

She paled, and her silvery eyes flashed at the slur. "You forget yourself. Not every man has the advantage of possessing a fortune from the day he is born. I wonder how well you would have done had you been born in Evan's circumstances."

Charles shrugged that off, as if to say that it was too improbable to be considered. "What is your father thinking of to let you make such a match?"

"Of my happiness." Unable to stop herself, she said, "He respects Evan, and he's delighted to have him in the family."

Charles laughed humorlessly. "I doubt that very much. My guess is that your father is no more able to control you than he ever was. Now, if you'd had the sense to accept my proposal . . ."

She bridled. "How fortunate that I would never have entertained even the slightest possibility of that. You and Evan are nothing alike."

"You think not?" Charles asked. His hand lashed out, closing around her wrist. Cat had been about to walk away. She was caught off balance and would have fallen if he hadn't jerked her against him.

Oblivious to the passersby, some of whom were beginning to glance in their direction, he said, "Your Irishman imagines himself to be strong and determined, but he has no real idea what those qualities entail. He would be very well-advised not to let his reach exceed his grasp."

"What is that supposed to mean?" Cat demanded. He was hurting her, but she was determined not to show it. A spark of fear darted through her as she saw the fevered light burning in his eyes. Belatedly she remembered his temper and realized that she had, however inadvertently, provoked it.

Charles smiled. It was a particularly unpleasant expression that sent a shiver down her back, as though a cold finger had pressed against every nerve-ending in her spine.

"Only that it takes very little effort to crush an upstart such as Evan O'Connell. There are more than a few of us who would enjoy doing it."

"You can think that if you like, but you'd be a fool to try it. Evan is more than a match for you."

Abruptly he let go of her. She fell back against the wall of the building and stared at him. His face was an expressionless mask. Even the demonic light she had glimpsed in his eyes was gone. He looked so calm that she wondered if she had somehow imagined it.

"Perhaps you're right," he said with a shrug. "At any rate you've made your choice, and you'll have to live with it."

"Thank you," she muttered sarcastically, "for your good wishes."

For a moment he looked almost pleased. "You always did have spirit, Cat. That can be a troublesome quality in a wife, but it would have been excellent in a son." With what seemed like genuine regret, he added, "Too bad that's all to be wasted now."

He inclined his head slightly and, with rigorous politeness, raised his hat. Then he was gone, striding away into the crowd while Cat stared after him, telling herself that there was no reason to take his words as a warning.

Charles was merely a selfish, arrogant fool who felt driven to strike out at her because she was marrying a man he deluded himself into thinking was his inferior. If she allowed him to upset her, she would be giving him exactly what he wanted.

Which she had absolutely no intention of doing. She straightened, her head tilted proudly, and resolved to forget about the incident as quickly as possible.

By the time she reached the Louisburg Square house, she had virtually done so. She entered to find the place in turmoil. A thin, beak-nosed fellow stood in the entry hall, waving his arms and terrorizing two young women who appeared to be his assistants.

He was complaining vociferously in French, which Cat understood only imperfectly. Still, she gathered this was Monsieur François, the latest French couturier to take Boston by storm, and that he was none too pleased to have been kept waiting.

Elizabeth was attempting to soothe the fellow while also directing the servants where to put various packages, which had apparently been delivered during Cat's absence. When her eyes fell on her daughter, she gave a visible sigh of relief.

"There you are, dear. I was concerned that you might have forgotten."

Before Cat could comment, Monsieur François began to flail about again. "*Mademoiselle*, I am not a—how do you say?—a miracle worker. We 'ave very little time to create a suitable gown. Every moment is precious. *Every* moment."

"I'm terribly sorry," Cat murmured as she removed her hat and placed it on the hall table. Absently she smoothed her golden hair as she tried hard to restrain a smile. "I . . . uh . . . ran into someone. But I'm here now, so let's begin."

Monsieur François appeared barely mollified, but he did agree to follow her and Elizabeth upstairs. His hapless assistants trailed after them, their arms laden with bolts of cloth and other supplies.

Cat's room, the one she had occupied since she and Jimmy turned twelve and left the nursery on the upper floor, was large and airy. It was furnished with a four-poster canopied bed covered in soft, rose-hued damask. A Persian rug, in muted tones of ivory and rose was laid over the parquet floor. Tall windows looked out on the garden behind the house. A full-length mirror in a gilt frame stood nearby.

"Eef *mademoiselle* will stand 'ere," Monsieur François said, indicating a spot in front of the mirror. He snapped his fingers imperiously at one of the assistants. "Quickly, Janine, ze first of ze silks. *Non, non, pas comme ça.* 'Old eet up higher. We must see ze fabric against ze skin."

A corner of the bolt caught Cat in the arm. She winced but kept her mouth firmly closed. Obnoxious Monsieur François might be, but he was said to be superb at his craft. She wanted so badly to look beautiful for Evan on their wedding day that she was willing to suffer, at least a little, toward that end.

Bolt after bolt of silks, satins and taffetas were waved away by the persnickety Frenchman. "*Non*, non, zat is affreux. Try ze other. *Ah, non, c'est plus mauvais. Mademoiselle*, you 'ave not been taking care of ze skin. Eet is—" he pronounced the word in tones of doom. "—sallow."

Cat's eyes widened. She had never been particularly vain about her looks, but she did know her own appearance well enough to be certain he was wrong. Far from being sallow, her skin had an ivory hue touched with color at the cheeks and lips.

"Never mind," Monsieur François rattled on. "We will contrive something. All my skill will be needed, and so short a time. So fortunate you for zat I am 'ere."

"Fortunate indeed," Cat murmured. Anxious to have the whole business concluded, she said, "Perhaps we could take a look at some designs before trying to select the material."

The couturier frowned, as though he didn't approve of anyone attempting to direct him, no matter how discreetly, but after a moment he acceded.

"Eef zat is vat you vish, but I must tell you, many of the designs will not be appropriate. Zey are for ze smaller women, delicate, doll-like." He waved his hands to sketch in the air the sort of female he had in mind. *"Vous comprenez?"*

"I think so," Cat said. She exchanged a glance with her mother, who was frowning.

"My daughter is hardly large, Monsieur François. I'd say she's about average height for a woman, and rather slender."

"Non, non, she is *plus* tall and ze carriage, ze shoulders, ze walk . . . all very—how do you say—aggressive." Turning to Cat, he said, "You were ze tomboy, *n'est-ce pas?"*

She shook her head. His comments no longer perturbed her. Instead she was beginning to smile. An idea had occurred to her that would rid her of the tiresome Monsieur François and solve the problem of a wedding gown all at the same time.

"No, not really. I'm sorry you're having such difficulty with this. Perhaps it would be better for us to make some other arrangement."

He stared at her blankly. "*Autre* arrangement? Vhat are you suggesting?"

Her mind made up, Cat walked over to the bedroom door. "Only that it has occurred to me that we really are placing too great a demand on you. After all, as you said, you aren't a miracle worker. Thank you for coming by, *monsieur*, but there is no need for you to trouble yourself further."

As it dawned on him that he was being dismissed, his thin face turned bright red. "Vell, eef zat is vhat you think, I vish you luck. No one else can do for you vhat Monsieur François can. But I go."

He snapped his fingers again at the assistants, who scrambled to pick up the bolts of material. Grimly he inclined his head to Elizabeth, who was trying very hard not to laugh.

"*Au revoir, madame.* Pleeze do not disturb yourself to see me out. Monsieur François does not stay vhere he is not appreciated."

"Oh, darling!" Elizabeth exclaimed as she collapsed on the bed following his departure and that of the assistants. "I'm so sorry I inflicted him on you. What a pompous little man, and without even the sense to appreciate how beautiful you are. But what," she added with some concern, "are we going to do now? You have to have a dress."

"It occurred to me," Cat said with a grin, "that I already have one. Or, at least, so I've always been given to understand."

Elizabeth needed a moment to realize what she meant. "You mean the dress I wore when I was married? Your grandmother's dress?"

Cat nodded happily. "That's the one."

Elizabeth's brow creased. "I'm not sure it will be suitable."

"Why not?" Cat asked.

"Because it was made a very long time ago, in 1859 to be precise, when styles were very different. When I wore it twenty-five years ago it was difficult enough for me to manage." She smiled at the memory. "I had to wear hoops. It took me days to get used to them. Not only that, but if you think the corseting today is bad, it's nothing compared to what women went through back then. I was so tightly laced that I don't think I took a breath from the moment I put on the dress."

Cat had listened carefully, but made only one comment. "Do we have any hoops?"

"Do you mean you'd seriously consider...?"

"Absolutely. I've decided I'm all for fine old family traditions. If that means I don't breathe on my wedding day, so be it. After all," she added with a smile, "I probably wouldn't have been able to breathe anyway."

"It is liable to be a bit tense," Elizabeth murmured.

Cat sat down beside her on the bed and put her arm around her shoulders. She had always loved her mother dearly, but never more than at that moment. There was so much Elizabeth could have said about her lack of consideration in deciding to be married so quickly, never mind her choice of a husband.

She could have lectured her interminably, raising all sorts of problems and barriers to the wedding. Instead she had thrown herself into the business of ensuring that her daughter had a wonderful day to remember.

"I'd love to wear the dress," Cat said softly, "no matter how uncomfortable it is. When I walk down the aisle to Evan, I want to think of you and Grandmother, of everything you've accomplished in your lives. If I can do as well, I'll feel extremely fortunate."

There were tears in Elizabeth's eyes as she touched her daughter's cheek softly. "I do so want you to be happy. Evan seems to be a genuinely good man, so I've hesitated to say anything, and I won't now, except for one bit of advice. The early days of marriage are seldom easy. There are often misunderstandings, but if you can hold fast to the love you share, it will all work out in the end."

"I'm certainly going to try," Cat said. She blinked rapidly, fearing that she was going to cry. Which would have been ridiculous, since she was so very happy.

Distantly she thought of the allusions Charles had once made to the state of her parents' own marriage at its beginning. With a watery smile she asked, "You and Father made it, so I imagine Evan and I can, too."

"You know about that?" Elizabeth asked, surprised.

Cat shrugged. "Not really, but I have the impression you went through some stormy times together."

Elizabeth laughed softly. "That's certainly the truth. I wouldn't have admitted it at the time, but we were virtually strangers to each other when we married. I thought he was the prince on the white horse, and he thought I was a tractable little female."

Cat joined in her mother's laughter. "He was certainly wrong about that, wasn't he?"

"As I was about him." Suddenly serious, Elizabeth took her daughter's hand in her own. "I'm sure you think you know Evan very well, and that he knows you, but that isn't the case. You've barely begun to get acquainted. There are going to be surprises along the way, some of them not very pleasant. If you expect each other to be perfect, you'll be set up for disappointment before you even begin. But I'm sure,'' she added quickly, ''that you're both far too smart for that.''

Cat nodded. She had no intention of contradicting her mother, even though she privately thought her concern was misplaced. Of course Evan wasn't a prince on a white horse. Oh, he was strong, tender, brilliant, stalwart, all those things. But this wasn't a fantasy; this was real. How very lucky she was to have found such a man and to be marrying him.

It all just went to show that differences in people's backgrounds were inconsequential. As she had said to her father, the past didn't matter. Only the future counted. And she could hardly wait for it to begin.

Chapter Twenty-two

TO THE MEASURED PACE of Mendelssohn's "Wedding March," Cat walked down the aisle on her father's arm, her grandmother's gown swirling about her. Elizabeth had related the story of how three seamstresses had labored for a fortnight to create it. No one remembered how many yards of silk and satin had been required, but the amount must have been considerable. In addition, there were vast quantities of seed pearls embroidered onto the bodice and sleeves, as well as the flounced and pleated skirt.

As luxurious as her life had always been, Cat had never before worn such a gown. She delighted in every step she took even as she gave respectful regard to the hoops she had only begun to master. After several days' practice, she was confident that she wouldn't disgrace herself.

Still, she could hardly claim to be comfortable. Between the need to manage the hoops and the tight corseting necessary to squeeze herself into the infinitesimal waist, she was amazed that she had any attention left for the wedding itself.

When she at last caught sight of Evan, she almost regretted it. His expression was unaccountably grim, hardly that of a man overjoyed by the sight of his bride. On the contrary, he looked as though he were plotting either mayhem or revenge, possibly both.

Baffled by the waves of anger she felt coming from him, she trembled slightly as Drake placed her hand in Evan's and stepped back. As he did so, the two men exchanged a glance. Drake frowned.

As the Episcopal priest who had agreed, with some persuasion, to marry them began intoning the ritual, Cat stole a look at her about-to-be-husband. She thought him devastatingly handsome in a formal dark cutaway coat, gray trousers and a white silk shirt.

His thick ebony hair was brushed back from his forehead, and his lean cheeks had been freshly shaven; she caught the merest hint of a mild after-shave. Beneath his straight brows, his light blue eyes gleamed. As he felt her looking at him, he turned. His expression softened a fraction, enough for her to relax a bit.

When the time came to exchange vows, her voice was soft and precise, his deep and firm. There was no hint of wavering on either of their parts. Evan slipped the sapphire-and-diamond band they had selected together onto her finger. She, in turn, slipped a plain gold band onto his.

The priest smiled, a bit nervously, Cat thought. Then she lost all awareness of the man, and, for that matter, everyone else, as Evan bent and kissed her gently.

For a moment their bodies pressed close together, presaging the passion they would share in a few short hours. She closed her eyes against a surge of yearning that left her feeling hot and flushed.

Walking down the aisle on Evan's arm, she caught a glimpse of her mother and father. Elizabeth was dabbing at her eyes with a lace handkerchief. Drake's features were tightly drawn. She looked away quickly and managed to exchange a shaky smile with Jimmy.

Outside, in the bright spring sun, she and Evan accepted the congratulations of the small number of guests. Carmody was there, looking very fine in his formal dress. He had been hesitant about attending, but Evan had insisted.

"You're the closest friend I've got in Boston," he had said, "and I'll be damned if I'm getting married without you being there."

Maude was there, as well; Cat thought her beautiful in a gown of light blue silk that perfectly offset her Titian hair and sparkling eyes. She had left the children with her husband in order to accompany Carmody. Despite her shyness in the presence of such august personages as the Benningtons, she was enjoying herself.

"It was a lovely service," she told Cat. Candidly she added, "I've never been to a Protestant church before. We're not supposed to go, you know. I must say, I can't see why." She leaned forward slightly and dropped her voice to a whisper. "It really isn't all that different."

"I'm glad you enjoyed it," Cat said with a smile. She'd only met Maude for the first time a few moments before, but she had already decided that she liked her. The young woman was intelligent and unpretentious; moreover, it was clear that she had a sisterly affection for Evan. Cat would have approved of her for that reason alone, if for no other.

"Congratulations, little sister," Jimmy said as he hugged Cat and shook hands with Evan. "Now do me a favor and have a couple of grandchildren quick, so the folks won't get any ideas about my providing them."

Cat blushed, but Evan merely laughed. "That might not be a bad idea," he said. Nothing in his tone revealed what was going through his mind at that moment: the thought of his children's grandfather being Drake Bennington did not sit at all well with him.

His eyes darkened as he looked in his father-in-law's direction. Drake was chatting with the priest and didn't see him, but Evan had time to take note of the other man's apparent calm and marvel at it.

He had resolved during the long hours of the night not to say anything to Cat about what had happened the other evening. There was still a possibility that he was mistaken.

He hadn't been precisely sober as he returned to his hotel from the bachelor party Carmody had organized. But then, he hadn't been drunk, either. If he had been, the men who came at him out of the alleyway might have had better luck.

It had come very close to being a repeat of the incident five years ago. All that had prevented it was his own wariness. Ever since breaking the news of their impending wedding to Drake, Evan had been watching his back. He'd gone nowhere unarmed, and he'd never for a moment lost sight of any potential danger that might be awaiting him.

Still, it had been a shock to realize that he'd been right to be so cautious. Now, standing in the bright sunlight outside the church, dark currents whirled through his mind.

He consoled himself with the thought that he and Cat were safely wed. Whatever emotions might be festering in Drake's soul, surely he would have the sense to give up now.

At the small reception afterward, Drake gave every appearance of being reconciled to events. He led the way in proposing a toast to his daughter and her husband, and even went so far as to formally welcome Evan into the family.

Evan was convinced his father-in-law was engaging in hypocrisy, but he gave no sign of his thoughts. On the contrary, he made it a point to appear perfectly happy and at ease.

He almost succeeded. Only Cat was not fooled. She told herself that she must be mistaken, but she continued to believe that something was seriously wrong.

The dining room of the Louisburg Square house had been filled with flowers and a sumptuous meal laid on. In between bites of lobster and sips of champagne, Cat cast the occasional cautious glance at her husband.

Their eyes met across the table, and Evan smiled provocatively. Cat felt a rush of warmth as she looked ahead to their wedding night.

When she had told Charles that the wedding was to be strictly a family affair, she hadn't been quite accurate. Some two dozen friends, of both the bride and groom had been invited. They made up a merry party that ate, drank and danced its way through to early evening.

As the sun was beginning to set, turning the sky radiant, Cat slipped upstairs. She gave an audible sigh of relief as Tilly, her mother's maid, helped her out of the dress.

"It's wonderful," Cat said, "and I love it. But oh, Lord, it feels good to take it off."

Tilly smiled as she carefully folded the gown over a chair. Cat watched as she did so. "Do you think," she asked softly, "That it might hold up for one more wearing?"

"That depends, missy."

"On what?"

"On how long you take to get yourself a daughter and raise her up," Tilly said flatly. She fingered the silk and lace gently. "They used truly fine material back then. Your momma and I found some yellowing when we took it out of the trunk, but a bit of soap and lemon juice took care of that. It should be good for at least another fifty years."

"I don't think I'll take that long," Cat said with a laugh. She wasn't in any rush to have children, but she was realistic enough to know that unless she and Evan took precautions, they would probably come along in fairly short order.

Her mother had told her frankly how to prevent that, but Cat hadn't yet been able to bring herself to discuss the matter with Evan. She supposed she'd have to fairly soon.

"I wish Grandmother and Grandfather could have been here," Cat said softly as she stepped into the dress Tilly held for her. "I would have loved for them to see me married in that gown."

"I'm sure they would have loved it, too," Tilly said gently. "But this isn't the time of year for them to be leaving the plantation. Besides, at their ages, it's not a good idea to be gadding about too much."

"Don't ever let them hear you say that," Cat admonished. "They think they really are as young as they used to be."

"No, child," Tilly said with a shake of her head. "They've both got more sense than that. But they take good care of each other, so there's no reason why they both won't be here for a while yet."

"We'll see them soon," Cat said as Tilly fastened the buttons up her back. "Evan understands how I feel about that. He says we'll go down as soon as we pick out a place to live."

"He's a good man. Though I have to admit," Tilly added with a grin, "I never really thought that a Connemara lad would be marrying into this family."

"Times are changing," Cat said confidently. "It's a whole new world. All sorts of things are happening that never did before."

"Still," Tilly cautioned, "old prejudices die hard. It's just as well you never cared for all those fancy society toffs and their doings."

"Because you don't think they'd welcome me anymore?" Cat asked mildly.

"I didn't say that, only..." The maid hesitated a moment, then said, "Only don't let anyone make you question your own heart, Miss Catherine. It's always your best guide through life."

"My mother told me much the same," Cat said. "For that matter, so did Mari."

"Then you remember what they told you." Briskly Tilly finished the buttons and sat Cat down in front of the dressing table. She pulled the pins from her golden hair and brushed it thoroughly before swiftly swirling it up again in a soft French twist. That done, she looked in the mirror critically.

"You're a bit pale, but I imagine that will change quickly enough."

True to her expectation, Cat promptly flushed. "Get along with you, then," Tilly said softly. As Cat rose, she put her arms around her and hugged her. "Be happy, Miss Catherine. That's all any of us wants for you."

But not, Cat thought as she walked slowly down the steps to rejoin the guests, all she wanted for herself. Her ambitions far exceeded mere happiness.

She wanted to have an impact on the wonderful new age she had spoken of to Tilly. To stretch the limits of what a woman could be in the hope that the hypothetical daughter she might one day have would find the world an even better place than Cat herself had.

With that thought in her mind, she smiled. Watching her from the foot of the steps, where he waited with the guests, Evan could not tear his eyes away. He had always known that Cat was beautiful, but at that moment she had an ethereal loveliness he had never before glimpsed. For an instant he had the sense of looking directly into her soul.

The moment passed. Cat stopped halfway down the stairs and, amid the laughter and cheers of the guests, tossed her bouquet. As the young women scrambled for it, she came down the rest of the way into Evan's arms.

He embraced her gently, conscious of holding something that was infinitely precious to him. They stood close together, apart from the surrounding tumult, until the world swept them up once again.

Cat had a quick, staccato sense of images—her mother and father with their arms around each other; Jimmy hoisting a bottle of champagne and laughing; Mari smiling tenderly.

Rice kernels showered the air as they left the house. A gleaming black-and-tan Pierce Arrow, complete with chauffeur, waited at the curb. Evan had purchased the automobile the day before but had said nothing about it to Cat, wanting to surprise her.

"Heavens," she said admiringly as the chauffeur opened the door for them, "is this yours?"

"Ours," he corrected. "Saunders here will drive it to New York for us. It will be waiting when we get back."

Cat turned to wave out the window. Her vision was slightly blurred, but she chose to attribute that to the slanting rays of the setting sun. She blinked back tears as the car pulled away. Evan put his arm around her shoulders and held her gently.

He respected her feelings but couldn't quite contain a twinge of resentment as he considered the hold her family still had on her. Under ordinary circumstances he would never have been so selfish as to want her to care only for him. But given his suspicions about Drake, he needed reassurance that he came first with her.

After a few moments she sat up and gave him a smile that was only slightly tremulous. "Well, that's done, thank heavens."

"It was very nice. Your mother did a marvelous job."

"Yes," Cat agreed, "she did. But I'm still glad it's over." She looked at him directly as she asked, "It's been . . . a long time."

Her slight hesitation and the flush that warmed her cheeks made it clear to him what she meant. He grinned delightedly. "For both of us, sweetheart. But that's all done with." He glanced out the window, gauging how far they were from their destination. "Or almost."

A short time later the car pulled up in front of the gracious hotel that fronted the Public Garden. The chauffeur tipped his hat as Cat and Evan stepped out. Bellboys hurried to claim their luggage as the hotel manager himself came forward to greet them.

"Mr. and Mrs. O'Connell," he said with a smile, "we're delighted to have you staying with us. May I be among the first to offer my congratulations?"

Cat made an appropriate response, though she was far more tempted to laugh. The man's respectful courtesy had surprised her somewhat, since she had presumed that her marriage would be viewed with at least a modicum of censure by proper Boston society.

After telling herself stalwartly for the past several days that she didn't care, she was mildly taken aback to discover her relief. Hard on it came a realistic assessment of its source: Boston might set great importance on propriety, but money counted for even more.

"Not to be vulgar," she murmured as she and Evan rode up in the elevator, "but Texas must have been extremely good to you."

He grinned. "That fellow downstairs sure seems to think so. Not too many years ago he would have thrown me out of here."

Cat wondered at how easily he could say that. It seemed as though the hardships of his earlier life had been completely forgotten. Certainly she caught no hint of lingering bitterness, except where her father was concerned. Determined not to think of that, she asked, "How long are we staying here?"

"Until tomorrow." They got off the elevator and walked down the corridor, following the bellboy. At the door to their suite, Evan tipped the young man and sent him on his way. He lifted Cat into his arms, kicked open the door and carried her inside.

Holding her with infinite tenderness, he asked, "Have I told you, Mrs. O'Connell, that you made a lovely bride?"

"No," she said, her full mouth curving in a smile. "However, you're welcome to do so now." On a note of daring, she added, "Better yet, you can show me."

Evan laughed softly. Her sensuality delighted him. He lowered his head and claimed her mouth with devastating thoroughness.

Cat gasped at the frank demand of his caress, even as her own passion rose to meet his. She parted her lips willingly for the thrust of his tongue, savoring the warm, moist taste of him.

Cradled in his arms, she felt totally protected and desired. She wrapped her arms around his neck. His crisp ebony hair was slightly rough beneath her fingers. She remembered the way it felt against her naked breasts and trembled.

Evan broke off the kiss to swiftly carry her into the adjoining bedroom. The satin spread on the large bed had already been turned back. Cat stared at the snow-white linen covering the plump pillows. She thought of their heads lying side by side and stirred with impatience.

"Evan," she said breathlessly, "I'm not a virgin."

He shot her a quizzical look. "Darling, I, above all men, am well aware of that."

She bit her lip, uncertain of how to express what was in her mind. "I meant that..." Words failed her. Self-consciously, she looked away.

Evan smiled tenderly. He put his hands on her shoulders and drew her to him. "You meant that I don't have to take as much care as I did before?"

"Something like that," she murmured against his shoulder.

"On the contrary," he whispered softly as he ran his hands along her back to the curve of her waist and hips. "That first time, in the hut, was not at all as I would have liked it. Even more recently in New York, there could have been more."

When she looked up at him in surprise, he added, "Let me show you, Cat."

She was hardly in a position to say no, especially not when her heart was beating wildly and her entire body felt suffused with heat. She stood as still as she could manage as he slowly undressed her.

When her jacket, skirt and blouse were gone, Evan gathered her to him. His lips were firm yet gentle as they moved along the sensitive line of her throat from behind her ear to the scented hollow between her collarbones. She moaned with delight as he bent her back slightly and caressed her breasts through the thin silk of her camisole.

When she was all but mindless with pleasure, he set her down on the edge of the bed and removed her shoes and stockings, his fingers running lingeringly over her calves to the delicate arches of her feet.

"Raise your arms," he murmured huskily as he at last stood up. She obeyed, and he pulled the camisole off, exposing her bare breasts, the nipples already hard with anticipation.

Naked from the waist up, with only the froth of her petticoats and pantaloons to hide her from him, she watched with mingled excitement and apprehension as he stripped off his own garments.

Her silvery gaze devoured the hard, taut virility of him, from the broad sweep of his hair-roughened chest to his narrow hips and long, muscular legs. His manhood, jutting from the nest of dark curls at his groin, drew her irresistibly.

Whatever fear she might once have felt at the sight was long since gone. She recognized the perfect compatibility of their bodies, meant to join together in a celebration of both love and life.

Rising up on her knees, she held her arms out to him. "Come to me, Evan," she breathed softly.

He caught her around the waist and with a hungry growl buried his head against her soft, fragrant skin. His tongue ran over her in long, lingering strokes, curling around her turgid nipples, licking at the undersides of her breasts, tracing the faint shadows along her ribs.

Drunk with the feel of her, he lowered her back onto the bed and let her experience the full force of his strength. His hands tangled in her honeyed hair as their gazes met.

"I want you, Cat, every inch of you, every tiny, secret part. I want you mindless, crazed with need. The same way you've made me."

She felt as though she were already at least halfway there, but when she tried to tell him so, he only shook his head and laughed. "Oh, no, my love, not yet. But you will be. That and more. I promise."

He slipped his thumbs beneath the waistband of her petticoat and pulled it down, along with her pantaloons, but only as far as the cleft between her hips. Smiling at her wide-eyed gasp, he moved lower in the bed and ran his hand over her belly from one hip to the other, just below her navel. Instantly she cried out, and her body stiffened.

"So responsive," he murmured with intense satisfaction. Slowly he slipped her last garments off completely and let them fall to the floor. When she was completely bare to his gaze, he moved over her, gently separating her thighs with his hands.

As his callused thumbs stroked the sensitive inner skin, Cat cried out. She tried to rise, but Evan would not permit it. He held her tenderly but firmly as he drove her to a peak of pleasure so explosive that she doubted her ability to survive it.

When she had at last floated back down to earth, her skin shone with a fine sheen and her bones felt as though they had turned to water. Dazedly she looked up at him through the thick fringe of her lashes. His eyes glittered fiercely, and his face was tautly drawn with the force of his own as yet unreleased passion.

Understanding rippled through her. She raised her hips slightly at the same time that she reached for him. Their joining was swift and complete. She held him in her arms almost protectively as he shuddered at the peak of his fulfillment.

Love for this man, for the beauty of what they shared, for the life they were beginning together, overflowed in her. She gave a silent prayer of thanks for the beneficence of creation that permitted such joy and purpose.

It was only much later, as Cat lay in Evan's arms, drifting between sleep and wakefulness, that something occurred to diminish her utter contentment. As her hand wandered caressingly down his broad chest, he winced slightly.

"Is something wrong?" she murmured.

He shook his head, breathing in the perfume of her hair. She lay against him like warm, honeyed silk. Her slender body with its high, firm breasts, narrow waist and rounded hips felt unutterably delicate in his arms. Again he was swept by the need to cherish and protect her. Because of that, he lied. "Everything is fine."

Cat snuggled down again, but her eyes remained open. They had left the lamps unlit, but sufficient light streamed in through the high windows for her to be able to see him.

Earlier, when they were making love, she had been oblivious to everything except the hard, taut perfection of him. But now, as her gaze wandered over him, she breathed in sharply. Dark splotches of bruises showed along his ribs.

"What ... ?" She reached out, brushing her fingers over him.

Evan muttered a silent curse. He had truly not wanted her to know that he was injured, but now that she did, he could hardly refuse to tell her what had happened. He could, however, minimize it.

"You should see the other guys," he said with a smile.

Cat's usually soft and generous mouth had thinned to an angry line. "There were more than one?"

He shrugged. "There usually are in a situation like that." Immediately, he regretted the ill-chosen words. She would undoubtedly be led to think of the incident five years before.

"This wasn't just a random occurrence, was it?" Cat asked as she sat up in the bed and looked at him. "It was another deliberate attack."

"These things happen. I've hardly gone through the years without making a few enemies."

She stared at him steadily for several moments before she said, "You think my father was responsible again."

"I didn't say that." He sat up, too, and reached for the silver cigar case on the table beside the bed. Gesturing to it, he asked, "Do you mind?" When she shook her head, he removed a cheroot, lit it and took several puffs before attempting to discuss the situation further.

"It is possible," he acknowledged, "that Drake is involved. Certainly, it would be consistent."

"Yet you don't seem to be quite certain."

It was true; he wasn't. Slowly he said, "I know he was hardly enthusiastic about our marriage, but there were many ways he could have tried to stop it short of sending goons after me again."

"The same could be said of the earlier attack," Cat reminded him. "There were other possible remedies then as well as now, possibly more."

"Of course," Evan said with a shrug, "he's accustomed to taking decisive actions, so perhaps he thought it was best to simply sweep me out of the way."

Cat was unconvinced. She had never shared Evan's conviction regarding her father's guilt, though she hadn't known what else to think, either, and now she was more certain than ever that something didn't fit.

Granted, Evan had seen a side of her father's character that she had never experienced. Yet she still could not see him acting in so low and brutal a fashion.

"Did these men say anything?" she asked.

He bared his teeth in what could have been mistaken for a smile. "All they expressed was their desire to get away from the Luger I happened to be carrying."

Cat's mouth formed a round O. She knew very little about firearms, but she had the sense to realize that a Luger was hardly a weapon intended for sport. "Are you still carrying it?"

He shot her an amused look. "Not at the moment." In fact he had removed it only a few hours earlier when Cat had briefly excused herself to change into her negligee. The pistol now resided in the drawer next to him. He had no intention of letting it get any further away until he was certain exactly who was stalking him, and why.

Carmody was already making discreet inquiries on his behalf to identify the men. The older man would have that information in hand when they returned from their honeymoon, possibly before.

"Evan," Cat said softly, "what are you thinking?"

Not about to let her into his thoughts, he sought refuge in equivocation. "Why do you ask?"

"Because you look very fierce all of a sudden." So fierce that he frightened her, though she was not about to tell him that.

Immediately his expression softened. "I'm sorry, sweetheart. Put this out of your mind. Whoever was responsible, I'll get it straightened out."

Cat didn't believe for a moment that he was as unconcerned as he was trying to sound, but she was glad enough to put the subject aside, if only temporarily. There were far more pleasant things to concentrate on as she let the sheet drop and moved back into his arms.

_____ *Chapter Twenty-three*

CATHERINE WIGGLED her bare toes in the warm sand and stared out across the sparkling water at the distant horizon. It was late afternoon. She and Evan had spent the past several hours on the deserted beach beneath their honeymoon cottage.

They had gone for a long walk, talking about nothing in particular, and had ended up in a grove of pine trees, where they had made love. After a short doze, they returned along the beach to sit in the shelter of a low hill and watch as the sun began its retreat.

It had, in her estimation, been a perfect day—the latest of the six they had shared together.

"I wish we could stay here longer," she said softly.

He smiled sympathetically. "So do I, but we can come back."

She didn't comment, although they both knew that it wouldn't be the same. Like it or not, the pressures of life would shortly intervene. They would be drawn once more into the world, and this blissful interlude that marked the beginning of their marriage would become only a cherished memory.

Still, she was glad enough to have that. "I would never have thought of this place," she said with a smile, remembering her surprise when, on the day after their wedding, he had told her where they were going. "But it's perfect."

Evan agreed. Together they glanced up at the two-story white clapboard house he had rented. Compared to the mansions of Newport, it looked austere. But they had both come to love the house in the short time they'd been in it. Alone, without servants, except for a local boy who brought them groceries, they had been free to discover each other without hindrance.

"Shall we walk out to the point tomorrow?" Evan asked as he helped her to her feet.

She dusted the sand off her navy blue skirt and nodded. "I'd like that."

They shared a private smile. The house was only a mile from the point where Evan had found Cat during the storm five years before. The hut they had shared that night still stood. They had rediscovered it together the day after they arrived at the house, and had put it to good use.

Hand in hand they climbed up the hill and walked across the flat expanse of sand to the house. Cat didn't bother to put her shoes or stockings back on. She felt wondrously free and unfettered. Her hair tumbled around her shoulders; the top buttons of her blouse were undone, and she had a smattering of freckles across the bridge of her nose to testify to her disregard of the sun.

She laughed as Evan plucked a Shasta daisy growing near the house and tickled her under the chin with it. When she attempted to retaliate, he dodged out of the way. They ran, laughing, up the steps and into the house.

Evan caught her near the kitchen, spun her around and kissed her soundly. Cat melted in his arms, utterly yielding and responsive. The hardening of his body sent a surge of anticipation through her. She was happily sinking into the hazy mists of pleasure when he abruptly let her go.

Looking down at her with a grin, he said, "So what's for dinner?"

Cat blinked rapidly. "Dinner?" He might have mentioned some exotic object with which she had no familiarity.

His amusement deepened. "A man has to keep up his strength."

"Are you sure," she demanded glumly, "that you really want me to try cooking again?"

"It can't be as bad as the last time," he told her reassuringly. "Besides, I'm tired of doing it. We've been living on fried eggs and baked beans for the last five nights. Anything's got to be better than that."

Cat had to agree, even though she privately doubted her ability to improve on what had been, admittedly, a limited diet. "I like eggs," she hedged, "and baked beans are good for you."

He leaned forward, his lips brushing warmly against her ear. "Steak," he murmured seductively. "Baked potatoes, fresh green beans, apple pie."

Cat's stomach growled. "Hmm, sounds good. Are we going out to dinner?"

Evan laughed and swatted her behind lightly. "You're cooking. I'll lend moral encouragement." He laid a firm hand on her shoulder and propelled her into the kitchen.

"It's going to take more than that," she told him.

"Nonsense, you're better at this than you know. All you have to do is relax and follow your instincts." In fact he didn't feel as confident as he sounded, but after the debacle of the first meal she had tried to prepare—burned chicken and shapeless lumps of dough that were supposed to be biscuits—he sensed that her pride needed restoring.

Actually he thought there was at least a chance that Cat knew something about cooking, since she had been a frequent visitor to the kitchens of her family's homes. She and Jimmy had both been favorites of the various cooks who had come and gone over the years. She couldn't have been around them so much without picking up some skill.

But when he told her this theory, Cat disagreed. "If I learned anything, it's long since been forgotten. Didn't the chicken prove that?" She had actually cried over the miserable mess she had made of that meal. Which, now that she thought about it, hadn't been all bad, since Evan had found a most satisfactory way to comfort her.

"Forget the chicken. This will be different."

"Not if it's instincts you're relying on."

He went over to the counter, where the delivery boy had left a basket of nonperishables. From it, he withdrew a book and brandished it triumphantly. "We also have a cookbook to fall back on. *Mrs. Peterson's Guide to Homemaking for the Twentieth-Century Wife and Mother.* Sounds like it should fit the bill, doesn't it?"

Cat remained skeptical, but she acquiesced enough to put on a long white apron while Evan riffled through the book. "Steak, preparation of. Here it is. Let's see now, it says that you—"

"Wait a minute. We don't start with the steaks. They won't take long. We have to make the pie first."

Evan glanced up and frowned. "We?"

She tilted her head to one side and smiled encouragingly. "Why should I have all the fun? Besides, this was your idea."

"All right," he relented. "I'll supervise."

She snorted delicately, took the cookbook from him and paged through it until she found a recipe for pie.

"All right, we'll need . . ." As she rattled off the ingredients, Evan assembled them on the wooden counter. He peeled the bright red apples and sliced them while Cat made the crust. She was surprised by how much she remembered, even down to flouring the rolling pin so that it wouldn't stick to the dough.

By the time she had ladled the mixture of apples, raisins and cinnamon into the pie pan, she was feeling a definite sense of accomplishment. The fact that the top crust was a bit ragged didn't deter her. Perhaps she could cook, after all.

While the pie and the potatoes baked, Evan got a fire going in the dining room. Although it was late spring, the nights were cool enough to make some extra warmth welcome. Cat sat peacefully watching the flames leap and dart until the aroma wafting from the kitchen warned her that the pie was done.

With some trepidation, she took it out, only to breathe a sigh of relief when she saw that it appeared quite presentable. While Evan was still in the dining room, she took a quick look at the cookbook, then put it back on the shelf. She was forking the steaks into a cast-iron skillet when he returned to the kitchen.

"All set?" he asked.

She shrugged lightly. "Of course, there's nothing to it."

He grinned and sat down on a stool to keep her company while the steaks cooked. "There's something very nice about this," he said softly. "Very homey."

She looked at him and nodded. "I know what you mean. Sometimes my parents, Jimmy and I would all go off someplace on our own. We'd be together like an ordinary family, without servants or fancy parties or anything like that." A reminiscent smile flickered across her face. "That was always a special time for us."

Evan frowned slightly. He knew he was wrong to begrudge any mention of her family, but it rankled nonetheless. He didn't like to think about what they had left behind in Boston. Much as he wanted to believe that the trouble would be over, doubts lingered. He wasn't absolutely convinced that even the move to New York would put an end to it.

Cat had turned back to the stove to check the steaks and didn't see his expression. When she glanced at him again, he seemed perfectly content. A deep sense of satisfaction welled up in her. It was such a simple thing—to cook dinner for her husband—yet she savored the accomplishment.

In the back of her mind there had always been a niggling fear that if she wasn't very careful, she might amount to no more than a pretty, somewhat spoiled young woman, incapable of making any real contribution to the world.

Her refusal to become what she feared had prompted her early disinclination for marriage and, after Evan's disappearance, had driven her to work for Mari. She didn't regret the path she had followed, but she was also glad to know that she could succeed in more traditionally feminine ways.

Her satisfaction increased when Evan dug into the meal with relish. Though she was a bit more tentative herself, she had to admit that it wasn't bad. The steaks were somewhat overdone, but that was nothing experience wouldn't remedy. She relaxed and thoroughly enjoyed herself as they disposed of the better part of a bottle of red wine while talking about their life together.

"You'll like the house in New York," Evan said. "It's three stories, well made, all the latest conveniences, and in a very fashionable area."

"Where is it?" Cat inquired softly. She didn't really care at that moment, but she liked the sound of his voice—deep and soft, with the vestiges of the accent he had almost but not quite lost.

"In the Fifties off Fifth Avenue," he told her. "All the best people are moving up there. I was lucky to secure the property."

Cat frowned slightly. "I thought you weren't going to buy it until I'd had a chance to take a look."

"I haven't," he assured her. "I've merely put down a deposit. That's the way it's done."

Cat knew perfectly well how real-estate transactions were conducted, having handled several for Mari, but she refrained from telling him that. Unwilling to spoil the mood between them, she said only, "I'm sure it's lovely, but don't you think someplace more convenient would be better?"

"It's true my offices will be on Wall Street," he agreed, "but I don't mind going back and forth. Saunders can drop me off in the morning and pick me up at the end of the day. In between you can have him for shopping and the like."

Cat took another sip of her wine. She set the glass down very carefully. "As long as Saunders will be taking you downtown, he can do the same for me." Quickly, she went on, "Remember when I mentioned moving to New York fairly soon? I wasn't making that up. Mari wants me to open an office for her there and take on more responsibility." She couldn't restrain an eager smile. "I'm very excited about it."

Evan was far less enthused, but he was no less anxious to spoil the mood than was she. Slowly he said, "We can work all this out later, can't we?"

"It's not very complicated. Our offices will be close together, so we can travel back and forth at the same time. It will be perfect."

He forced a smile even as his mind tried to grapple with the idea of his wife working anywhere at all, much less amid the rough-and-tumble of Wall Street. As absurd as he knew the idea to be, he was loath to spoil her dream. Perhaps the wisest course would be simply to let her try, and find out for herself how impossible it was.

"We'll discuss it later," he said again. "In the meantime, what do you say we hold off on dessert for a while?"

She saw the gleam in his eye and nodded. The pie would keep, the passion between them would not. They found assuagement together on the soft Persian carpet in front of the fire.

Their lovemaking was by turns fierce and tender. Cat had become more assertive; she rejoiced in her ability to drive him to ever greater heights of pleasure. Her instinctive shyness dissolved as she explored his body as thoroughly as he did hers.

When at last they lay quiet in each other's arms, their earlier discussion was all but forgotten. Beside the totality of their love, any disagreements were surely inconsequential.

The next day they walked out together to the point and made love again in the tiny hut. "No matter who this place really belongs to," Cat said afterward, "it will always be ours."

"True enough, mavourneen," Evan murmured against her breasts. He was torn between regret at the end of their idyll and eagerness to return to New York. Challenges awaited him there. He was looking forward to matching himself against them, confident that he would come out on top.

As he smoothed her hair gently away from her face, he smiled. She was so beautiful, so elegant, so utterly feminine; he wanted to give her everything. At last he was in a position to do so.

She would be the most bejeweled woman in New York, the envy of the glorious Five Hundred, society's elite. He would swathe her in silks and drape her in furs. She would be the shining symbol of his own success. Surely she could want nothing more?

"What are you thinking?" Cat murmured. She traced one of his straight black brows with her fingertip as she gazed into his sapphire-bright eyes. Sometimes she could guess what was going on in his mind, but more often than not his thoughts were still a mystery to her.

She told herself it was because they were as yet newly married. Complete understanding would come in time, as it had with her parents and grandparents.

"About you," he murmured. "How lovely you are, and how fortunate I am."

Her mouth—soft and moist from his kisses—curved upward at the corners. "I can hardly disagree with that."

"Sometimes," he said with sudden candor, "I can still hardly believe this has happened. I wake up occasionally in the middle of the night, thinking I'm back in Ireland or the North End. Sometimes I've been dreaming about Texas, so I think I'm there again. Then I feel you in my arms, and I know where I am."

"Where," she whispered against his mouth, "is that?"

"Home," he said softly. "I'm finally home."

Cat clasped him to her, swept by the need to give him everything he had been denied by a harsh and precarious life. "You are," she said, her throat tight, "I'll always be your home, Evan."

"And I will be yours, Cat. We belong together." With a touch of humor, he added, "Sure and if we didn't, we would never have made it this far."

She had to laugh at that, if a bit shakily. Beyond the problems they had faced, shadows lay over the future. On the eve of their return to the real world, she was vividly aware of his suspicions about her father. But more even than that, she was terribly afraid that the most recent attack on him might not be the last.

"Evan," she said softly, "promise me that once we're in New York you'll continue to be very careful. At least until we've gotten this mystery cleared up."

"Mystery?"

"About who attacked you. I know," she went on hastily, "that you believe it's Father, but I just can't convince myself—" She broke off, concerned that her conflicting loyalties would anger him.

"It's all right, mavourneen," he said gently, his lips touching hers. "I'll take care of everything. Put it out of your mind."

She couldn't, and she resented his suggestion that she do so. She wanted to discuss the situation with him, to hear his thoughts and tell him her own. But Evan was shutting her out. She supposed he was doing it for the best of motives—to spare her distress—but his attitude still rankled.

She did, however, have better things to think about. They lingered in the hut, making love again and dozing for a while, before heading back to the house late in the afternoon.

Cat cooked dinner again, achieving even greater success than the night before. As they ate together in front of the fire, she said teasingly, "Perhaps I should hold off hiring a chef. In fact, perhaps we could get along without any servants at all. It could be just the two of us, alone together every evening and every n—" She stopped, coloring slightly at the direction of her own thoughts.

Evan laughed. After all these days of unbridled passion, she still blushed as easily as a virgin. Not that he minded. He regarded her mixture of unfettered sensuality and decorous propriety as ideal.

"It's a sweet notion, love," he said gently, "but you'd tire of it quickly enough. By all means cook the occasional meal, if you will, but save your energies for more important things."

"It's true I'll be very busy," she began.

He nodded quickly. "Especially once the children start coming."

Cat's eyes widened. She glanced at him cautiously. "There's no hurry with that, is there?"

"Of course not. A year or so to ourselves would be fine."

"A year? But . . . that's not very long."

Evan frowned slightly. He reached over and took her hand. "Cat, I'm not pushing you to have children. Far from it. I lost a sister in childbirth, and ever since, I've had my doubts about the whole process."

"Oh, I know," he went on when she would have interrupted, "you'll have the best medical care, but frankly, I'll still be glad when the whole business is done with. As for putting it off, I understand what you're saying about being young, but surely it won't get any easier for you."

"I have some time yet," she murmured. "I understand your concerns, but I really don't think we have to rush into anything."

He shrugged, not disagreeing with her, but not agreeing, either. "Let's talk about it again in a few months. You may find by then that you'd welcome a child. If nothing else, it would be something for you to do."

Her eyebrows rose. "I expect to be quite busy as it is."

He let go of her hand and reached into his jacket pocket for the silver cigar case. As he flipped it open, he said mildly, "I know your job is important to you, Cat, but you shouldn't set too much store by it."

"Why not?"

Through a haze of smoke, he looked at her. "You're an intelligent woman. You must understand the difficulties."

"You mean the prejudice? Yes, I do, and so must you, since what you encounter isn't really all that different."

He shook his head. "Granted, I haven't been welcomed with open arms by the financial establishment, but that doesn't matter. There are more than enough opportunities today for a man to make his way without help. But the same is not true for a woman."

"I admit it may be more difficult, but that's no reason for not trying."

"Perhaps not," he said quietly. "But why should you want to?" When she looked at him blankly, he said, "If you doubt my ability to give you the sort of life you're accustomed to, I assure you there's no need."

"That isn't why I want to work," Cat said, surprised that he hadn't already understood that. There had never been any question in her mind about his ability to support them both. Her confidence in him was absolute.

"I have no concern at all about that," she told him. "In fact I have to admit that I never gave it any thought."

He smiled as though she had proved his point. "Because you've never had to think about money. You've never had to go out into the world and work for your daily bread. To strain and struggle, to see your illusions and your dreams crumble and still keep fighting. You have no idea the depths people will sink to, the things they will do to achieve their own ends. And I'd just as soon keep it that way."

"I'm hardly a child to be protected," Cat said stiffly. "I'm well aware that there are unpleasant elements in the world, but I feel confident that I can deal with them."

When he looked blatantly skeptical, she added, "The last five years haven't been a picnic, Evan. I've been in that real world you think I know nothing about. I've had a few shocks, but I haven't done at all badly. Ask Mari if you don't believe me."

He was silent for a few moments, studying her, before he said, "Has it occurred to you that everyone you came in contact with knew that you were Drake Bennington's daughter and was therefore disposed to treat you more kindly than would otherwise have been the case?"

"Yes," Cat replied candidly, "the thought crossed my mind. I'm sure that was true, at least in the beginning. In addition, Mari has a certain reputation of her own that makes many people loath to cross her."

"In Boston. She has considerably less clout in New York."

"Which is exactly why we're opening up an office there."

Evan repressed a sigh. He was growing weary of the discussion, seeing no point to it, since Cat was clearly not going to be convinced. She was blindly stubborn in her outlook, to such an extent that he was more certain than ever that only experience could teach her the error of her ways. Much as he would have liked to spare her the disappointment he was sure was coming, he did not believe that was possible.

Upon reflection, he thought it might not really be such a bad thing for Cat to learn that the world would not always bend to her desires. Her parents had not completely spoiled her, but they had come close. He could hardly blame them, since he intended to do virtually the same. But first she had to learn to be content within her proper sphere.

"You have a beautiful mouth," he said softly as he snuffed out the cigar, "but just now I'd like to put it to better use." He ran the back of his hand down her bare arm and was pleased to feel her tremble in response.

Despite the warmth flowing through her, Cat hesitated. She had the sense of something important being left unresolved and felt that she should try harder to get him to see her point of view. But that was extremely difficult when he was driving every thought from her mind.

He stood, drawing her upright with him. Pressed against the length of his body, she felt a surge of passion so overpowering that she almost cried out. Silk rustled softly as he pulled her long skirt up, sliding his hands over her buttocks. His fingers probed lightly between her thighs as she trembled spasmodically.

"This is where you belong, Cat," he whispered softly. "With me, apart from the rest of the world." His hand moved again, and this time she did cry out. His mouth caught the sound as his tongue plunged deeply.

Cat's knees gave way before his sensual onslaught. She sagged against him as his steely arm caught her around the hips. He carried her a short distance away and lowered her in front of the fire.

Neither could bear to delay long enough to undress. Evan pushed her skirt farther up and stripped off her pantaloons as Cat fumbled with the buttons of his trousers. They moved together in a fierce rush, mindless of everything except their need for each other.

Long after their passion was spent, Cat lay with Evan's head on her breasts, staring into the fire. A soft smile curved her swollen mouth as she thought how foolish she was to have any concerns about their future together.

Evan might not fully understand her need to work, but he would never attempt to stop her. Of that, at least, she was sure. She stroked his dark hair tenderly as she considered how fortunate she was. There were times when she thought she must have been born under a lucky star.

Only a single, niggling doubt disturbed her contentment: that so many blessings would ultimately have to be paid for. Jimmy would have said that was the Irish in her, seeing trouble where there was none; but her concern lingered.

Long after she drifted into sleep, her dreams were troubled, shot through with fragmented images of her parents, Mari, and a man she had never met but still felt as though she knew.

Chapter Twenty-four

"I'M VERY PLEASED," Mari said with a smile. "You've made great progress, more than I could ever have expected."

Cat laughed, a bit wryly. The two women were seated in Cat's office on the third floor of a building that looked out over Wall Street. The office was part of a larger suite Cat had rented two months before. In the outer room half-a-dozen bright, ambitious young people worked. She had deliberated long and hard before hiring the four men and two women whom she thought had the qualities necessary for spotting good investment opportunities and pursuing them aggressively.

The women were, like her, from wealthy families. They had grown up fascinated by the world of their fathers and brothers, but had been denied access to it by virtue of their sex. Cat was giving them a chance to prove the folly of such prejudice. So far, she was not disappointed with the results.

"I'm not kidding myself," she said as she leaned forward slightly to refill their coffee cups. "Right now a tailor's dummy could come out ahead in the market. My guess is that that will continue for a while, but eventually some of the excesses will catch up with us."

"How long would you advise we wait?" Mari asked.

Cat thought for a moment before she said, "I think we should be safe for another year or so. But I wouldn't want to delay much longer than that before moving us into the most conservative securities, the kind of investments that could ride out any trouble that might come."

"That sounds fine to me," Mari said. She looked at the younger woman with unconcealed approval. "If you don't mind my saying so, I'm a bit surprised by your perceptiveness. I agree that the financial markets are due for a shake-up, but I wouldn't have expected you to have already tumbled to that."

Cat flushed slightly. She was very tempted to let Mari think that she had come to the conclusion on her own, but innate honesty prevented her from doing so. "Actually," she said slowly, "Evan is quite blunt in his assessment of the market. He's been saying for several weeks that it's fine for the short term, but eventually the chickens will come home."

"Evan's a smart man," Mari murmured. "The problem is that whatever happens in the next year or two, that won't be the end of the matter. So long as the government looks the other way, excesses are going to occur."

"That's also what Evan says."

Mari smiled gently, making Cat wish she could withdraw the words. She must sound like a parrot, mentioning her husband every other minute and making him the authority for everything she thought and did.

It wasn't really like that. In the two months since her marriage to Evan, they had largely gone their separate ways, to such an extent that Cat was concerned about it.

They saw each other only in the morning, when they drove to work together, and in the evening, when they returned the same way. Both were so busy that they tended to do paperwork during the ride back and forth rather than talk. Four or five times a week they went out socially, often not returning to the East Fifty-third Street house until the wee hours.

They still made love almost every night, but aside from that, it seemed to Cat that they had virtually no contact. She was finding the situation increasingly difficult, even as she had no idea what to do about it.

"I should be getting myself together," she said as she glanced at the watch pinned to her jacket. As always, she dressed elegantly but quietly for the office. She tried to set the right tone by wearing muted colors and conservative styles, but nothing could conceal the radiance of her beauty.

Occasionally one of the young men in the office would glance at her admiringly, or she would be the recipient of such looks from fellow Wall Streeters. She ignored them. Not only did she lack the inclination to do otherwise, but she also understood that if she for a moment unbent enough to acknowledge such male approval, she would have lost vital ground. It was essential that she be seen strictly as a colleague, one whose competency had to be respected.

Still, it was a strain never to feel that she could let down her guard and relax. She went home exhausted every evening. More than once she had been tempted to suggest to Evan that they forego the social round and stay home. But she hadn't done so, because she wasn't sure what the results would be if they actually had time to talk to each other. Her doubts saddened her, and she was unable to banish them.

"Are you sure," she asked Mari as she stood up and began gathering her papers, "that you won't join us this evening?"

The older woman shook her head. "Thank you, dear, but I'll be taking the early train back to Boston in the morning. I'm going to have a quiet dinner at my hotel and turn in.''

"You know," Cat said as they left the office together, "you would have been more than welcome to stay with us. We have plenty of room. In fact, the house is so big that we all but rattle around in it.''

"That will change when you've settled in more. But in the meantime, only an insensitive boor would impose on a newly married couple. No, dear,'' she went on as Cat started to protest, "I may be getting on in years, but I remember perfectly well what the early months are like.'' She chuckled softly as Cat flushed. "You give Evan a hug for me and tell him I'll see him soon.''

After Mari had driven off in a cab, Cat stood for a moment looking after her. The summer heat had prompted many to leave the city, so the homebound crowd was lighter than usual. Nonetheless Cat was jostled sufficiently to break off her thoughts. She spotted Saunders waiting patiently at the curb and hurried over to him.

They collected Evan on the next block. He got into the back of the Pierce Arrow without waiting for Saunders to open the door. His quick glance surveyed Cat before he smiled. "Good evening, mavourneen.'' Lightly he touched his mouth to hers before settling back against the leather seat.

For once Cat did not open her briefcase and begin reading. She glanced out the window for several minutes, watching the passing parade of buildings without really seeing them. Her mind was on Mari.

She had seemed well enough, but she also gave the impression of being deeply tired, something Cat could certainly understand.

"Gideon's at it again," she murmured.

"What was that?" Evan asked.

"What? Oh, I was just thinking."

He put the papers he'd been reading aside and gave her his full attention. "About Gideon?"

Reluctantly Cat nodded. "He's threatening to take Mari to court yet again over some paltry matter. She knows she'll win, but the endless harassment wears her down."

Evan rubbed the back of his neck. He had spent a hectic day and was not in the best of moods, but the knowledge that Gideon Mackenzie was up to his old tricks worried him.

"What do you know about him?" he asked.

"Not much. He's my great-uncle, Josiah Mackenzie's eldest child. He expected to inherit everything, but most of the estate went to Mari instead, and he hates her for it." She was silent for a moment, then murmured, "He's almost as old as she is, but he still seems to have some fantasy about ultimately taking over from her."

"That's hardly likely," Evan said. "Mari will pick her own heir when the time comes."

Cat hesitated again. Quietly, not looking at him, she said, "She already has. That's part of what she came to discuss with me."

"I see," Evan said slowly. Mari's decision was hardly unexpected; he just hadn't thought it would come so soon. "How do you feel about that?"

Cat shrugged. "I can't really conceive of it. To begin with, I'd have to imagine Mari dead, and that's impossible."

Evan placed a hand over hers and squeezed it lightly. "Everyone comes to an end eventually."

"I know," she murmured, "but Mari has always been so indomitable." Despite her concern, a smile tugged at the corners of her mouth. "She claims that inside she's always been mush, but not too many people would agree with that."

"No," Evan said, thinking of some of the things he had heard about Mari Mackenzie, usually from irate men who'd had the misfortune of tangling with her, "they wouldn't. She's carried a tremendous amount of responsibility over the years, but she's handled it well."

"I only hope," Cat said softly, "that I can do the same."

Evan's hand tightened on hers. He was no more resigned to his wife's involvement in business than he had been two months before, but he had to admit to a certain pride in her success.

Through his own rapidly growing network of businesses, he kept a discreet eye on her. Several times he had thought she was about to stumble, but she'd always managed to pull herself up. It couldn't have been easy. He kept waiting for her to ask him for help, but so far she had refrained from doing so.

The papers on his lap were forgotten as he watched the play of light and shadow across her face. She looked tired, though that in no way detracted from her beauty. Her hair was coiled at the nape of her neck, but a few stray wisps had slipped free. He caught one around his finger and twined it slowly.

"Cat . . . what do you say we stay home tonight?"

Her eyes widened. "We're supposed to go out." They had been invited to a dinner being given by business associates, hardly a crucial event, yet she had supposed he would still want to go.

"Do you have your heart set on it?" he asked, raising her hand to his lips. He turned it over and touched his lips to the center of her palm. Instantly a shimmery bolt of pleasure rippled through her.

"No," she murmured, "I don't."

His smile was purely male. "Good, then we'll send our excuses."

"I'm not sure there are any that would be thought acceptable."

"Perhaps—" he added provocatively "—we should simply tell them the truth."

"W-what's that?"

He leaned forward, his breath warm against her flushed cheek. "That I prefer to stay home and make love to my wife. Would that shock them very much?"

"I'm afraid so," Cat murmured, knowing that she sounded breathless, and not caring. Self-consciously she glanced toward the front seat, where Saunders had his eyes fixed rigidly ahead. If he had any idea what was going on behind him, he certainly gave no sign of it.

Evan laughed softly. He released her hand and moved a small distance away, though his eyes remained on her. "I suppose we're enough of a shock as it is," he said quietly, "without adding to it."

"Perhaps," she acknowledged. "But it doesn't matter. I've never been particularly concerned about what other people think."

He wasn't absolutely certain whether or not to believe her, but he found the temptation too great to resist. Nonetheless he said, "I don't want you to lose out in any way by our marriage, Cat. You're used to being received by everyone in society, and I intend to see that doesn't change."

"I think you're far more concerned about it than I am," she murmured. "Anyone who doesn't care to receive Mrs. Evan O'Connell is someone I don't care to associate with."

He laughed softly, pleased by her response, even though he automatically discounted it. They had only been married for two months; there hadn't been time for her to discover what social ostracism meant. The vast wealth he was rapidly accumulating would ensure that she never did.

"We'll have to start doing some entertaining," he said as the car drew up in front of their elegant stone residence. It had been built about ten years before by the scion of an old shipping family. No extravagance had been spared in creating a masterpiece of gracious living. The style was Greek revival, with a touch of Italianate. Wide stone steps led to the double-door entrance, where a butler, alerted to their arrival, awaited them.

"Good evening, madam," he intoned. "Sir. A pleasant day, I hope?"

"Very nice," Cat murmured as she handed him her hat and gloves. "Were there any callers?"

"Indeed, madam," he said, inclining his head toward the silver tray that reposed on the hall table. A single card lay in it.

Cat picked it up and glanced at it for a moment before she frowned.

"What is it?" Evan asked.

"Nothing," she said, frowning. "Charles van Rhys dropped by."

"What for?"

"I have no idea." She couldn't imagine why he would have come, given the tone of their last meeting. "Did he say what he wanted?" she asked the butler.

"Unfortunately not, madam, though I did get the impression that he had called to see you, rather than Mr. O'Connell. I explained that you were at work."

"Did he leave a message?"

"Only that he would be in touch again."

"I wonder what brings him to New York," Evan said as they walked up the curving marble staircase together to the second floor. His hand was on the small of her back, his fingers warm and firm through the fabric of her jacket.

"Business, probably. What else?"

"What else indeed?"

"Evan, you aren't suggesting that I have anything to do with Charles being here?"

"It's a possibility, isn't it?"

"I don't think so."

They walked down the corridor together to the suite of rooms they shared. When the door was closed behind them, Evan said, "It was hardly a secret in Boston that he was very interested in you."

Cat stiffened slightly. "I assure you it was not reciprocated," she said quietly.

"That's reassuring to hear," Evan said with a slight smile. He pulled at the knot of his tie to loosen it, then removed his jacket and hung it over the back of a mahogany chair.

Cat had gone to the large windows that looked out over the garden behind the house. She began to draw the curtains, and Evan came to help her. When the room was plunged into a soft half-light, they stood in the center of the room and embraced.

Evan's arms were strong yet tender as he held her. She relaxed against him and let his strength surround her. The cares and tensions of the day began to fade. She cupped his face between her hands, feeling the slight scratchiness of his cheeks, and laughed softly.

"The maids will be shocked when they come to turn down the bed and find we've already done it for them."

"Our scandalous behavior," he murmured as he nuzzled her throat, "enlivens what would otherwise be a tedious job."

"If we miss dinner again, Cook will quit."

"No, she won't. Mrs. Mulroy likes us."

"True," Cat said. She'd had the great good sense to hire an Irishwoman as cook instead of bowing to fashion and employing a Gallic tyrant. Barely had Mrs. Mulroy arrived on the scene than she'd produced three nieces and two nephews, all of whom Cat had also hired. The problem of finding household staff had thus been quickly solved. As yet she'd had no reason to regret her haste.

Much later she and Evan finally emerged from the bedroom to venture downstairs in search of something to eat. They had been making love for hours, but felt no urge to sleep. Food, however, was a different matter.

"Let's see," Evan said as he opened the icebox door and took a look inside. "Here's a roasted chicken, some potato salad, and it appears Mrs. Mulroy made her excellent coleslaw." He emerged holding several platters and bowls in his arms, with a definite look of satisfaction.

"I found a plate of brownies," Cat said, "and, oddly enough, someone seems to have left a bottle of champagne chilling in that bucket over there."

"You'd almost think," Evan said with a grin, "that they expected us to do this."

With the guilty pleasure of children, they hauled everything upstairs and proceeded to devour it sitting picnic fashion on the bed. Evan nibbled at a chicken leg Cat held for him while she sipped champagne from his glass. In between, they kissed.

"You taste delicious," he said softly.

She leaned back against the pillows, drawing him with her. "That's the brownies."

He tried again, as though to be sure. "No, it's you."

They smiled at one another, enchanted with pleasure given and received, heedless, for the moment, of whatever awaited them beyond the sanctuary of their love.

Chapter Twenty-five

IT WAS RAINING when Cat got up the following morning. Evan had gone on ahead with Saunders, while she stayed behind to keep an appointment with an antique dealer. The house was as yet only partially furnished, and she was anxious to complete the job.

The dealer's store was located only a few blocks away on Madison Avenue. She decided to walk over despite the inclement weather and was putting on her boots in the hall when the doorbell rang.

"I'll get it," she called, seeing no reason to stand on ceremony, particularly when that would simply keep her visitor waiting on such a soggy morning.

When she opened the door to discover Charles, her first impulse was to regret her haste. He also appeared startled to see her, rather than the butler he had expected, but recovered quickly.

"Good morning, Catherine," he said as he stepped inside and doffed his hat. "I trust I haven't come at an inconvenient time?"

"Actually, I was just going out." She hesitated, stymied by the courtesy that was so much an inbred part of her nature, yet bewildered as to why he should be there.

"I have an appointment to view some furnishings," she said, hoping that would discourage whatever notion he had of lingering.

That was immediately dashed when he said, "If it wouldn't be too much to ask, I'd be very pleased to accompany you. You know," he went on as he took the coat from the butler who had appeared to assist her and held it out himself, "I've regretted our last meeting very much. I was unforgivably rude, though I hope you may still find it in your heart to pardon me."

Embarrassed by his apparent sincerity, she attempted to reassure him. "Please don't give it any further thought. I fully realize that my marriage came as a surprise to many people."

"That's certainly true," Charles said as they left the house and walked down the steps together. He took her arm, a gesture she could hardly resist, since any gentleman would do the same under the circumstances.

The rain had tapered off, though the sky remained overcast. Passersby hurried along, heads down against the unseasonably brisk wind blowing off the Hudson.

"It will be an early fall, I think," Charles said as they turned south along Madison Avenue, past the row of elegant shops that were beginning to spring up to serve the wealthy clientele residing nearby. "In Boston everyone seems to be coming back to town early. Is it the same here?"

"I suppose," Cat said, glad of an innocuous topic of conversation, even though it held no interest for her. "The Vanderbilts are back, so I suppose the rest of the Five Hundred must be, too."

"It's the times. No one knows what Mr. Roosevelt plans next, except that it will be ill-advised."

Cat kept silent. She was a supporter of Teddy Roosevelt, seeing beneath the blustery exterior a keen intellect and a determination to restore the country to a more even moral keel. Had she been permitted to vote, he would have been her choice.

But she could also understand why certain people were distressed by a president determined to smash class privileges and do away with the blatant inequities that had allowed the top reaches of the business world to remain a private club. Only a very few men, such as Evan, had broken into it, and then only by virtue of extreme hard work coupled with fierce determination. It was time, she thought, for a more equitable system.

Not, of course, that she was about to say so to Charles. The last thing she wanted was to get into yet another argument with him. Unbidden, the recollection rose of Evan's suggesting that Charles nurtured a long-held desire for her. If it did exist, it certainly did not rest on their having anything in common.

"What brings you to New York?" she asked as they paused at the corner to let several cars and a lone horse-drawn carriage pass.

"Business, mainly. There are several matters that need attention. Telephone and telegraph are fine, but I still think face-to-face contact works best."

"Oh, I agree," she said with a smile. "There's no substitute for it."

"That's right," Charles said thoughtfully. "I understand you're working. How does Evan feel about that?"

"He thinks it's fine." Feeling mildly guilty for having exaggerated her husband's position, to say the least, she added, "Of course, it's an adjustment for both of us."

"Yes," Charles said slowly, "I imagine it must be. Evan's doing great things on Wall Street, I hear."

Cat nodded. "He has the knack, which isn't to say that he doesn't work very hard."

"I'm sure he does. Do you see much of each other?"

The question was asked innocently enough, but Cat was still reluctant to answer it. She would have hesitated before confiding in her mother about the strains in her marriage. She most certainly was not going to do so with Charles.

"Everything is fine with us," she said at length. "Really, Charles, marriage is wonderful. You should give it a try."

"So my parents keep telling me," he said with a slight laugh. "They're anxious for grandchildren, but I admit to being less eager to oblige them."

"The right woman will change that," she said softly.

He cast her a quick, sharp glance but did not respond. Instead he gestured toward the shop ahead of them. "Is this the place?"

Cat nodded. Before she could enter, Charles drew her to one side. He gazed down at her intently as he said, "You really do love Evan, don't you?"

Surprised that he should raise so personal a subject, she nonetheless answered matter-of-factly. "Yes, I do, with all my heart."

For an instant she thought she saw a flash of pain cross his narrow, aristocratic features. But the impression was so fleeting that she couldn't be certain she hadn't imagined it.

With a wry twist of his mouth, Charles released her hand. "Your husband is a very lucky man. You must tell him that for me."

They both knew that she would do nothing of the sort, but Cat still felt compelled to make it clear to him that she would not keep secrets from Evan. "I'll mention that you stopped by again," she said quietly. "Perhaps the next time you're in town, you'll be our guest at dinner."

Charles was noncommittal on that point. "I'll keep it in mind. In the meantime, take care of yourself, Catherine."

They parted a few moments later, Charles catching a cab at the corner to take him downtown and Cat proceeding into the shop. The antiques dealer hurried out to greet her and immediately began extolling his wares.

She gave him as much of her attention as she could muster, but even as she nodded approvingly at a Sheraton breakfront and a Louis XV desk, she was thinking about her encounter with Charles.

In the back of her mind she still found it difficult to believe that he had simply happened to stop by to apologize for his earlier rudeness and renew their acquaintance.

The Charles she remembered was far too volatile for any such courtesy. He had never taken at all well to being thwarted. His temper was notorious, as was his willingness to exercise it.

All too clearly she remembered the incident at Carmody's. Jimmy had once admitted to her that he believed Charles had provoked the fight. Certainly relations between the two young men had been cool before then and even more so afterward.

Cat trusted her twin's judgment. He had never liked Charles, had in fact always been suspicious of him. She couldn't quite convince herself that she was wrong to feel the same way.

Yet by the time she got to her office several hours later, she had put Charles firmly out of her mind.

Amid the ringing telephones, the clacking of the Teletype machines and the constant comings and goings of both employees and visitors, she managed to get through her own work. At least enough of it so that by five o'clock she was feeling satisfied with herself and eager to turn her thoughts to Evan.

When he called to tell her that he would be delayed and therefore couldn't drive home with her, she felt a sharp stab of disappointment.

"Are you sure?" she asked. "It's nothing you could put off until tomorrow?"

"I'm sorry," he said softly, "but it isn't. I'll be home as soon as possible."

"All right," Cat murmured. After a moment she added, "I'll be waiting for you."

There was silence on the other end until Evan said quietly, "I love you, Cat."

Startled by the sudden intimacy, especially over the telephone, to which she was not yet accustomed, she laughed. Her voice was very gentle as she said, "I love you, too, Evan."

"Wait up for me?"

"Oh, my, you do expect to be late."

"Not necessarily, but if I am . . ."

"I'll be up. Not only that, but I'll see if I can't convince Mrs. Mulroy to cook another chicken."

He gave a deep chuckle that reverberated all the way through her. When they had both hung up, she stared at the phone with a bemused smile. Not until her secretary put her head in the room to remind her that Saunders was waiting did she manage to tear her attention away.

EVAN SET DOWN the phone with similar reluctance. He leaned back in his leather desk chair and stared pensively at the opposite wall for several moments before he recalled himself to the matter at hand.

With palpable aversion, he pressed a button on his desk and spoke into the speaker. "You may show Mr. van Rhys in now."

Evan stood up as Charles entered the room. The two men eyed each other warily as they shook hands.

"O'Connell," Charles said with a smile. "I've been looking forward to meeting you."

Evan gestured to a chair in front of his desk as he resumed his own seat. "What can I do for you, Mr. van Rhys?" His formality was deliberate; he wanted to make it clear to the other man that he was well aware of the differences between them and was not about to engage in any false cordiality for the sake of appearances.

"You can begin by allowing me to congratulate you on your marriage," Charles said smoothly. "Catherine is a wonderful woman."

"Yes," Evan agreed, "she is."

"I suppose you know there was a time when I had thoughts in that direction myself?"

Surprised by the other man's frankness, Evan nodded. "I believe I heard something to that effect." He leaned back and watched his visitor carefully. Charles had sat down and was smoothing his trousers. His brown hair was unruffled by the wind Evan could hear immediately beyond the office windows. He was immaculately dressed, down to the starched whiteness of his cuffs and the perfect Windsor knot of his tie. His expression was calm to the point of complacency, and utterly confident.

"Yes, I'm sure you did," Charles said with a smile that invited Evan to see the humor in the situation. "But Catherine is very independent. She made her choice, and we must all abide by it."

"I'm glad to hear that," Evan said dryly. He cast a surreptitious glance at the clock on his desk as he wondered how long Charles would take to get to the reason for his impromptu visit.

"I mention my fondness for her only because I want you to understand that I wish both of you well. It would sadden me greatly if anything untoward were to happen to Catherine."

Evan's sapphire eyes narrowed to a brilliant intensity. His long fingers drummed on the arm of his chair. "I have never appreciated innuendo and allusion, Mr. van Rhys. I prefer plain speaking. If you have something to say regarding Catherine, spit it out."

"Plain indeed," Charles murmured with a faintly condescending smile. He let the silence drag out a few moments longer before he said, "You are, I presume, acquainted with Gideon Mackenzie?"

Evan shook his head. "Not exactly. I've never met the man."

"No, I didn't really think you had. What I meant was, you know of him?"

"By reputation, which to say the least is not good."

"I agree that Gideon has a somewhat checkered past. However, he is still regarded by many to be a very astute businessman. Enough so for me to have had some dealings with him in the past few years."

"Is there a point to this?"

Charles frowned. A flash of temper darkened his cheeks. "The point, O'Connell, is that I am no stranger to Gideon Mackenzie. I know the man, what he wants, how he thinks. Above all, I know the obsession that has ruled his life these many decades."

"You are referring to the business with his stepmother, Mari Mackenzie?" When Charles nodded, Evan went on. "I imagine most of Boston knows about that, but what has it got to do with Catherine?"

"She is Mari Mackenzie's heir."

"May I ask," Evan inquired quietly, "how you came by that information?"

Instead of answering directly, Charles said, "Are you denying it?"

"On the contrary, I'm perfectly willing to confirm it. But Catherine only learned of this recently herself. How did you know about it?"

"Before she left Boston, Mari Mackenzie had a new will drawn up in which she names Catherine as her primary beneficiary," Charles explained somewhat grudgingly. "Gideon Mackenzie has kept a paid informer in the offices of Mari's attorney for some time now. He got word of the new will before the signatures on it were dry. I might add that it made him absolutely furious."

Evan shrugged. He was unconcerned about the reaction of an aged, unbalanced misogynist, except insofar as it might affect Catherine. "He can always challenge it in court, if he lives long enough."

"That's the problem," Charles said. "Gideon is hardly a young man. He realizes that while he may outlive Mari, he can't count on many years beyond that. He's afraid everything he's fought for for so long will be denied him in the end. That is absolutely unbearable to him."

"What," Evan asked carefully, "does he intend to do about it?"

"I don't know," Charles said. "If I did, I would tell you. All I can say is that I think you should make clear both your willingness and your ability to protect your wife. If he understands that you will strike hard and fast at any threat to her, he may be persuaded not to try anything."

"I see. How do you suggest I go about this?"

"By confronting him directly. Gideon doesn't understand or respect anything else. See him face-to-face, tell him you know he intends to make trouble, and that at the first sign of it, you will make sure that he profoundly regrets his actions."

With a confidential air, Charles went on. "Gideon has a deeply rooted fear of men like you, O'Connell. Men who make their own rules and don't much care how they get what they want."

Evan's eyebrows rose mockingly. "Is that how you imagine me to be?"

"Aren't you?"

"That depends, Mr. van Rhys. In business I am probably a good deal more scrupulous than you. I have to be, since at the first sign of impropriety, men like yourself would be lined up to knock me down. However, private affairs are a different matter entirely."

"I thought they might be," Charles said with a hint of smugness. "You'll do what's necessary, I'm sure."

"I'll see to it that Catherine won't be endangered," Evan agreed as he rose to show his visitor out. His dislike of Charles van Rhys was no longer impersonal. Having met the man, he felt almost as though he had come into contact with something unclean.

He told himself that he was merely experiencing a combination of jealousy and his own insecurities. Charles van Rhys was wealthy, cultured and socially acceptable in every way. He had the background Evan would once have given almost anything to have himself.

Over the years, he had come to realize that being born to great wealth was not necessarily an advantage. Too often it prevented any real sense of accomplishment and the pride that went with it. What he had, he had earned for himself.

He paused in the midst of closing his briefcase. Was that what compelled Catherine to fight so hard for success in a world where she was expected to have none? Until that moment, it had not occurred to him to equate his own driving determination with hers, even though she had tried to make him see the similarity.

Always, in the back of his mind, he had wondered why she couldn't be content to enjoy the life he was able to give her instead of always striving for something of her own. He had resented the subtle implication that what he gave her somehow wasn't good enough. Now, for the first time, he felt compelled to reassess his views and consider that what she was doing had nothing at all to do with him. It was something she needed to do for herself.

Considering that, he left the office and took a cab home. Cat was upstairs in their bedroom. She had changed out of her business suit and was wearing a thin silk wrap. As he entered, she was seated at her dressing table, brushing out her hair.

"Evan," she said with a smile, "I thought you'd be held up longer."

"It turned out to be a short conversation," he replied as he bent and kissed the back of her neck. Their eyes met in the mirror. "You're looking very lovely."

"Thank you," she murmured, "but actually, I was just thinking that I was beginning to look a bit worse for wear."

"I don't agree," he said as he sat down on the edge of the bed. "But we have both been working very hard. What would you say to a holiday?"

"I'd say wonderful, except that I have a full schedule of appointments next week." Reluctantly she said, "I'm afraid it's too late to cancel them."

"That's all right," Evan said. "I'm in much the same position. What I had in mind was a weekend in Boston. We could take the train up tonight, if we hurry, and stay until Sunday."

"I'd like that," Cat said slowly. She was surprised that he had suggested Boston, thinking that he would opt to go just about anywhere else. Boston meant her parents, in particular her father, and Evan's unresolved suspicions concerning him.

Carefully, she said, "If we go, I'd like to see my parents."

"Of course," Evan said immediately. "There's no reason for you not to." Ignoring her startled glance, he pressed the button beside the bed to summon Cat's maid. "Sheila can pack for us while you get dressed. I'll telephone the station and reserve a compartment."

Before she could comment further, he kissed her again and left the room. Downstairs, where the telephone was kept, he paused for a moment before picking up the receiver. The plan, thought up during the drive home, satisfied him. He would be able to confront Gideon Mackenzie while being sure that Cat was safe with the only man he trusted to look after her as scrupulously as he would himself. With a soft laugh, he accepted the irony of the situation and made his call.

Chapter header

_____ *Chapter Twenty-six*

"I'M SURE YOUR PARENTS will understand," Evan said. "Make my excuses and explain that I'll be by later."

Cat bristled at his peremptory tone. This trip wasn't working out at all as she had expected. They hadn't even left the train station, and already they were arguing.

"I don't understand why you can't come with me, at least for a few minutes, long enough to say hello and get settled in. Surely this business you have to take care of, whatever it is, can wait that long?"

It rankled that he had made her believe the trip was purely for pleasure when apparently he'd had another motive.

"I'd rather get it out of the way now," he said as he led her toward a cab parked at the curb. "Then I can relax and enjoy the rest of the visit."

His behavior made no sense to her. Beneath her annoyance, she was becoming worried. "Evan," she said as the driver sprang out to collect their baggage, "you'd tell me if something was wrong, wouldn't you?"

He hesitated for barely a split second. "Everything is fine, Cat. I'll join you directly. In the meantime, you can catch up on family news with Elizabeth and Drake. After all, you haven't seen them in two months."

"Is that why you're doing this, so my parents and I will have some time alone?" Before he could reply, she went on, "If it is, it's very sweet, but unnecessary. You're part of the family now."

"I appreciate that," he said as he handed her into the car. He was trying very hard not to appear impatient, but he doubted that he was succeeding. Shutting the door behind her, he said, "Ask your parents if they would like to be our guests at dinner tonight. The three of you can pick out someplace nice."

"All right . . . but, Evan, I still think . . ."

Before she could say anything further, he gestured to the driver. As the car pulled away, Evan waved and gave her what he hoped was a reassuring smile.

That faded the moment the cab was out of sight. His face was set in hard, implacable lines as he waved down a second cab and quickly gave an address to the driver. The man looked startled.

"Are you sure that's where you want to go, sir? It's not exactly the best part of town, if you take my meaning."

Evan's mouth lifted wryly. The address was on the waterfront, not far from where he had bought the warehouse five years before. "I know where it is," he said quietly. "Take me there."

The driver shrugged. They set off through the crowded streets. Evan stared out the window sightlessly, his mind on the man he was shortly to confront.

It had not been difficult to learn where Gideon Mackenzie could be found, but the information had certainly been surprising.

Over the past decade or so, Gideon had all but withdrawn from the world. He belonged to no clubs and attended no social functions. During his frequent litigations against Mari, he didn't even appear in court, sending lawyers to represent him instead. He had become something of a mystery man, still known to be active in business, but never seen except by a handful of associates, such as Charles van Rhys.

Gideon ran his considerable holdings out of a ramshackle building near the wharves. It dated from the early part of the nineteenth century and looked the worse for wear.

Evan paid the cabdriver, then stood for a few moments on the sidewalk in front of the building, surveying it carefully. Several passersby took note of the tall, well-dressed man who inevitably stood out among the scruffy, somewhat surreptitious denizens of the docks. When he became aware that he was an object of their unwanted attention, Evan went up and knocked on the door.

When there was no response he tried again. The sound of his knocking reverberated behind the door, but he could hear no one coming. He put his hand on the doorknob. Rather to his surprise, it turned.

Ahead of him was a large open space that ran the entire length and width of the building. It was empty save for a few dusty packing crates and a battered table and chair positioned near a grime-encrusted window.

Evan stepped inside gingerly. He heard the scurrying of rats off to the side, but otherwise there was only silence. His footsteps rang out sharply as he crossed the room. The air was rank with the smell of the nearby water. With an expression of distaste, he stopped and glanced around.

A rickety staircase led up to the second floor. The railing was missing, but the steps still looked usable. He tested each before putting his weight on it and reached the top without incident.

Several rooms opened off a narrow corridor. Evan glanced in each, finding them all empty. By the time he reached the last one, he had all but concluded that his errand was in vain. Either the information he'd been given was incorrect, or Gideon Mackenzie was elsewhere at the moment. He would have to try again.

But first he wanted to check the last room. As he stepped into it, he was startled to catch sight of a bright patch of color. In the gloom he could make out what appeared to be a woman lying slumped unconscious on the floor.

He crossed swiftly to kneel at her side and was about to turn her over when a sound behind him made him jerk his head back toward the door. There was just time to see the shape of a man in a dark suit before the door was slammed shut.

Evan jumped to his feet. He reached the door even as an iron bar was slammed into place across it, effectively imprisoning him.

"What in hell?" he muttered. Footsteps retreated down the corridor. When they had faded away, Evan returned to the woman. The moment he put a hand to her shoulder, he knew he had been fooled. A low, virulent curse escaped him as he turned the seamstress's dummy over. The feathered hat that had been stuck on its head fell off and rolled across the floor.

Evan wasted no time contemplating the trick that had trapped him. He rose with the lithe strength of a cat and began prowling around the room, looking for a way out. The single window was set high up in the wall. Thanks to his height and strength, he was able to get hold of the sill and pull himself up. The window was nailed shut, but he could break the pane of glass. There was no point, however, since the opening was far too small for him to squeeze through.

Dropping back to the floor, he glanced around again. The only other possibility was the door itself, which he quickly set about examining. Belatedly he realized that it was new, made of thick, solid wood, with the hinges on the outside, where he could not reach them.

Whoever had planned his capture had done a thorough job of it. It appeared that he had no choice but to wait until the purpose of his captivity was revealed to him.

"YOUR FATHER had to go out, dear," Elizabeth said as she greeted her daughter in the entry hall of the Louisburg Square house. "It seems there is some urgent business requiring his attention, but he said he should be back soon."

She stepped back a pace and surveyed Cat, smiling at what she saw. Despite the furrow between her brows, her daughter looked lovely. She radiated the contentment of a well-loved woman, if not one who was perfectly at ease.

"Evan also had business to attend to," Catherine said. "He'll join us shortly."

"I see." Elizabeth took Cat's arm and led her into the parlor. "Then it's just the two of us for a while. That's fine. We can have a nice chat. Tell me, how is the house coming along?"

"Fine," Cat murmured absently. She supposed it was merely a coincidence that her father and Evan were both absent at the same time. Certainly there was no reason to think otherwise. Yet suspicion lingered.

"Mother," she asked when they were seated together on the parlor couch, "did Father say where he was going?"

Elizabeth shook her head. "Only that he didn't think he'd be long. Why?"

"I was just wondering. It's probably my imagination, but something seems to be troubling Evan. He suggested this trip on the spur of the moment. Frankly, it surprised me that he was so eager to visit Boston."

"Why? Surely his memories of this place aren't so bad?"

"Actually," Cat said slowly, "they aren't particularly pleasant." She hesitated, unsure how much to tell her mother, but deciding that the time had come for candor. "You know Evan left here rather precipitously five years ago?"

"I did have that impression," Elizabeth murmured. "I've also wondered if his departure didn't have something to do with you."

Cat shot her a startled glance. "You knew?"

Elizabeth laughed softly. "I'm hardly blind, dear. There was such a glow about you when you came back after that storm. It was perfectly clear what had happened."

"I suppose you thought it was awful."

"On the contrary. I was concerned, of course, but I also thought that Evan was a strong, sensible man who clearly loved you." Elizabeth put her hand over her daughter's as she added softly, "I fully expected him to propose marriage."

"He did," Cat whispered. "In fact, it was all settled between us before we returned to Newport. He waited a week to speak with Father only to give everyone time to settle down after the scare we'd had."

"That was very considerate of him. What went wrong?"

Briefly, Cat explained what she knew of Evan's interview with her father. "Everything seemed to be fine. Father wasn't delighted, to be sure, but he gave every evidence of being willing to at least consider the matter. Evan left his office feeling very hopeful.''

"And...?" Elizabeth prompted gently.

"That night he was attacked on the street. The men nearly killed him. While they were beating him, he heard them talking about the rich man he'd offended who had paid them to go after him."

"Oh, Lord." Elizabeth was genuinely shocked. She had always suspected that something was not quite right between Evan and Drake, but not until that moment did she realize what her son-in-law believed.

"Surely you don't think your father would do such a thing?"

"I have a great deal of trouble accepting it," Cat acknowledged. "But there's also the fact that the night before we were married, Evan was attacked again. This time he was prepared and ran the men off, but it seems clear that someone definitely wanted to prevent our marriage."

"Not your father," Elizabeth said firmly. "I can say with absolute certainty that he would never act in so heinous a fashion. He accepted your engagement to Evan, admittedly with some reservations, but also with all honesty. He is not the sort of man who says one thing and does another."

"I know that," Cat said. "I also think that as Evan has thought about it more, he's had trouble believing Father guilty. But that doesn't explain who was behind the attacks."

"At any rate," Elizabeth said, "they occurred, and so you were surprised when Evan seemed eager to visit Boston."

Cat nodded. "He came here for some purpose he hasn't revealed. I'm sure of that. I only wish I knew what it was."

Both women were silent as they contemplated the situation. At length Elizabeth said, "It's possible that he's concerned about you for the same reason that your father and I have been."

"You don't mean that business with Gideon?"

"That's exactly what I mean. You've seen Mari by this time?" When Cat nodded, Elizabeth went on. "She came to tell us that she was going to make you her heir. We all agreed that there could be a potential problem with Gideon, but that there's nothing to be done for it except to be cautious.

"At least," she added slowly, "that's what Mari and I agreed. Now that I think of it, your father was rather uncharacteristically silent on the subject."

"Perhaps he was keeping his own counsel."

"It wouldn't be the first time." Elizabeth smiled gently. "Despite your marriage, he is still very protective of you. It's possible that he may be planning to speak with Gideon himself, to warn him off, as it were."

The two women looked at each other. They nodded as one. "Evan would want to do the same thing," Cat said.

"Would they go so far as to join forces?"

"I doubt that. Evan may be willing to believe that Father was not responsible for the attacks, but I don't think he's ready to be allies. No, my guess is that they're acting separately."

"I don't agree," Elizabeth said. "At least, not completely. However, I suppose we'll find out soon enough."

Cat stood up decisively. She smoothed her skirt and began drawing her gloves back on. "You may be content to sit by and wait, but I'm not. This is my problem they're trying to solve. At the very least, I should be present when one or both of them sees Gideon.''

"Do you really think that's wise, dear?" Elizabeth asked doubtfully.

"Absolutely."

Elizabeth recognized that tone. She had used it often enough herself. With a resigned sigh, she also rose. "In that case, I'm going with you."

"There's only one problem," Cat said with a slight smile. "I'm not sure *where* we're going."

"I am," Elizabeth said. "Your father isn't the only one who's kept an eye on Gideon over the years. I know exactly where to find him."

EVAN HAD BEEN LOCKED in the room for a little more than an hour. He had paced its width and length so many times that he knew the measurements by heart. Several more times he had hoisted himself up to the window again, hoping for some sign of life in the alley below. But no one had appeared, and he had gradually abandoned his hopes of being able to call for help.

He did think at one point that he heard someone opening the door downstairs, but the sound was indistinct. It was followed by a series of dull thuds that brought him swiftly upright. In the space of a few seconds, he thought he could detect a struggle and a strangled cry, followed by silence.

He was leaning against the wall, his arms crossed over his broad chest, when he heard footsteps coming down the hall. Without moving, he waited as the iron bar was lifted and the door opened.

As he eyed his captor, he smiled faintly, without humor. "You know, while I've been waiting here, I've been trying to figure out who was behind all this. It's always nice to be right, even if belatedly."

"Not that it will do you any good," Charles said. He gestured with the gun he held. "Come on."

As they walked out into the corridor, Evan said, "I suppose that was Gideon I heard arriving a few minutes ago."

"You'll see."

Charles said nothing more as they went down the stairs to the main floor. He gestured again with the gun toward the back of the room. An old, disheveled man was sitting at the battered desk. He had scraggly white hair that hung to his shoulders, a deeply seamed face and wide, unblinking eyes.

"Strangled?" Evan inquired matter-of-factly.

Charles nodded. "With a piano wire. It's quite effective.

"I'll take your word for it," Evan murmured. He could see the red welt around Gideon's neck. As he watched, the body sagged and slipped to the floor.

"Get behind the desk," Charles said.

"I don't think so."

Charles's narrow face darkened. "Do as I say or I'll shoot you where you stand."

"Which just might make it a bit difficult for anyone to believe that you'd come upon me in the act of strangling Gideon Mackenzie and shot me in your own defense. That is the plan, isn't it?"

Charles looked taken aback, but recovered quickly. "It's flawless. I'll be a hero, and you'll be dead. Added to that, with Gideon out of the way, Cat will be safe. He really did want to kill her, you know. He talked about it to me. That's what gave me the idea in the first place."

"But you decided to get rid of me as well."

"She should have been mine," Charles spat. "I knew something had happened between you two. I was there, about to call on her, when your note arrived. I took it off the hall table and read it."

His mouth curled in a hate filled grimace. "No low-life scum should be able to take advantage of an innocent young woman. The moment I realized what you'd done, I knew I'd been right to want you dead. First you took a business deal I wanted, then you took Cat. I tried to stop you again before the wedding, but your luck held." He laughed. "It always has, until now."

"You've never taken defeat well, have you, Charles?" a low, steady voice inquired from the front of the building. Drake stood silhouetted in a beam of sunlight pouring in through the open door.

He stood firm and unmoving as he said, "The wharf property was your first try at business, wasn't it? When the New England Investment Association snatched it out from under you, you went to great lengths to find out who to blame. You couldn't stand the idea of a young, ambitious Irishman getting something you wanted for yourself."

"He had no right!" Charles shouted. He had whirled around to face Drake, the gun pointed directly at the older man. It went off even as Evan hurled himself through the intervening space and brought Charles down with a resounding thud.

"Close," Drake murmured as he walked over to where Evan was quickly subduing his would-be killer. Charles was hardly weak, and fury added to his power, but against Evan's implacable strength he was helpless.

"I've finally found a use for this thing," Evan said as he pulled off his tie and used it to secure Charles's hands behind his back. That done, he yanked him upright and grinned at Drake. "Is there any point asking what you're doing here?"

"After we spoke on the phone and you expressed such interest in locating Gideon, I decided to pay him a call myself." He glanced at the body lying on the floor. "He was a particularly treacherous old devil. I didn't see any reason for you to confront him alone."

"I assure you," Evan said mildly, "I was perfectly capable of handling the situation."

"Undoubtedly," Drake agreed. "However, there was no reason for you to do so. After all, you're part of the family now."

The words echoed what Cat had told him earlier, but for the first time Evan truly believed them. He laughed as he held out his hand to Drake. "It isn't often that I'm delighted to admit I've been wrong, but I had suspicions about you that were completely unfounded. I hope you'll accept my apology."

"I had a few doubts about you myself," Drake said as the two men shook hands. "Let's put them behind us, too."

They were smiling at each other, satisfied with the morning's work, when Charles made his move. With a surprising suddenness, he yanked free of Evan and ran for the door.

Taken by surprise, Evan and Drake delayed a moment before following him. By the time they did so, he was rounding the nearby corner. The silk tie had proved insufficient for the purpose to which it had been put. It lay forlornly on the sidewalk, where it had dropped.

The two men ran after him. They got as far as the next block, in time to see a car pull up suddenly at the curb. A young woman leaped out. As Charles tried to evade her, she stuck out her foot and brought him down in a heap.

"Nice work, dear," Drake said approvingly.

"What are you doing here?" Evan demanded.

"Helping you," Cat said. She glanced at Charles, who was attempting to scramble back to his feet. He was assisted by Drake and Evan, who then made sure to hold on to him securely. "What did he do?"

"Quite a bit," Evan said looking at his wife. Her cheeks were flushed, and her breasts rose and fell rapidly. She looked very beautiful, if rather fierce. Slowly he smiled. "I'll tell you all about it."

"I ALMOST FEEL SORRY for him," Cat said softly. She turned over in the bed, propping herself up on her elbow so that she could look at Evan.

"Don't," he said as he watched a smoke ring float up toward the ceiling. "He'll end up in some nice, discreet sanitarium instead of the prison he deserves."

"The judge made sure he'll never be eligible for release," she reminded him. "Surely that's enough."

Evan shrugged. His body felt utterly content, replete with the intense satisfaction of their lovemaking. But his mind remained restless.

Charles van Rhys's trial had concluded earlier that day. Both Evan and Cat had given testimony, as had Drake and Elizabeth. The jury had been swift in delivering its verdict, and the judge had not needed to deliberate long before sentencing Charles to confinement for life. He had, however, accepted the judgment of doctors hired by Charles's family, who contended that he was certifiably insane and should be placed in an institution.

"If he'd come from any other background," Evan said, "he would have been put on a chain gang. Privilege endures, no matter what the circumstances."

"You resent that, don't you?" she asked softly. "No matter how much money you make, you're still angry that some people have everything handed to them from birth."

"Yes," he admitted, "I am. I don't think I'll ever forget the injustices I saw in Ireland, or right here in Boston, for that matter."

She ran a pale hand down his chest, her long fingers tangling in the dark curls she found there. "Why should you? If people forget, nothing will change."

He raised an eyebrow, studying her. "Do you want it to?"

She lay back against the pillows, looking up at the ceiling. "The night I met you, I was filled with excitement about the new century we were entering and all the possibilities it held.

"Now," she added with a slight smile, "I'm a bit older and wiser. I know there are no simple answers, and that nothing will happen automatically. We have to work for it."

Her silvery eyes were dark with emotion as she turned her head to meet his gaze. "My grandparents came of age amid terrible violence and injustice that almost destroyed this country. My parents saw the Industrial Age explode and transform the way we all live. In both cases, they struggled long and hard to make things better for their children. Now it's our turn."

"We don't have any children," he reminded her.

Her smile deepened. "That can be remedied." At the quick flash of concern across his face, she felt a stab of sympathy for the fear she knew he felt. "Trust me, Evan," she said softly. "It will be all right."

"Will it?" he asked softly. He reached out and touched her cheek lightly, feeling the petal-smooth skin beneath the roughness of his fingertip.

His eyes were pensive as he said, "We come from such different backgrounds that it's remarkable we ever see anything the same way. I'm always going to have an urge to put you up on a pedestal, and you're always going to want to jump off.''

''Probably,'' she admitted quietly. ''I used to think that I wanted a placid, happy marriage, like the one I imagined my parents had. I thought that being in love meant that all conflicts were resolved, all misunderstandings settled. But do you know something? It means nothing of the sort.''

She took the cheroot from him and laid it in the crystal ashtray beside the bed. Her lips touched his lightly as she said, ''You'll have your ideas about what's right, and I'll have mine. There will be times when we disagree, possibly loudly. We'll have to learn to compromise.''

''Aye, mavourneen,'' he murmured as his hands closed over her milky shoulders, ''that we will. But I'll tell you a secret. There's nothing an Irishman likes better than a good argument.'' With a flash of candor he added, ''You're not the only one who's getting wiser. I used to want a wife who wasn't much more than a symbol of my own success. Now I prefer for her to be a human being instead, with all the faults and foibles that implies.''

''In that case, Evan O'Connell,'' she murmured as she moved against him provocatively, ''you have nothing whatsoever to worry about. Your future happiness is assured.''

''*Our* future happiness,'' he corrected her gently, his passion rising to meet hers.

The shadows deepened across the room as the figures on the bed entwined. The night faded slowly, unnoticed by the man and woman joined in a love that overcame all barriers and made them, together, vastly more than they ever could be apart.

Shannon OCork

Turning Point

A novel of passion, power, wealth and deadly secrets . . .

A young woman is suddenly cast into a world where beautiful faces hide daring lies, shocking truths . . . perhaps even murder.

A chilling novel of mystery, suspense, reincarnation and a love so powerful it survives time...and even murder.

FOREVER LOVE

Margaret Chittenden

An author makes a startling discovery during a tour to promote her latest novel when she realizes that the same book was actually written by a woman who was murdered years ago.

MAURA SEGER

Be a part of the Callahan and Gargano families as they live through the most turbulent decades in history. Don't miss these sweeping tales of destiny and desire by Maura Seger!

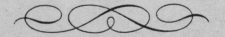

Award-winning novelist Maura Seger has captured the hearts of romance readers everywhere!

A compelling family saga spanning the Civil War to the twentieth century and chronicling the lives of three passionate women.

SARAH is the story of an independent woman's fight for freedom during the Civil War and her love for the one man who kindles her pride and passion. $3.95 ☐

ELIZABETH, set in the aftermath of the Civil War, is the tale of a divided nation's struggle to become one and two tempestuous hearts striving for everlasting love. $3.95 ☐

CATHERINE chronicles the love story of an upper-class beauty and a handsome Irishman in turn-of-the-century Boston. $3.95 U.S. ☐

   $4.50 Cdn. ☐

SEG-1

Order your copies by sending your name, address, zip or postal code along with a check or money order for the total amount payable to Worldwide Library (add 75¢ for postage and handling) to:

In the U.S.

Worldwide Library
901 Fuhrmann Blvd.
Box 1325
Buffalo, NY 14269-1325

In Canada

Worldwide Library
P.O. Box 609
Fort Erie, Ontario
L2A 5X3

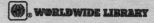 WORLDWIDE LIBRARY

Patricia Matthews, America's most beloved romance novelist and author of sixteen national bestsellers, has written a novel of compelling romantic suspense.

Patricia Matthews
Mirrors

After a young woman discovers she is to inherit an enormous family fortune, her identical twin sister stops at nothing—even murder—to assume her sister's identity and become sole heiress.

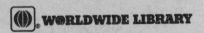